I0670414

GALACTIC TRAP LORDS

———— ✦ ————

Book One

BLOOD

IN THE

STARS

✦ ✦ ✦

a novel by

Lampert x Griffin Urban Universe™

First Edition

Trade Paperback Edition

ISBN: 978-1-969709-29-6

For everyone who grew up in the struggle
and dared to dream beyond the stars.

✦ ✦ ✦

✦ ✦ ✦

CHAPTER 1

Drive-By at Dock C-13

The bass from my Caprice was hitting so hard it made the whole damn dock vibrate. I had her hovering about six feet off the platform, that slime-green underglow painting everything underneath like toxic waste. This wasn't just any ride—this was a 2084 Stellar Caprice Classic, straight from Earth before the colony wars, retrofitted with ion thrusters and a sound system that cost more than most people's yearly income.

My boy Lil Zeno had chopped and screwed the engine till it purred like a big cat getting its belly rubbed. The candy paint—this deep blue that looked black until the light hit it right—was so wet and fresh you could see your reflection better than in a mirror. Chrome everywhere. Twenty-four inch rims that cost me three months of moving weight. This was hood royalty, and everybody knew it.

"Nova, quit playing with these motherfuckers," Trixx said from the passenger seat, her purple legs crossed, that glitter dress riding up her thighs. She had a bottle of Remy Martian between her knees—that expensive shit from the distilleries on Mars that ran about two hundred credits a bottle. She took a long pull straight from the bottle, no glass, and wiped her mouth with the back of her hand. "Either we doing this or we ain't."

I loved watching her. Everything about Trixx was extra—from the glow-ink tattoos that covered her arms and shoulders to the way she walked like she owned every room she entered. We'd been fucking around for about six months now, nothing official, but the type of situation where we both knew what it was. She was ride-or-die, and in the Verge, that's the only type of woman worth your time.

"Two minutes," I told her, hands light on the wheel. I was rocking the Caprice side to side on the thrusters, just showing off. If you ain't styling in space, you just another broke motherfucker trying to get from point A to point B.

From the backseat, OG Hark leaned forward. His metal knuckles—the ones the prison surgeons had grafted on after he lost his real fingers in a fight on Titan Penitentiary—rapped against my headrest. "Young blood," he rumbled, voice sounding like gravel in a blender, "you sure you ready for this? Once we light this warehouse up, ain't no going back."

I glanced at him in the rearview. Hark was fifty-something, looked seventy, but could still outfight men half his age. Prison barcodes ran up his temple like ladder rungs. His left eye was glass—some crystal shit that the prison doctors installed after an inmate stabbed the real one out. The glass eye moved slower than the real one, giving him this crazy, unsettling look. People called him a cyborg. He said he was just a man who refused to die.

"I'm sure," I said. My thumb traced the scar on my left hand—the one I got when Ky and I blood-brothered ourselves when we were kids. Ky. My little brother. My heart. The kid who used to follow me around the Block like a shadow, talking about how he was gonna be just like me when he grew up.

He'd loved my copper-wrapped braids, was always asking when he could get his own. And he'd been fascinated by my eyes—those blue-edged Xytherian eyes I got from our mama, proof of the mixed blood Vale and his type hated so much.

Vex had spaced him. Put him out an airlock without a suit over some bullshit about territory and respect. They found Ky's body floating near Dock Seven, frozen solid, eyes still open. I hadn't slept right since the funeral. Every time I closed my eyes, I saw my little brother's face, that look of terror frozen on it forever.

"This for Ky," I said, more to myself than anyone else.

Trixx put her hand on my knee and squeezed. Her nails were long and sharp, painted that holographic purple that shifted colors under different lights. "In and out, baby," she said softly. "We smoke these fools and bounce. No hero shit."

"No hero shit," I repeated, but we both knew I was lying.

I sparked up a Black Death cigarette—that harsh tobacco they grew on the dark side of Luna—and let the smoke fill my lungs. The nicotine hit my system like an old friend. In the backseat, Hark was rolling up something stronger, that Nova Dust mixed with crushed dream-chips. The smell was sweet and chemical, like burnt sugar and ozone.

"Want a hit?" he asked, offering me the blunt.

"After," I said. "Need my head clear for this."

The Dock C-13 warehouse sat ahead of us, looking like every other piece-of-shit building in Nova Block Six-Nine. On paper, it was registered as a herb farm—they grew oxygen moss and some legal prayer vines for the religious folks. In reality, everybody knew Vex used it to cook Nova Dust and package dream-chips for rich assholes from Echelon Prime who came slumming in the Verge looking for thrills.

Nova Dust was the drug of choice out here. It was synthetic, made from processed stardust and some chemical shit I couldn't pronounce, and it made you feel like you were flying through space without a ship. The high lasted for hours, and the crash was brutal—people said it felt like your soul was being pulled out through your chest. But that didn't stop motherfuckers from spending their whole paycheck on it.

Vex controlled the Nova Dust trade in our sector. He also controlled the dream-chip trafficking, the illegal weapons shipments, and had his hands in about a dozen other dirty businesses. The Federation turned a blind eye because he paid the right people. But he'd fucked up when he touched my brother.

I checked the duffel bag on the floor between my feet. Three pieces: a Laser Glock .45LX with the red targeting stripes that made it look like something out of a comic book, a Hi-Tek 9 laser machine gun with a clear barrel that glowed blue when it powered up, and the crown jewel—a Plasma Uzi 9K. The Uzi was all chrome, vented barrel, military-grade shit that I'd gotten from a weapons dealer who owed me a favor. Zeno had tuned the coils until the hum it made sounded like music.

"Check your piece," I told Trixx.

She pulled the Glock from her purse, checked the charge pack, and nodded. Trixx could shoot better than most men I knew. She'd grown up in the Rings, that rough section of stations orbiting Saturn where you either learned to handle yourself or you became a victim. She'd told me once, pillow talk after we'd finished fucking, about how her daddy had taught her to shoot when she was eight. He'd been killed in a territory dispute when she was twelve. She didn't talk about him much after that.

Hark already had the Hi-Tek 9 in his lap, his metal fingers stroking the barrel like it was a woman. "Let's get this money," he said with that dead smile of his.

I killed the exterior lights on the Caprice, leaving just the underglow. We were a ghost now, sliding through the dark like a rumor. The music—some old Earth trap shit from the 2020s that Zeno had programmed into the sound system—kept thumping. I let the beat set my heart rate.

The warehouse had these long tinted windows running along the side—cheap security glass that was supposed to stop laser fire. It wouldn't. I'd made sure of that when I'd bought these weapons.

"Now," Hark said.

I tapped the ion pads with two fingers, and the Caprice moved sideways like she was on hydraulics. I'd spent hours practicing this move in empty sectors, learning to control the thrusters with the delicacy of a surgeon. The ship crabbed sideways until we were parallel to the warehouse, maybe twenty feet away. Close enough.

I grabbed the Plasma Uzi, felt its weight in my hands. The grip was warm, almost alive. I thumbed off the safety, and the coils inside started spinning with that musical hum. Zeno was an artist.

"Three, two, one," I counted down, watching the warehouse windows. Inside, I could see shadows moving—Vex's crew, the Null-boys, going about their business like they weren't about to have a very bad night.

On one, I squeezed the trigger.

The Uzi came alive in my hands, kicking like a wild animal, spitting out bolts of superheated plasma that lit up the darkness like lightning. The first shot hit the window and spider-webbed it. The second shot punched through. By the third shot, the whole window exploded inward in a shower of glittering shards.

Inside the warehouse, people started screaming.

"Light 'em up!" I shouted.

Hark leaned out the back window, the Hi-Tek 9 chattering in his hands. Lines of blue laser fire stitched across the warehouse bay, sparking off metal, setting shit on fire. I saw a Null-boy in cheap armor trying to run for cover, and Hark's lasers caught him in the back. The man dropped like somebody cut his strings.

Trixx was more precise. She lined up her shots carefully, taking her time. Two quick pulls of the trigger, and a guy manning a console went down with smoking holes in his chest. She blew him a kiss. "Rest in piss, bitch."

I kept the Caprice moving, juicing the thrusters to slide left, then right, never staying still. That was the key to a drive-by in space—

motion is life. You stop moving, you become a target. Return fire started coming our way, but it was sloppy, panicked. These weren't soldiers; they were street dealers playing gangster.

"Side door," Hark called out. "Four of them."

I swung the nose of the Caprice toward the side entrance and let the Uzi sing. The plasma bolts hit the door's hinges, melting through the metal like butter. The door sagged, then fell inward. Three Null-boys were behind it, caught in the open. Trixx got one. Hark got two. The fourth threw a grenade—one of those old-school fragmentation types—and it bounced off my front bumper.

For a second, my heart stopped. Then the grenade just floated away, tumbling in the low gravity, before it detonated about fifty feet out. My shields absorbed the shock wave like it was nothing.

"That all you got?" I shouted at the warehouse.

That's when the roof opened up, and Vex himself appeared.

He was standing on a scissor lift, rising up like he was some kind of god. Vex was a tall motherfucker, mixed race—part human, part something else I could never quite figure out. He wore this expensive suit, the kind with the woven-in power cells that could stop small arms fire. His smile was all teeth and no warmth. Dead eyes. Shark eyes.

In his hands was a rail pistol—military-grade hardware that could punch through starship hulls. He aimed it right at my windshield.

"Drive!" Hark yelled.

"Nah," I said. "Let him see me."

I wanted him to know who was killing him. I wanted him to see Ky's big brother, the one he thought he could disrespect. I wanted him to understand that you don't touch my family and live.

Our eyes met through the windshield. My eyes—the blue-edged Xytherian eyes I'd inherited from my mother's side, the alien DNA that made people call me hybrid, mutt, half-breed—stared into his human ones. I could see his lips moving, probably saying some racist shit about how mongrels like me didn't belong in the Verge.

I didn't give him the satisfaction of hearing it.

"Vex!" I shouted into the comm, my voice amplified across the dock. "You remember Ky? That kid you spaced? He says hello, bitch."

I pulled the trigger, and the Plasma Uzi roared.

Blue fire streaked across the distance. Vex's rail pistol coughed once—a shard of metal screamed past, kissing my hood and leaving a scar—but he was already moving too slow. The plasma caught him in the shoulder, then the chest, then the throat. His expensive suit didn't mean shit. The plasma ate through it like it was tissue paper.

Vex's body jerked once, twice, then he slumped forward. The scissor lift, stupid and automated, kept rising for a few seconds before its safety protocols kicked in and it stopped. Vex's body hung there, smoking, dead.

The Null-boys inside the warehouse just froze. They'd never seen their boss drop. They didn't know what to do.

I didn't wait to find out. I goosed the thrusters, and the Caprice arced up and away, bass still thumping, underglow still painting the darkness green. Behind us, alarms finally started going off, lights flashing red.

"That's how you do a drive-by," Hark said, laughing that broken-glass laugh of his. He sparked up the blunt he'd rolled earlier, took a long hit, and passed it forward to Trixx.

She hit it, held the smoke in her lungs for a long count, then exhaled slowly. "Nova, baby," she said, voice soft and dreamy from the drugs, "you just painted a target on your back the size of a moon."

"Good," I said. "Let them come."

I took the blunt from her and took my own hit. The Nova Dust hit my system like a warm wave, making everything feel floaty and distant. The edges of my vision got soft, and for a moment, the grief that had been sitting on my chest like a boulder felt lighter.

"Where to?" Trixx asked.

I grinned. "Club Nebula Nights. We earned a drink."

.   .   .

Club Nebula Nights floated off Axis Street like a neon wet dream. The building was all curves and glass, with holographic palm trees that swayed to invisible wind. The sign flickered between a dozen languages before settling on English: MONEY.

To get inside, you had to fly through the entry tunnel—this narrow passage lined with projected images of lips. Every time you passed through, it cost twenty credits. Stupid tax for stupid people, but everybody paid it because Nebula Nights was the spot.

I set the Caprice down in the docking bay, making sure to park her where I could see her from inside. The hood had a fresh scar from Vex's rail gun, but otherwise, she was perfect. I ran my hand over the dash like I was saying goodbye to a lover.

"Be good, baby," I told her.

Inside the club, the heat hit me like a wall. Bodies everywhere—dancing, drinking, fucking in the dark corners. The air was thick with smoke—tobacco, weed, vaporized dream-chips. Purple fog machines were working overtime, making everything look like a fever dream.

The bass here was different from my car—longer, deeper, the kind that made your chest vibrate. Lights swept across the crowd in time with the music, catching skin, chrome, glass, making everything look wet and alive.

Trixx grabbed my hand and pulled me toward the bar. Her glow-ink tattoos were reacting to the club lights, pulsing in waves under her skin. She looked like a goddess, and every head in the place turned to watch her move.

"Two Remy Martians," I told the bartender drone. "And a bowl of those meteor limes."

The drone—a floating sphere with mechanical arms—chirped acknowledgment and went to work. A minute later, it came back with three bottles instead of two.

"Smart machine," I said, tipping it an extra credit.

Hark had already posted up in his usual spot—back corner, left side of the stage, where he could see both exits. He set his metal hand flat on the table so everybody could see it. Fear tax, he called it. People saw that hand and remembered the stories. They remembered OG Hark, the legend, the man who'd survived Titan Penitentiary and come out harder than he went in.

I leaned on the rail and watched the club do its thing. On the center stage, a six-armed dancer—some kind of genetic mod job— was working the pole like it owed her money, all those arms moving in impossible patterns. In the smoking section, a kid from the South Rings was selling counterfeit catalysts, trying to look tough. A group of rich boys from Echelon Prime sat in the VIP, slumming it, their faces lit up with guilt and thrill.

And in the far corner, parked like a threat, was a Space Hellcat Charger. Midnight chrome body, red velvet cockpit, Federation decals on the doors. My heart did something complicated in my chest.

"That's Vale," Trixx said, sliding up next to me. She'd already finished half her bottle, and her eyes were bright with alcohol and trouble. "The Fed. What's he doing here?"

Lieutenant Vale. The Federation officer with the purity speeches and the hard-on for hybrids like me. He was inside the club somewhere, probably sitting in the VIP with his badge making him untouchable.

Vale was the type of cop who believed in purity laws—the outdated bullshit regulations that said humans and aliens shouldn't mix. He'd made it his personal mission to make life hard for people like me, people with mixed DNA, people who didn't fit into his narrow idea of what humanity should be.

I'd seen him roughing up a hybrid kid once, just because he could. I'd been too far away to stop it, but I'd remembered his face. Now here he was, drinking in our club, breathing our air.

"What's the play?" Trixx asked.

I drained my bottle, felt the Remy Martian burn down my throat like gasoline. "We wait," I said. "Let him have his fun. Then we make sure he remembers who owns this neighborhood."

My earbud buzzed. Zeno's voice came through, excited and high. "Nova! Baby! You're trending on the mesh! Vex's people are chirping everywhere. You wrote a whole damn hymn tonight, my boy!"

"Any heat coming my way?" I asked.

"Some pings, nothing direct. You got maybe twenty minutes before somebody official shows up. But yo—" His voice dropped conspiratorially. "That Hellcat Vale's driving? She's talking to me. I can ghost her limiter for sixty seconds if you can get close enough to scratch the belly camera. But Vale's got the ignition set to blood recognition. You'd have to make him bleed on it to steal her."

"He'll bleed," I said.

Zeno giggled like a kid on Christmas. "That's my dog. Hit me when you need me."

I looked at Trixx, at the glow pulsing in her skin, at the way her dress clung to her curves. I looked at Hark, posted up like a gargoyle, metal hand gleaming. I thought about Ky, about my little brother floating frozen in the void.

Tonight, we'd painted the first line. Tomorrow, the Federation would paint back. But right now, in this moment, with expensive liquor in my system and my crew around me, I felt untouchable.

"Another round," I told the drone. "And keep them coming."

The music shifted, the bass dropping into something darker, heavier. The club pulsed like a heartbeat. Somewhere in the crowd, Vale was watching. Somewhere in the city, people were talking about what I'd done.

Good. Let them talk. Let them all know that Nova ain't the one to fuck with.

I raised my bottle toward the ceiling, toward the stars beyond. "This one's for you, little brother," I said softly.

Then I drank, and let the night take me wherever it wanted.

✦ ✦ ✦

CHAPTER 2

Stealing Thunder

Lieutenant Vale didn't walk toward me—he glided, like a shark that had just smelled blood in the water. Everything about him was precise: his uniform pressed sharp enough to cut, his hair lined up perfect, his smile calculated. He was the type of Fed who believed he was better than everyone in the Verge just because he wore a badge and had access to Echelon Prime bathrooms.

I hated him on principle.

He set his badge on the bar next to my empty bottle, making sure I could see the serial number, the rank insignia, all that official bullshit that was supposed to make me nervous. It didn't. I'd been nervous before—when my mama died, when Ky got spaced—but this motherfucker wasn't worth the adrenaline.

"Evening," he said, voice smooth as expensive whiskey. He had that Echelon accent—proper English with just enough street vernacular thrown in to show he'd "spent time" in the hood. Like tourism gave him a pass. "Mr. DeLeon, isn't it? Kash. Though I believe your friends call you 'Nova.' Very... dramatic."

Trixx laughed, low and dangerous. "His friends call him whatever they want. You ain't his friend."

Vale's eyes slid to her like she was a piece of art he was considering buying. "You glow beautifully," he said, and the way he said it made my jaw tighten. "Does it do anything useful, or is it just for decoration?"

Trixx's smile could've frozen the sun. "Come closer and find out, baby."

I set my bottle down carefully and kept both hands visible on the bar. I had the Hi-Tek 9 tucked in my waistband under my jacket, but pulling it in a club full of witnesses—especially with Vale's badge sitting right there like a threat—wasn't the move. Not yet.

"What brings a Federation officer to our humble establishment?" I asked, keeping my voice level. "You slumming, or you actually got business?"

"I'm here for balance," Vale said, leaning against the bar like he owned it. "This station's ledger is off. Your... community... takes more than it contributes. Crime is up. Respect for law is down. And people like you—hybrids, half-breeds, genetic mistakes—you're at the center of it all."

There it was. The purity talk. Vale was one of those Feds who believed in the old laws, the ones that said humans and aliens shouldn't mix, that children like me—born from human fathers and Xytherian mothers—were abominations that needed to be regulated, controlled, eliminated.

My mother had been beautiful. She'd died when I was twelve, some bullshit illness that the Echelon doctors could've cured but wouldn't, not for a hybrid family in the Verge. I remembered her laugh, her blue-edged eyes that I'd inherited, the way she'd sung old Xytherian songs when she cooked.

Vale's smile said he didn't think people like her deserved to exist.

"Funny," I said, my voice cold. "The ledger I read says y'all took my brother. Spaced him without a trial. So I'd say we're about even."

Vale's jaw flexed—just a twitch, but I caught it. "Waste floats," he said. "Sometimes it takes a body to remind the rest of the trash where they belong."

My hand moved toward the Hi-Tek 9 on instinct. Trixx caught my wrist before I could do something stupid. Her fingers were cool, gentle but firm. She leaned close, lips brushing my ear without touching.

"Not yet," she whispered, and the sound of her voice pulled me back from the edge. "Not here. Not like this."

Vale saw the exchange and smiled wider. He leaned in closer, close enough that I could smell his cologne—something expensive and overpowering. "Here's some advice," he said. "Echelon's justice moves slow, but it moves. Your little vandalism tonight—shooting up Vex's warehouse—it won't feel clever when the paperwork finishes processing. Walk carefully, Nova. Stop pretending you're a king. You're a footnote in a book you can't even read. And that book is mine."

"Your book boring as hell," I shot back. "Probably why nobody reads it."

He smirked. "Cute." His eyes flicked back to Trixx, lingering on the way her dress hugged her curves. "If you ever want a man who can actually take care of you, who can buy you out of this dump—"

Trixx's laugh cut him off. It was the kind of laugh that had sharp edges. "If I ever want a man who needs his ego stroked more than his dick, I'll let you know," she said sweetly. "But until then, why don't you run along and find someone desperate enough to pretend they're impressed?"

The glow-ink on her throat pulsed brighter, and Vale actually took a step back. For all his talk, he recognized danger when he saw it. Trixx wasn't just pretty—she was lethal, and he knew it.

Vale tapped the bar twice with his knuckles. "Enjoy your evening," he said, voice tight. "And enjoy my car while you can. I'll be getting it back. Along with everything else you think you've stolen."

"I'll enjoy it," I said. "Might even fuck in it, just for you."

His eyes went cold, dead. He picked up his badge and walked away without another word.

I exhaled slowly, realized I'd been holding my breath. My heart was pounding, adrenaline making my hands shake. Trixx squeezed my knee under the bar.

"You good?" she asked softly.

"Yeah," I lied.

My earbud buzzed. Zeno's voice, excited and breathless. "Yo, Nova! You're trending hard on the mesh right now. Everybody talking about what you did to Vex. They got your face on murals, baby! You're a fucking legend!"

"Any heat?" I asked, keeping my voice low.

"Some pings, nothing direct yet. You got maybe twenty minutes before somebody official shows up looking for you. But yo—" His voice dropped, conspiratorial. "That Hellcat Vale's driving? She's connected to my network. I can ghost her security limiter for sixty seconds if you can scratch the belly camera. But the ignition's locked to his blood. You'd have to make him bleed to steal her."

I looked across the club at Vale. He was talking to one of the bouncers, probably running his mouth about order and purity and all that bullshit he believed in.

"He'll bleed," I said quietly.

Zeno giggled like Christmas came early. "That's my boy. Call me when you're ready."

I looked at Trixx. At the glow pulsing in her skin. At the way she was watching me with that mix of concern and excitement that meant she knew I was about to do something stupid.

"We stealing that Hellcat," I told her.

She closed her eyes and laughed. "Of course we are. Because why would we do anything smart when we could do something that gets us killed?"

"You don't have to come," I said.

She opened her eyes and the look she gave me could've melted steel. "Baby, if you think I'm letting you do this alone, you're dumber than you look. And you look pretty fucking dumb right now."

From his corner, Hark had been watching the whole exchange. He walked over, his metal hand clinking against his glass. "Y'all about to do what I think you're about to do?"

"Probably," I said.

He grunted. "Hemocode lock means you need his blood."

"I know."

"You planning to cut him?"

"Something like that."

Hark sighed like a father disappointed in his son. "You gonna start a war you ain't ready for."

"I'm not starting anything," I said. "I'm finishing what Vex started. What Vale's been pushing for months. They want to treat us like animals? Fine. I'll show them what happens when you back an animal into a corner."

Hark studied me for a long moment. Then he nodded once. "Then let's do it smart. We got one shot. If we fuck this up, we're dead or in custody. Probably both."

• • •

The plan was simple, which meant it would probably go wrong.

I'd approach Vale, extend my hand for a handshake—some bullshit about no hard feelings, respect between men, all that fake-ass peacekeeping. While we were shaking, I'd use my ring to cut my own finger, get some blood on my hand. Then I'd make sure some of that blood got on him, on his hand, where I could use it later.

It was a stupid plan. But stupid plans were the only kind that worked in the Verge.

I walked up to Vale while he was still talking to the bouncer. Up close, I could see the lines around his eyes, the way his jaw was set tight. He was older than me—maybe thirty-five—and he had that hardness that came from years of believing he was right about everything.

"Hey," I said, interrupting his conversation. "Forgot to say thank you."

He turned, eyebrows raised. "For what?"

"For the advice," I said, and extended my right hand. "No hard feelings. Yet."

His eyes went to my hand like it was a trap. His training probably told him not to shake. But his pride—that masculine need to never back down—told him to do it anyway.

Pride won.

His palm was warm, rough with calluses. He squeezed hard, trying to prove something. I let my ring—the one with the sharp edge I'd filed down specifically for situations like this—bite into my own finger. A bead of blood welled up under the metal, mixing with sweat.

I squeezed back, making sure that blood got on both our hands.

"Catch you outside," I said, smiling.

He glanced down, saw the red crescent on my ring finger. His eyes widened as he realized what I'd done. He looked at his own hand, saw the smear of blood there.

"You—" he started.

But we were already moving.

Trixx was already crossing the floor, hips swaying like she had all the time in the world. Hark blocked two security guards who hadn't realized yet that they were too slow. I pushed through the exit door into the docking bay, cold air hitting my face like a slap.

The Hellcat sat there, purring like it knew we were coming. All midnight chrome and red velvet, looking like money and power and everything Vale thought made him better than us.

"Zeno," I hissed into my earbud. "Ghost me. Now."

"Scratching the bellycam," Zeno sang. "Limiter goes dark in three... two... now."

I dropped to the ground, slid under the Hellcat's nose, and dragged my blade across the tiny camera lens Zeno had marked on my HUD. It squealed and died. The Hellcat's lights flickered, amused.

Behind me, I heard the club door bang open. Vale's voice, sharp and commanding: "Stop! Federation authority!"

I didn't stop.

I popped the driver's door and dropped into the velvet cockpit. The seat was butter-soft, expensive, the kind of luxury poor kids like me only saw in vids. The steering wheel glowed faintly, waiting for a blood signature.

"Sixty seconds," Zeno said in my ear.

I pressed my bloody finger to the wheel's hub. The metal drank the blood like it was thirsty. A tiny light shifted from red to amber.

"Fifty seconds."

The door on the passenger side opened and Trixx slid in, breathing hard, eyes bright with adrenaline. "Vale's coming. We got maybe ten seconds."

Hark materialized at the rear door, moving faster than a man his age should be able to. He dropped into the back seat with a grunt.

"Forty seconds."

The wheel's light shifted from amber to green. The Hellcat's engine roared to life, a deep, throaty sound that was pure power. Every system came online at once—targeting computers, shield generators, weapons systems. This wasn't just a car. This was a military-grade interceptor with a luxury package.

"Thirty seconds."

"Drive!" Trixx shouted.

I slammed my foot on the thruster pad. The Hellcat launched forward like she'd been shot from a cannon, pinning us back in our seats. We screamed out of the dock, leaving a trail of exhaust and burning rubber-substitute.

Behind us, Vale ran into the bay, gun drawn, shouting orders that nobody was listening to. His face was twisted with rage, with humiliation. I'd stolen his ride, his pride, in front of witnesses.

He'd never forgive me for this.

"Twenty seconds."

I pushed the Hellcat hard, threading through the dock traffic like a needle through cloth. Other ships scattered, pilots cursing on the open channel. An alarm started blaring somewhere, but it was distant, someone else's problem.

"Ten seconds."

"Where we going?" Hark asked from the back.

"Home," I said. "We drop this beauty off with Zeno, let him strip the good parts before Vale tracks her. Then we lay low for a minute."

"Timer's up," Zeno said. "Limiter's back online. She's gonna start screaming to the Fed network in about three minutes. Get her to me fast."

I punched it, and the Hellcat sang.

•　•　•

We dumped the Hellcat at Zeno's chop shop—a converted cargo bay on the edge of Nova Block where he did his best work. He was practically drooling when we pulled in.

"Oh, baby," he whispered, running his hands over the chrome like it was a woman. "This is beautiful. This is art. Nova, you just brought me Christmas."

"Strip her fast," I said. "Vale's gonna be looking."

"Already on it. I'll pull the weapons systems, the shield generator, maybe the entertainment console if I'm feeling greedy. Then I'll dump the husk in a scrap yard and let them think she got parted out by randoms."

"How long?"

"Two hours. Maybe less if she cooperates."

We left Zeno to his work and caught a ride back to my place in the back of a delivery drone. My apartment was small—two rooms, a bathroom that barely worked, and a kitchen that I never used. But it was mine. I'd paid for it with money I'd earned moving weight for the local dealers before I'd gotten smart enough to go independent.

Ky's jacket still hung on the hook by the door. I touched it like a ritual, felt the worn leather under my fingers. Some days I swore I could still smell him—that mix of cheap cologne and smoke he always wore.

"Don't," Trixx said softly. She knew where my head went when I looked at that jacket too long.

I pulled my hand back.

The mesh was still buzzing with news about the warehouse shooting. Pictures of Vex's body, smoking and slumped. Videos of the Hellcat theft spreading like wildfire. My face was everywhere—some artist had turned it into a stencil, and now kids were spray-painting it on walls all over the Block. Nova the rebel. Nova the hero. Nova the fool who'd just painted the biggest target on his back that the Verge had ever seen.

I sparked up another Black Death cigarette and let the smoke fill my lungs. Trixx poured us drinks—more Remy Martian, because why not?—and collapsed onto my beaten-up couch. Her glow-ink was pulsing slower now, less excited, more tired.

Hark stood by the door like furniture with opinions. "You know what comes next," he said.

"Retaliation," I said.

"Be specific."

"Vex's boys are gonna hit back. They'll burn a corner store, shoot up a few stalls, make noise. The Feds will swoop in pretending to save us while they're really just looking for an excuse to crack skulls. Vale gets a warrant with my name on it. Rich folks in Echelon read about it over breakfast and feel good about keeping the Verge under control. Business as usual."

Hark nodded. "So what are we changing?"

"Timing," I said. "We don't wait for them to come to us. We make them react to us."

My earbud buzzed. Zeno's voice, excited enough that his words were running together. "Yoyoyoyo—boy, I got something. Off-world job. Pays stupid money. Risk is even more stupid. Perfect for you."

Hark groaned. "If it smells like a trap and pays like a dream, it's both."

"It's a run," Zeno said. "Not drugs. Not guns. Mem-bricks."

My mouth went dry. Memory bricks. The hottest commodity in the galaxy. Little clear chips that recorded a person's most intense experiences—joy, pleasure, victory, sex—and let other people relive them like they were their own. They were addictive as hell. Rich people in Echelon paid fortunes for them. And running them was dangerous as fuck because everybody wanted to steal them.

"From who?" I asked.

"Auntie Rhys."

The name hung in the air like smoke. Auntie Rhys. The broker, the fixer, the woman who moved everything from weapons to drugs to information. She was small, soft-spoken, and absolutely fucking terrifying. She paid well, but she also had a reputation—you didn't cross her, you didn't steal from her, and you didn't fail her. If you did any of those things, your body ended up floating in the void with a note attached explaining what you'd done wrong.

"What's the route?" I asked.

"Gravebend to the Ashwind Corridor," Zeno said. "Through the Red Choir nebula. It's a shortcut that cuts past Fed checkpoints and rival territory. But it's dangerous—plasma storms, space pirates, and some weird gravitational shit that'll tear your ship apart if you don't know what you're doing."

"Payout?"

"Two-fifty upfront. Two-fifty on delivery. Clean credits, Auntie's signature. She wants someone young, someone loud, someone who's trending right now. She wants to use your reputation as cover."

I looked at Trixx. She was biting her lip, running the numbers in her head. Two hundred and fifty thousand credits was enough to get us off Nova Block, maybe buy our way into one of the safer stations. Or it was enough to die trying.

"When?" I asked.

"Corridor's quiet in eight hours. After that, Fed patrols cross it for a full day cycle. Auntie will hold the job for you, but not the window."

I looked at Ky's jacket. At Trixx sitting on my couch with her glow dimming. At Hark standing by the door like a gargoyle waiting for bad news.

"We're in," I said.

Trixx closed her eyes. When she opened them, the glow was brighter. "Then we do it clean. No hero shit. No scenic routes. We get in, deliver, get paid, get out."

"Amen," Hark said.

✦ ✦ ✦

CHAPTER 3

Red Choir

Eight hours later, we were prepping the Caprice for the run. Zeno had already installed his cloak-mesh—a rough net of sensors and scramblers that made our outline fuzzy on scanners. It wouldn't fool military-grade equipment, but it would make patrol drones second-guess themselves long enough for us to slip past.

"This net gonna hold?" I asked, running my hand over the installation. It felt like cheap fabric, nothing that could actually save our lives.

"Baby, I'm offended," Zeno said, not looking up from his work. He was under the Caprice's belly, wiring something that sparked and hissed. "This is artistry. This is science. This is me keeping your ungrateful ass alive."

"I'm grateful," I said. "Just making sure I ain't about to die because you were high when you built this."

"I'm always high," Zeno said cheerfully. "That's when I do my best work."

He crawled out from under the car, face smudged with grease. Lil Zeno was twenty, looked sixteen, and had the kind of genius that would've made him rich in Echelon but kept him broke and brilliant in the Verge. He wore his hair in locks, had cybernetic implants running up both arms that let him interface directly with machines, and spoke in run-on sentences when he got excited.

Which was always.

"Threnody's loaded and ready," he said, pointing to the Ak-4700 Rail Blaster he'd built custom. The gun was pure chrome, with a coil system that hummed even when it was off. "She'll punch through armor, shields, and bad attitudes. Just don't fire her near anything you like, because the magnetic pulse will fuck up electronics for about fifty feet."

"Noted," Hark said, picking up the weapon and checking the sights. He handled it smooth and careful, the way a man who knows guns is supposed to.

Trixx was in the back of the shop, changing into something more practical. When she came out, I forgot how to breathe for a second. She'd swapped the club dress for tactical gear—armored leggings that hugged her legs, a cropped jacket with impact plates hidden in the lining, and boots that looked cute but could probably crush a man's windpipe. Her glow-ink was still visible at her throat and arms, pulsing soft purple.

"Stop staring," she said, but she was smiling.

"Can't help it," I said.

She walked up and kissed me quick, lips tasting like mint and something sweeter. "Stay focused. We got a job to do."

"I'm focused," I lied.

We loaded up. Food packs, water, extra charge packs for the weapons, a medical kit that Hark insisted on even though we all knew if we got hurt bad enough to need it, we were probably already dead. I stashed a bottle of Remy Martian under my seat—for luck, I told myself, though really it was because I didn't trust luck without a little chemical assistance.

Hark brought out his armor. Old military-grade stuff from his days before prison, dented and scarred but still functional. He strapped the plates on over his clothes, checked his sidearm—a nasty plasma pistol that could melt through bulkheads—and nodded once.

"Ready," he said.

I looked at my crew. Trixx, beautiful and deadly. Hark, old and harder than coffin nails. Zeno, young and crazy and too smart for his own good.

This was my family. The only family I had left after Ky.

"Let's get this money," I said.

·   ·   ·

The flight to Gravebend took two hours through the back routes, the paths only locals knew about. We flew dark—no running lights, no transponder signal, just the Caprice and the void. The cloak-mesh made us look like debris on most scanners, just another piece of junk floating through space.

I sparked up a Black Death and let the smoke curl around the cockpit. Trixx cracked the bottle of Remy and took a pull, then passed it to me. The liquor burned going down, settled warm in my stomach.

"You scared?" she asked quietly.

"Always," I said. "Fear keeps you sharp."

"Fear also keeps you alive," Hark added from the back. He'd lit up his own smoke—something herbal that made the air smell sweet and chemical. "But too much fear makes you freeze. And freezing gets you killed."

"Balance," I said.

"Balance," he agreed.

We passed through a debris field—wreckage from some old battle, ships that had died before I was born. The Caprice threaded through the hulks like a ghost, quiet and careful. Out here, the

Federation didn't patrol. This was the forgotten space, the place where laws went to die.

My earbud buzzed. Zeno's voice, crackling with static. "Yo, you're about twenty minutes from Gravebend. Sensors show it's quiet, but quiet don't mean safe out there. Keep your eyes open."

"Copy," I said.

Gravebend appeared on the horizon like a bad memory. It was an old mining station, built back when corporations thought they could strip-mine asteroids for profit. They'd given up after a decade, left the station to rot, and now it was home to the kind of people who didn't want to be found. Smugglers. Pirates. People running from debts or warrants or their own pasts.

Zaz Station was the main hub—a ring of metal and rust that looked like it was held together by prayers and spite. Lights flickered. Dock arms twitched. As we got closer, I could see ships parked in various states of disrepair, from sleek racers to hulking cargo haulers that probably hadn't moved in years.

"Bay Seventeen," I said, reading the coordinates Zeno had given me. "That's where we're meeting Auntie's guy."

We docked smooth, magnetic clamps grabbing the Caprice with a metallic clunk. I kept the engine running—just in case we needed to leave in a hurry. Through the canopy, I could see the bay: empty except for a single crate and a man standing next to it.

The man was small, tidy, wearing a suit that looked expensive but old. His hands were in his pockets, and he watched us with the kind of patience that came from seeing too much shit to be impressed by anything.

"That's Kess," I said.

We exited the Caprice, weapons concealed but ready. The bay smelled like machine oil and ozone. The air was thin, recycled too many times, tasting like metal.

Kess didn't move as we approached. "You're the bell," he said, looking at me. His voice was smooth, educated, the kind of voice that belonged in board rooms, not smuggler dens. "And your chaperone. And your insurance."

"Good morning," Trixx said, because apparently someone needed to have manners.

Kess inclined his head. "Good morning. I am Kess. Auntie Rhys sends her regards and her impatience. You will take this crate. You will not open it. You will not look at it too long. You will not apologize to it if it hums. You will transport it through the Ashwind Corridor to Bay Twelve on the far mouth. There, you will leave it and depart. Quickly. Without questions. Without curiosity."

"Why's it hum?" I asked, because I've never been good at following directions.

Kess smiled slightly. "Because memory bricks record joy, Mr. DeLeon. And joy doesn't like to be contained. It leaks. It sings. It tries to seduce you into opening the box to experience what's inside. Do not do this. The memories inside are not yours, and stealing joy has a price."

"Poetic," Hark said. "Put it in the car."

Kess snapped his fingers. Two loader drones—floating spheres with mechanical arms—lifted the crate and carried it to the Caprice's cargo hold. The car sagged under the weight, complained with a hydraulic hiss, then adjusted.

I could already feel it. A vibration. A hum. Not a sound, exactly, but a feeling—like standing next to a speaker playing bass so low you couldn't hear it, only feel it in your chest. The memory bricks were awake, sensing us, wanting to share their stolen experiences.

Kess produced a credit chip with a flourish, held it out. "Half now. The other half arrives when you arrive. If you don't arrive..." He shrugged. "Then the money won't matter."

I took the chip, felt its weight. Two hundred and fifty thousand credits. Enough to change everything or bury us trying.

"Any trouble we should know about?" I asked.

"Wrecker Flock has been active in the Corridor," Kess said casually. "Salvage pirates. They worship something they call the Great Repair. They believe disassembling ships makes the universe whole. Also, there's a Federation patrol that crosses the Corridor every few hours. Young officer. Ambitious. Angry about something."

He didn't say Vale's name, but we all knew.

"Anything else?" Trixx asked.

"Yes," Kess said. "Don't listen to the bricks. They'll offer you things. Promises. Experiences. Ignore them. They lie."

"Thanks for the warning," I said.

We loaded back into the Caprice. The crate hummed louder now, like it was excited to be moving. Hark secured it with cargo straps, double-checking everything.

"Ready?" I asked.

"No," Trixx said. "But let's go anyway."

I fired up the thrusters and we undocked, leaving Gravebend behind.

•   •   •

The Ashwind Corridor opened up ahead of us like a throat. The Red Choir nebula hung to our left—massive clouds of red and purple gas, glowing with plasma storms that could fry a ship's systems in seconds. It was beautiful and deadly, like everything worth looking at.

"Nav says the route is clear for now," I said, checking the HUD. Zeno had loaded a song-map—a path through the Corridor that changed constantly, updated by smugglers and runners who'd survived the trip. "But clear don't mean safe."

"Nothing in the Verge is safe," Hark said. He'd loaded Threnody, the rail gun resting across his lap like a sleeping animal. "Safe is for rich people in Echelon."

"Real talk," I agreed.

The Corridor was narrow, twisting between asteroids that had been here since before humanity left Earth. Some of them were the size of cities, big enough to have their own gravity wells. Others were just chunks of rock, tumbling through space like dice waiting to land wrong.

I flew careful, watching the instruments, feeling the ship respond to my touch. The Caprice handled smooth, Zeno's modifications making her dance through tight spaces. We were halfway through when Hark's voice came from the back.

"We got company."

I checked the scanner. Three ships behind us, closing fast. They weren't Federation—their signatures were all wrong, patched together from different vessels, illegal configurations.

"Wreckers," Trixx said, voice tight.

"Fuck."

The three ships—sleds, really, more engines and weapons than hull—came at us from different angles. Their hulls were decorated with prayer flags and scrap metal shaped into symbols I didn't recognize. One of them opened a comm channel, and a voice filled with religious fervor came through.

"Vessel with the singing cargo," the voice said. "We hear the Great Repair calling from within your hold. Surrender the vessel. Let us disassemble it. Let us return it to component form. The universe hungers for wholeness."

"They're fucking crazy," Trixx said.

"Yeah," I agreed. "Hark, you ready?"

"Always."

The Wreckers opened fire. Laser cannons and plasma rounds lit up the void. I juked hard left, rolling the Caprice through a gap between two asteroids. The shots missed, splashing off rock instead of shields.

"They're trying to box us in!" Trixx said.

She was right. The sleds were moving to cut off our escape routes, herding us toward the Red Choir nebula. Smart tactics for crazy people.

I gunned the thrusters, pushing the Caprice faster. The engine whined in protest. One of the sleds got close enough for me to see the pilot through the canopy—face painted white, eyes wild with whatever drug they were on.

Hark opened the top hatch and climbed out. The wind from our speed whipped around him, but his magnetic boots kept him locked to the hull. He brought Threnody up, aimed at the closest sled.

"Hold her steady!" he shouted.

I did my best. The rail gun fired with a sound like thunder, the slug punching through space at hypersonic speed. It caught the sled square in the engine block. The ship exploded in a bloom of fire and debris.

"Good shot!" I said.

"Two more!" Trixx warned.

The remaining sleds were still on us, hooks extending from their hulls like grasping fingers. They wanted to latch on, tear us apart piece by piece. I couldn't let that happen.

I dove under an asteroid, came up on the other side, and spun the Caprice in a full rotation. The Wreckers followed, but they were slower, less maneuverable. It gave Hark another shot.

He took it. The second sled took a hit to the cockpit, spinning out of control, smashing into an asteroid.

The third sled backed off, reconsidering. Then its comm channel crackled to life again.

"We will find you," the voice said. "The Great Repair is patient. All things return to component form eventually."

Then they were gone, accelerating away into the void.

"That was too close," Trixx said.

"Yeah," I agreed, hands shaking on the controls. "But we're clear."

Hark climbed back inside, armor scorched from the plasma fire. "Next time, let's pick a route with less religious fanatics."

"I'll make a note," I said.

We pushed on through the Corridor. The Red Choir loomed larger now, close enough to feel the heat bleeding through the shields. Close enough to hear the static hiss of interference on the comms.

And then the scanner lit up again.

Not Wreckers this time. Something worse.

A Federation Interceptor. Sleek, fast, armed to the teeth. And I recognized the ship's signature from the data Zeno had pulled.

Vale.

"Of course it's him," Trixx said. "Of course he followed us."

The Interceptor hailed us on a secure channel. Vale's voice came through, smooth and controlled. "Mr. DeLeon. I believe you have something that belongs to me. My dignity, perhaps. My car. Certainly my patience."

"Your car's in pieces," I said. "Dignity was already gone. And your patience ain't my problem."

"Everything about you is about to become my problem," Vale said. "I'm bringing you in. Theft of Federation property. Assaulting an officer. And whatever's in that crate you're carrying. Pull over and surrender. This is your only warning."

"How about you fuck off instead?" I suggested.

The line went dead. Then the Interceptor opened fire.

Laser fire streaked past us, red lines cutting through the void. I yanked the controls hard, rolling the Caprice into a dive that made my stomach try to exit through my throat. The lasers missed, splashing off an asteroid behind us.

"He's serious!" Trixx said.

"Yeah, I noticed!" I shouted back.

The two escort ships—smaller Fed patrol vessels—moved to flank us, trying to box us in like the Wrecker sleds had. But these pilots were trained, professional, not religious fanatics with more faith than sense.

I pushed the Caprice hard, weaving through the asteroids. The cloak-mesh helped, making our outline fuzzy, but it couldn't hide us completely. Vale was too good a pilot, too experienced. He stayed on us like a shadow.

"Incoming!" Hark warned.

A missile streaked toward us, contrail bright against the darkness. I punched the countermeasures, dumping a cloud of chaff and flares. The missile got confused, detonated early, the explosion rocking us but not hitting directly.

"That was close," I said.

"Too close," Trixx agreed. She was already climbing back out the top hatch, Uzi ready. "Keep him off our ass and I'll light him up!"

I did my best. Juked left, then right, then dove under an asteroid and came up the other side. Vale followed every move, matching me maneuver for maneuver. The man could fly, I'd give him that.

Trixx opened fire, painting the Interceptor with plasma bolts. His shields flared, absorbed most of it, but a few shots got through, scarring his hull.

"That's for my cousin, motherfucker!" she screamed into the void.

One of the escort ships got brave, tried to cut us off from the front. Bad decision. Hark leaned out with Threnody, took his time aiming, and fired. The rail slug punched through the escort's cockpit like it was made of paper. The ship went dark, tumbling away.

"Good shot!" I said.

"I know," Hark replied calmly.

But we weren't out of it yet. Vale was still on us, closer now, his weapons cycling up for another shot. The Red Choir nebula loomed ahead—a massive wall of plasma that no sane pilot would fly into.

"Nova," Trixx said slowly. "Please tell me you're not thinking what I think you're thinking."

"We fly through it," I said.

"That's suicide!"

"So is staying here!"

I aimed the Caprice straight at the plasma wall and punched it. We hit the edge of the nebula and everything went red. Alarms screamed. Shields flared. The temperature inside the cockpit spiked instantly, sweat beading on my forehead.

Behind us, Vale hesitated. Just for a second. But a second was all we needed.

We plunged into the Choir, and the universe screamed.

•   •   •

Flying through the Red Choir was like flying through hell. The plasma storms battered us from all sides, lightning arcing across our shields, radiation fucking with every system. My instruments were going haywire, readings spiking and crashing.

"This was a bad idea!" Trixx shouted over the alarms.

"I know!"

But it was working. Vale had followed us in, but the storms were hitting him just as hard. His Interceptor was tougher than the Caprice, military-grade, but even he couldn't shrug off this much punishment.

And then the crate started singing.

Not humming anymore. Singing. A chorus of experiences, of memories, all crying out at once. The plasma storms were exciting it, waking up all the joy and pain and pleasure locked inside those bricks. I could feel it washing over me—someone's wedding night, someone's victory lap, someone's last kiss before they died.

"Don't listen!" Hark shouted. His face was twisted, jaw clenched so hard I thought his teeth would crack. "It's not real! It's not yours!"

But god, it felt real. It felt better than real. It felt like everything I'd ever wanted—

Trixx slapped me. Hard. The sting brought me back, cleared my head.

"Fly!" she screamed in my face. "Fly or we die!"

I flew.

We burst out the other side of the plasma wall like a cork from a bottle. The alarms stopped. The singing faded to a hum again. We were through.

Behind us, Vale's Interceptor emerged, smoking, shields flickering. He'd taken damage. Real damage. His ship was limping.

But he was still coming.

"Bay Twelve!" I said, seeing it on the scanner. "That's the drop point!"

I pushed the Caprice toward it, ignoring the protesting engines, ignoring everything except getting this fucking crate off my ship.

We slid into Bay Twelve, mag-clamps grabbing us. I popped the cargo hold, and the crate slid out onto the bay's loading platform. The second it was off the ship, the singing stopped. The pressure in my head released.

"Payment received," an automated voice said. "Thank you for your service."

Two hundred fifty thousand credits appeared in my account.

"Let's go!" I said.

But as we were pulling out, Vale's Interceptor appeared at the mouth of the bay. And so did the Wrecker Flock—three sleds, hooks extended, seeing both a Fed and a smuggler as targets.

Vale had to choose: chase us or deal with the pirates.

He chose the pirates. Probably because they were shooting at him.

We punched out of Bay Twelve, leaving the chaos behind. As we accelerated away, I heard Vale cursing on the open channel, heard the sounds of weapons fire and prayer flags whipping in the void.

"We made it," Trixx said, laughing with relief and disbelief.

"We made it," I agreed.

Hark lit up another smoke and took a long drag. "Don't do that again," he said.

"No promises," I said.

We set course for home, five hundred thousand credits richer and very lucky to be alive.

✦ ✦ ✦

CHAPTER 4

After the Storm

We made it back to Nova Block without any more drama. The Caprice limped home, her paint scorched from the plasma storms, shields flickering, but alive. We were alive. That's what mattered.

The docking bay at our Block was quiet—it was early morning, that dead time when even criminals were sleeping off their sins. I set the Caprice down gentle, killed the engines, and just sat there for a minute, hands still on the wheel, heart still racing.

"We did it," Trixx said softly. She was looking at me, glow-ink pulsing slow at her throat. "Five hundred thousand credits. We're actually rich."

"For now," Hark said from the back. But even he couldn't hide the relief in his voice. "Till we spend it on something stupid."

"Or invest it in something smart," I said.

He laughed. "You? Smart? That'll be the day."

I checked my account on my wrist display. The numbers were there, real, not a dream. Five hundred thousand credits. More money than I'd ever seen in my life. More than my mama had made in her entire life working in the recycling plants. More than Ky would ever see.

The thought of my brother brought the grief back, sharp and sudden. But the money helped. Money always helped. It couldn't bring him back, but it could make sure his death meant something. It could buy revenge, or at least the tools for it.

"Let's get inside," I said. "I need a drink and about twelve hours of sleep."

"I need a shower," Trixx said. "I smell like plasma storms and fear."

"You smell good to me," I said.

"That's because you got no taste," she shot back, but she was smiling.

We climbed out of the Caprice. Zeno was waiting by the dock entrance, practically vibrating with excitement. He'd monitored the whole run from his workshop, probably watching our vitals spike every time we almost died.

"YO!" he shouted, running up and throwing his arms around me. "You made it! You actually made it! I thought for sure when you flew into the Choir you were dead, but you came out the other side like— like—"

"Like an idiot who got lucky," Hark finished.

"Exactly!" Zeno laughed. He pulled back, looked at all of us. "Drinks on me. Well, drinks on Nova since he's the one with half a million credits now."

"Drinks on me," I agreed.

•   •   •

An hour later, we were back at my apartment. Hark had gone to his own place—the old man needed his rest—but Zeno had followed us up, bringing two bottles of something expensive he'd been saving for a special occasion.

"Lunar Reserve," he said, showing me the label. "Real shit from the dark side distilleries. Costs about a thousand credits a bottle."

"Open it," I said.

He did. We passed it around, drinking straight from the bottle like we were broke kids instead of newly rich criminals. The liquor was smooth, smoky, tasted like money and bad decisions. I loved it.

My apartment felt different now. Smaller, somehow, like I'd outgrown it in the space of a day. Ky's jacket still hung on the hook. The furniture was still beaten up and cheap. But I had money now. I could move. Could buy something better.

But not yet. Not until I'd finished what I started.

"So what's next?" Zeno asked. He was sprawled on my couch, cybernetic implants glowing faintly. "You gonna retire? Buy a nice place in the outer rings? Live the quiet life?"

I laughed. "You know me better than that."

"Yeah," he said. "I do. Which is why I'm asking what crazy shit you're gonna do next."

Before I could answer, my comm buzzed. A message from Auntie Rhys. I opened it, read the brief text.

Bay Twelve. Payment delivered. Additional opportunity available. Interested?

"She's got another job," I said.

Trixx groaned. "Nova, baby, we just survived one job. Can we enjoy being alive for like, a day, before you sign us up for more danger?"

"She pays well," I said.

"She always pays well," Trixx countered. "But money ain't worth shit if you're dead."

She had a point. But I also knew that sitting still wasn't an option. Not with Vale hunting me. Not with Vex's crew still out there. The only way forward was through more jobs, more money, more power. Enough that people would think twice before fucking with me.

"Let me see what she wants," I said. "We don't have to say yes."

Trixx rolled her eyes. "You're gonna say yes."

"Probably," I admitted.

Zeno finished the bottle, set it down with a satisfied sigh. "Well, I'm out. Got work to do. Your car needs fixing, and I got about six other projects calling my name. Hit me up when you need me."

He left, and suddenly it was just me and Trixx in the apartment. The silence felt different now, charged with something I couldn't quite name. Adrenaline, maybe. Relief. Desire. All of it mixed together.

She was looking at me with those eyes, the ones that said she knew exactly what I was thinking.

"You need that shower," I said.

"You offering to scrub my back?" she asked, voice low.

"Among other things."

She stood up, stretched, body moving in ways that made my mouth go dry. "Then stop talking and come here."

•   •   •

The shower in my apartment was small, barely big enough for one person, definitely not built for two. But we made it work.

The water was hot, steam filling the tiny bathroom within seconds. Trixx stepped in first, and I followed, closing the sliding door behind us. The space was cramped, intimate, our bodies pressed close by necessity.

I ran my hands down her sides, feeling the curve of her hips, the softness of her skin. Her glow-ink reacted to my touch, pulsing brighter, patterns swirling across her shoulders and arms like living art.

"I love when you do that," I said, tracing one of the glowing lines with my finger.

"Do what?"

"Glow for me."

She turned to face me, water streaming down her body, her purple skin glistening. "I can't help it. You make me react."

I kissed her, slow and deep, tasting the water on her lips. She pressed against me, soft and warm and perfect. My hands found her ass, squeezed, pulled her closer. She made a sound in the back of her throat, half-moan, half-laugh.

"We almost died today," she whispered against my mouth.

"I know."

"I need to feel alive."

"I know," I said again.

Her hand slid down my stomach, wrapped around me. I was already hard, had been since she'd suggested the shower. She stroked slowly, deliberately, eyes locked on mine.

"Turn around," I told her.

She did, bracing her hands against the shower wall. The water ran down her back, highlighting every curve, every line of glowing ink. I ran my hands over her ass, spreading her, admiring the view.

"You're perfect," I said.

"I know," she replied, looking back over her shoulder with that confident smile. "Now stop talking and fuck me."

I didn't need to be told twice.

I pressed against her entrance, felt her warmth, her wetness. She pushed back against me, impatient, wanting it. I slid inside slow, inch by inch, feeling her stretch around me.

"Fuck," she breathed. "Yes."

I gripped her hips and started moving, slow at first, then faster. The shower was too small, awkward, but we made it work. Every thrust made her gasp, made her glow brighter. The bathroom filled with purple light, reflected off the water, making everything look surreal.

"Harder," she demanded.

I gave her what she wanted, pounding into her, the sound of skin slapping skin mixing with the rush of water. She was tight, perfect, body moving with mine like we'd been doing this forever.

"Touch yourself," I told her.

Her hand moved between her legs, and I felt her shudder, felt her walls tighten around me. She was close. I could always tell—her breathing changed, got faster, more desperate.

"Nova," she moaned. "Don't stop. Don't fucking stop."

"I won't."

I kept the rhythm steady, deep strokes that made her whole body shake. Her glow-ink was blazing now, so bright I had to squint. She was beautiful like this, lost in pleasure, all that confidence melted into pure need.

"I'm—" she started, then cut off with a cry.

She came hard, her whole body tensing, squeezing me so tight I thought I'd lose my mind. I held on, kept moving through her orgasm, drawing it out, making it last.

When she finally relaxed, I pulled out, turned her around, and kissed her hard. She kissed back, breathless, satisfied, still glowing.

"Your turn," she said.

She dropped to her knees on the shower floor, water streaming over her, and took me in her mouth.

The sensation was intense—hot water, hot mouth, her tongue working magic. I braced one hand against the wall, the other tangling in her hair. She looked up at me with those eyes, challenging, teasing, knowing exactly what she was doing to me.

"Fuck, Trixx," I groaned.

She sucked harder, faster, one hand working what couldn't fit in her mouth. The pressure built fast, too fast. I tried to hold back but couldn't.

"I'm gonna—"

She didn't pull away. Kept going, kept sucking, kept looking at me with those eyes until I came hard, everything going white for a second.

When I finally came back to myself, she was standing up, smirking, water washing everything away.

"We're even now," she said.

"For what?"

"For you almost getting us killed today."

I laughed, pulled her close, kissed her forehead. "Fair."

•   •   •

Later, we were in bed, naked under the thin sheets, sharing a Black Death cigarette. The nicotine felt good after sex, settling my nerves, making everything feel distant and manageable.

"So what did Auntie want?" Trixx asked, her head on my chest, fingers tracing lazy patterns on my skin.

I pulled up the message on my wrist display, projected it on the ceiling so we could both read it.

Additional opportunity: Intelligence asset extraction. Target: The Black Book. Chaplain transport, Axis Ward. Two days. Payment: 750k credits. Interested?

Trixx whistled low. "Three-quarters of a million. That's real money."

"That's 'retire and never work again' money," I said.

"That's also 'probably die trying' money," she countered.

"Maybe."

She propped herself up on one elbow, looked at me seriously. "Nova. Real talk. We got half a million in the bank right now. We could leave. Go to one of the outer colonies, somewhere the Feds don't reach, somewhere Vale can't find us. Start over. Be normal."

"You want to be normal?" I asked.

She thought about it. "No. But I want you to be alive."

"I'm alive right now."

"For now."

I took a drag from the cigarette, held the smoke in my lungs. "I can't leave. Not yet. Not until I've made Vale pay for what he did to Ky. Not until I've made the whole fucking Federation understand they can't just kill us and expect no consequences."

"Revenge won't bring him back," she said softly.

"I know. But it'll make me feel better."

She sighed, laid her head back down on my chest. "Then I'm coming with you. Because someone needs to keep your stupid ass alive."

"I love you," I said. The words surprised me—I hadn't meant to say them out loud.

She was quiet for a long moment. Then: "I know."

Not 'I love you too.' Just 'I know.' But somehow, that felt right. That felt real.

We lay there in the dark, smoking, glow-ink pulsing soft purple like a heartbeat. Outside, Nova Block hummed and creaked and lived. Somewhere out there, Vale was planning his next move. Somewhere, Vex's crew was plotting revenge. Somewhere, Auntie Rhys was counting her money and calculating odds.

But right now, in this moment, none of that mattered.

Right now, I was alive, rich, and in bed with a beautiful woman who knew exactly who I was and stayed anyway.

That was enough.

. . .

The next morning, I sent Auntie my response.

Interested. What's the play?

Her reply came back in seconds.

Details in person. Bay Twelve. One hour.

I looked at Trixx, still asleep beside me, face peaceful in a way it never was when she was awake. I looked at Ky's jacket on the hook. I looked at my reflection in the cracked mirror on my wall—blue-edged Xytherian eyes, copper-wrapped braids, scars earned from living in the Verge.

"One more job," I whispered to myself. "Then maybe we can rest."

But I knew that was a lie. There was always one more job. That's how it worked in the Verge. You kept running until you couldn't run anymore, and then you hoped someone cared enough to remember your name.

I got dressed, left a note for Trixx, and headed out to meet Auntie Rhys.

Time to find out how much dying was worth these days.

✦ ✦ ✦

CHAPTER 5

The Black Book

Bay Twelve at Ashwind Station felt different this time. Last time I'd been here, I was dropping off stolen memory bricks and running from pirates. Now I was walking in like I had an appointment, which somehow felt more dangerous.

The bay was cleaner than most in the Verge—Auntie Rhys paid for maintenance that worked. The lights actually functioned. The air didn't smell like recycled fear. There was even music playing softly from hidden speakers, some classical shit that probably cost more per second than most people made in a day.

At the far end, sitting in a projected chair that looked more real than reality, was Auntie Rhys herself.

She was exactly how I remembered from the holograms: small, soft-looking, with a smile that made you think of grandmothers and poisoned tea. She wore velvet—always velvet—in deep purple today, with jewelry that caught the light and probably cost more than my entire neighborhood. Her hands were folded in her lap, patient, like she had all the time in the world and knew I didn't.

"Little bell," she said as I approached. Her voice was warm, musical, the kind of voice that could sell you your own funeral and make you thank her for the service. "You arrived promptly. I appreciate punctuality. It's so rare in the young."

"I appreciate money," I said. "That tends to make me prompt."

She laughed, a sound like wind chimes made of bone. "Honest. I like that. Sit."

A chair appeared next to hers—not projected, real, probably been there the whole time but hidden by whatever tech she used to control her environment. I sat. The velvet was soft, expensive. I felt out of place, like a rat in a jewelry store.

"You did well with the memory bricks," she said. "Very well. You survived the Corridor, evaded Vale, and delivered on time. That's... uncommon. Most runners I hire either die in the Choir or decide the merchandise is worth more than my payment. You did neither."

"I'm not stupid," I said.

"No," she agreed. "You're not. Reckless, perhaps. Angry, certainly. But not stupid. That's why I'm offering you this."

She made a gesture and a holographic display appeared between us. It showed what looked like a ship—specifically, a chaplain transport, one of those religious vessels the Federation used to move people and cargo while pretending everything was sanctified and holy.

"The Black Book," she said. "Have you heard of it?"

"No."

"Good. Most people haven't. It's Federation Intelligence's dirty little secret—a ledger of names, payments, informants, off-the-books operations. Everything they don't want the public to know. Everything they use to maintain control." She zoomed in on the ship. "This particular transport is carrying a portable copy of the sector's Black Book. Vale's unit moved it off Echelon Prime for security reasons, disguised it as religious research materials."

"You want me to steal it," I said.

"I want you to acquire it for me," she corrected. "Stealing implies we're doing something wrong. We're simply... redistributing information."

"For three-quarters of a million credits."

She smiled. "You read the offer. Good. Yes. Seven hundred fifty thousand credits. Half now, half on delivery. Clean, untraceable, Rhys-signed. Enough money to set you up for life if you're smart about it."

I thought about it. Thought about Trixx, about Hark, about the life we could build with that kind of money. Thought about Vale's face when he realized his precious intelligence had been stolen.

"What's the catch?" I asked.

"Several," she said, counting on her fingers. "One: the transport docks at Axis Ward in two days. That's your window. Two: Vale will be there personally, flying escort. He likes to be close to his secrets. Three: the transport is staffed by actual clergy—Pure Dawn priests who believe in what they're doing. I prefer not to have religious martyrs on my conscience, so no killing priests unless absolutely necessary."

"Anything else?"

"Yes. The Book itself is stored in a seed—a data crystal protected by biometric locks. You'll need to bypass hemocode security, prayer authentications, and probably a few other surprises Vale has installed. My man Zeno assures me he can handle the technical side, but you'll need to physically access the seed."

She leaned forward, eyes suddenly sharp despite the soft smile. "And Nova? Vale knows you stole his car. He knows you killed Vex. He's building a case, preparing something called Operation Exodus—a systematic purge of 'undesirables' in the Verge. If you don't take this job, he comes for you anyway. If you do take it, at least you'll have the money to fight back."

That's what decided it. Not the money, though that helped. The fact that Vale was coming regardless. The fact that doing nothing meant dying slow instead of dying rich.

"I'm in," I said.

"Excellent." She made another gesture and a credit chip appeared in her hand—a flower made of glass that glowed with internal light. "Three hundred seventy-five thousand. Half now, as agreed. The rest comes on delivery."

I took the chip, felt its weight, its warmth. More money than I'd ever held at once. It felt like power.

"One more thing," Auntie said. "You'll be working with someone. A consultant. He's... particular, but he knows the Pure Dawn protocols better than anyone."

"Who?"

The bay door opened behind me. I turned.

The man who walked in was tall, dressed in white and gray robes that marked him as Pure Dawn clergy. But it was his face that caught my attention—or rather, the lack of it. He wore a bone-white mask, smooth and featureless except for thin slits for eyes. The mask had a gold rim that caught the light, made it look like a halo made of wealth and threat.

"This is Bone Mask," Auntie said. "He's a former chaplain. Now he's... freelance."

"Heretic is the word most use," Bone Mask said. His voice was dry, precise, like pages turning in an old book. "I prefer 'disillusioned.'"

"He knows the transport layout, the security protocols, where the seed will be kept," Auntie continued. "He'll guide you through the heist. In return, he gets a percentage and certain... assurances about his safety."

I looked at the masked man. "You gonna be a problem?"

"Only if you make me one," he said. "I have no love for Vale or his crusade. The Pure Dawn once stood for something. Now it's just another tool for control. So yes, I'll help you steal their secrets. Consider it penance."

"Great," I said. "A thief, a heretic, and a Fed's worst nightmare walk into a church. Sounds like the beginning of a joke."

"Or an epitaph," Bone Mask said.

Auntie clapped her hands once, a sound that somehow echoed despite the soft acoustics. "Wonderful. You'll work together, steal my Book, and everyone walks away richer. Except Vale, who walks away embarrassed. I consider that a bonus."

. . .

I left Bay Twelve with the credit chip burning in my pocket and Bone Mask's words echoing in my head. Back at the Caprice, Trixx was waiting, leaning against the hood with her arms crossed.

"So?" she asked. "We doing this?"

"We're doing this."

"Of course we are." She pushed off the car, walked over, pressed herself against me. "You know this is crazy, right? Robbing a church? With a masked heretic as our guide? While Vale's watching?"

"I know."

"Just checking." She kissed me, hard and quick. "Let's go get drunk and plan how we're not gonna die."

. . .

Back at my apartment, we spread out. Hark showed up within an hour, took one look at the credit chip, and whistled low.

"That's real money," he said.

"Auntie doesn't deal in fake," I replied.

Zeno arrived next, practically vibrating with excitement. He'd already started working on the technical side—fake priest badges, holographic robes, prayer authentication spoofs. His cybernetic implants were glowing brighter than usual, data streaming through his nervous system like electric blood.

"Okay, okay, okay," he said, talking fast. "So chaplain transports have three entry points: one for clergy, one for government officials, one for maintenance. The maintenance door is our best bet—less security, fewer cameras. I can spoof a badge scan for about twelve seconds, which should be enough to get you inside."

"And then what?" Trixx asked.

"Then you walk like you belong there. The Pure Dawn priests won't question other priests. It's against their doctrine to assume deception in the faithful. As long as you look holy, they'll leave you alone."

"I don't do holy," I said.

"You do whatever pays," Hark corrected. "And this pays."

We spent the next few hours going over the plan. Bone Mask sent detailed schematics of the transport—where the reliquary was located, what kind of locks protected it, the patrol patterns of the security teams. The man was thorough, I'd give him that.

"The seed is kept in a shock-mounted case," Zeno explained, projecting the image on my wall. "Biometric lock requiring hemocode and prayer authentication. I can fake the prayer part—recorded some archdeacon's greatest hits and coded them into a priest glove. The hemocode is trickier."

"How tricky?" I asked.

"You'll need to touch the lock with warm, prayer-blessed hands. The glove will handle the warmth and the blessing. But if they've updated their security since Bone Mask left, we might have problems."

"Problems we can shoot our way out of?" Hark asked.

"No," I said firmly. "Auntie said no killing priests. We do this clean."

"Clean means harder," Hark said.

"Then we do it harder."

We drank while we planned. Not Remy Martian this time—we were saving the good stuff—but some cheap vodka Zeno had brought that tasted like industrial solvent and burned like revenge. By the time we'd gone through the plan three times, we were all pleasantly buzzed, the edges of fear softened by alcohol and confidence.

"Two days," I said, raising my glass. "Two days, we rob a church, steal a book, and embarrass Vale so bad he'll never recover."

"To embarrassment," Trixx said.

"To money," Hark added.

"To not dying," Zeno finished.

We drank.

∘   ∘   ∘

Later that night, after Hark and Zeno had left, Trixx and I lay in bed, not sleeping, just existing. The apartment was dark except for the glow from her skin, pulsing soft and steady like a heartbeat made of light.

"You scared?" she asked quietly.

"Terrified," I admitted.

"Good. Me too."

She rolled over, propped herself up on one elbow. In the darkness, with just her glow lighting her face, she looked like something out of a dream—beautiful and dangerous and mine.

"After this job," she said, "we should leave. Take the money and go somewhere Vale can't reach us. Somewhere we can just... be."

"Where would we go?"

"Anywhere. The outer colonies. Maybe one of the agricultural stations out past Jupiter. Somewhere quiet. Somewhere we don't have to look over our shoulders every five seconds."

I thought about it. Really thought about it. A life without the Verge, without the violence, without constantly waiting for the next person to try to kill me. It sounded like paradise.

"After this job," I said. The words came out slower than I expected, like my mouth was testing them before committing. "We finish this, get paid, and then we leave."

She waited, watching my face in the darkness. Looking for something. I don't know if she found it.

"Okay," she said finally. Not pushing. Not asking for more. Just accepting what I could give.

She kissed me, slow and deep, body warm against mine. We made love slowly this time, not the frantic, adrenaline-fueled sex from before, but something gentler, more real. Like we were trying to memorize each other's bodies, just in case.

When we finished, she curled against my chest, her breathing evening out as sleep took her. I stayed awake longer, staring at the ceiling, thinking about the job, about Vale, about the future we were trying to build from stolen money and stolen time.

Two days. Then everything would change.

Either we'd be rich and free, or we'd be dead.

In the Verge, those were the only two options that mattered.

*   *   *

The next morning, I woke to find a message waiting on my comm. No sender ID, but I knew who it was from.

I know what you're planning. Don't. -V

Vale. He knew. Of course he knew. The man was a Fed, after all. He had resources, informants, probably cameras I didn't even know about.

But knowing and stopping were two different things.

I deleted the message, got dressed, and met with my crew.

"Vale knows," I told them, showing them the message.

"Then we move faster," Hark said.

"Or we abort," Trixx suggested.

"We don't abort," I said. "We're too far in. He's trying to scare us off. We don't scare."

"Speak for yourself," Zeno muttered. But he kept working on the tech anyway.

That day, we prepared. Ran drills. Memorized the layout. Tested the holographic robes Zeno had acquired—they shifted colors at a button press, from lavender to gray to white, making us look like proper clergy. The veils covered our faces, made us anonymous. Perfect for a heist.

Bone Mask met us at an abandoned docking bay on the edge of the Block. He showed us exactly how Pure Dawn priests moved, talked, prayed. It was all performance, he explained. Ritual designed to project authority and piety.

"Walk slow," he said. "Keep your head bowed slightly. Hands together in prayer position. If anyone addresses you directly, respond with a blessing. They'll expect it, and it gives you time to think."

"What if they ask questions?" Trixx asked.

"They won't. Pure Dawn doctrine discourages questioning the faithful. As long as you look the part, they'll assume you belong."

We practiced until our movements were smooth, natural. Until we could walk like priests who believed in what they were doing.

The next day was for rest. We'd need our heads clear for the job. But rest didn't come easy. I lay in bed, Trixx beside me, both of us pretending to sleep while our minds raced through a thousand scenarios, a thousand ways this could go wrong.

"Nova," she whispered in the darkness.

"Yeah?"

"If this goes bad... if we have to run... promise me you'll run. Don't try to be a hero. Don't die for pride."

I didn't answer right away. We both knew what that silence meant.

"Nova."

"I hear you." I pulled her closer. "We're gonna be okay. We're gonna steal that Book, get paid, and get out. Then we're gone. New life. New names. Somewhere Vale will never find us."

"That's not what I asked."

"I know." I kissed her forehead. "But it's what I can give you."

"You really believe that?"

"I have to."

She was quiet for a long time. Then: "I love you."

It was the first time she'd said it. The words hung in the air like a prayer, like a promise, like a curse.

"I love you too," I said.

And then, finally, we slept.

✦ ✦ ✦

CHAPTER 6

Holy Heist

Axis Ward looked like a cathedral that somebody forgot to finish. White metal ribs arched overhead, cheap gold trim trying to make poverty look pious. Security cameras blinked like altar boys trying not to look at something dirty. Everything was designed to make you feel watched, judged, found wanting.

Perfect place for a robbery.

The chaplain transport sat in Dock H like it owned the place. Matte pearl hull, stained glass windows that probably cost more than my entire block, and a rail turret hidden under a projected halo that showed doves when it wasn't busy being a gun. The whole thing screamed "we're holy but we'll shoot you if necessary."

We'd parked the Caprice three docks over, in a maintenance bay that Zeno had reserved under a fake name. Now we were in the shadows behind a supply kiosk, changing into our disguises.

The holographic robes felt weird sliding over my clothes—like wearing light instead of fabric. They rippled from gray to lavender to white depending on how I moved, programmed to look like proper Pure Dawn vestments. The veil covered my face, turned my features into anonymous piety. I looked like every other priest in the station. That was the point.

Trixx adjusted her robe, glow-ink dimmed down to almost nothing. "I feel ridiculous," she muttered.

"You look holy," I said.

"Same thing."

Hark was already in character, moving with the slow, deliberate pace of an old deacon who'd spent too many years carrying coffins. His metal hand was hidden in his sleeve. Threnody was broken down in his bag, disguised as religious texts.

"Comms check," Zeno's voice crackled in my ear. He was back at the Caprice, running tech support. "Can you hear me?"

"Loud and clear," I said quietly.

"Good. Transport's crew change happened ten minutes ago. You got a window of about thirty minutes before the next shift. Badge scan spoofs are ready. Priest glove is calibrated. You're good to go."

"Copy."

I looked at my crew. Trixx, beautiful even under the veil. Hark, dangerous despite the holy robes. And somewhere in the station, Bone Mask was watching, making sure we didn't fuck up his carefully planned heist.

"Let's go steal a book," I said.

. . .

We joined a group of real priests heading toward Dock H—Pure Dawn clergy with their little pins shining, mouths set in that expression of judgment that holy people wore like armor. I kept my head bowed, hands folded in prayer position like Bone Mask had taught me.

A deck chaplain stood at the transport's ramp, waving a scanner over everyone entering. The device pinged green as the real priests passed through. When it got to me, it hesitated—yellow light, thinking—then Zeno's spoof kicked in and it turned green with a happy chirp.

"Blessings," the chaplain said, not looking up.

"And to you, brother," I replied, voice pitched lower, more formal.

We were in.

The interior of the transport smelled like wood polish and expensive lies. Everything was designed to look humble while screaming wealth—simple pews with magnetic locks that probably cost a fortune, icon panels cycling through holy symbols in high definition, a choir loft that looked like it belonged in a palace.

The ship was bigger than I'd expected. The main sanctuary took up the center, with pews arranged in neat rows. At the front, elevated on a dais, was a glass-walled chapel where Vale stood talking to a senior chaplain. I could see him through the transparent walls—uniform pressed perfect, jaw tight, scanning readouts like he was waiting for something to go wrong.

He was waiting for me. I knew it. He'd sent that message. He knew we were coming. But knowing and proving were two different things.

"Positions," I murmured into my comm.

Trixx peeled left, drifting toward the choir stairs like she belonged there. Hark moved to the back pew, settling in with the posture of a man who'd spent his life in churches. I stayed center, letting the robe make me invisible among the other priests.

"Security's heavier than expected," Zeno said in my ear. "Three tech-deacons in the console pit, two armed guards by the glass chapel, and... shit. That's Bone Mask. He's actually on the ship."

I spotted him—the bone-white mask standing out even among the clergy. He was near the reliquary at the front of the sanctuary, talking to another priest, perfectly calm. He saw me, gave the smallest nod. Ready.

"On your mark," Zeno said.

"Mark," I replied.

Trixx took a breath and began to sing.

The sound was beautiful—something between a hymn and a lullaby, voice carrying through the sanctuary like it was born for the space. Heads turned. People stopped what they were doing. Even Vale looked up from his readouts, curious.

And while everyone was distracted, I moved.

I slipped sideways through a gap between pews, heading for the crew door that would take me to the back corridors. My hand found the panel, pressed where Zeno had told me to press. The door blinked from red to amber to green.

I was through.

The corridor behind the sanctuary was utilitarian—none of the religious decoration, just metal walls and service panels. This was where the real work happened, where the machinery of faith met the machinery of control.

"Left past the holo-font, second hatch," Zeno directed. "You'll see a maintenance tech—that's Lazlo, my guy. He owes me for fixing his synth organ."

I found him exactly where Zeno said he'd be—lanky kid in coveralls, holding a wrench like he was supposed to be doing something important. He saw my robe, nodded respectfully, and stepped aside.

"Blessings, father," he mumbled.

"And to you, son," I replied, not breaking stride.

The second hatch opened with my spoofed badge. Cold air hit my face, smelling like recycled atmosphere and responsibility. I was close.

The reliquary wasn't gold—it was gunmetal gray with polite etchings, designed to look humble while hiding a fortune. Cases sat on shock mounts, each one holding something valuable that the Pure Dawn wanted protected. And in the center, in a cradle of black glass, was the seed.

The Black Book. Vale's dirty little secret. Every name, every payment, every off-the-books operation in the sector, all compressed into a ceramic wafer the size of my thumb.

"Beautiful, isn't it?" a voice said behind me.

I spun, hand going for the weapon I wasn't carrying.

Bone Mask stood in the doorway, calm as a statue. Up close, the mask was even more unsettling—smooth bone with a gold rim, eye slits that showed nothing but darkness.

"Relax," he said. "I'm not here to stop you. I'm here to make sure you do it right."

"You could've led with that," I said, heart still pounding.

"Where's the drama in that?" He moved past me, examined the seed cradle. "Biometric lock, just like I said. Press the glove here, let it read the prayer code. The cradle will open. Take the seed, leave the dummy Zeno made. You have sixty seconds before the dummy fails authentication."

I pulled on the priest glove Zeno had made—synthetic skin that hummed with warmth and fake piety. I pressed my palm to the cradle's halo. It shivered, thought about it, then opened like a flower.

The seed sat there, small and unassuming. It hummed—not a sound, but a feeling, like standing next to something that knew too many secrets.

For a second, I saw things. Flashes of information bleeding through. Names I recognized. Faces. Payments. Orders. And there, buried in the data like a knife in the heart—

Ky. My brother's name. The order that had him spaced. Vale's signature.

Rage hit me so hard I almost crushed the seed in my hand.

"Don't," Bone Mask said quietly. "Don't listen to it. Take it and leave."

I forced my hand to move, pulled the seed from its nest, slipped it into the velvet pouch Auntie had given me. The pouch hummed, out of phase, confusing the security sensors built into the wafer. I set down Zeno's dummy seed—a perfect copy that would pass inspection for exactly sixty seconds.

"Now run," Bone Mask said.

· · ·

I made it back to the corridor before the alarms started. Not loud sirens—nothing that would panic the congregation—but a soft, insistent chime that told security something was wrong.

"Vale knows," Zeno said in my ear. "The dummy just failed. He's mobilizing security. Get out. Now."

I walked fast but didn't run. Running was guilt. Walking was just a priest with somewhere to be.

I made it back to the sanctuary just as Trixx's song hit its peak. She held the note, perfect and pure, then broke it deliberately. The sound shattered into an overtone that made half the ship's microphones glitch. The console pit flooded red with error messages.

In the chaos, I slipped out through the same door I'd entered. Hark was already moving toward the exit, duffel bag in hand. Trixx descended from the choir loft, veil bright, acting concerned like everyone else.

We walked toward the ramp.

Vale appeared in our path.

He stood at the bottom of the ramp, uniform perfect, expression cold. Behind him, two armed guards with plasma rifles. To his right, a senior chaplain in elaborate robes—not Bone Mask, someone else. Someone official.

"Stop," Vale said. Not loud. He didn't need to be loud.

We stopped.

"You're making a mistake," he continued. "Whatever you think you're taking, it's not worth dying for."

"Everything's worth dying for if the price is right," I said through my veil.

His eyes narrowed. He knew my voice. "Mr. DeLeon. I'm disappointed. I expected you to at least try to be subtle."

"Subtle's boring."

"So is prison. So is execution. So is watching everyone you care about suffer because you couldn't resist playing hero." He stepped closer. "Return what you stole. Right now. And I'll consider your trespassing an administrative error. No charges. No consequences. You walk away."

"And if I don't?"

"Then you don't walk at all."

Trixx's hand moved inside her robe. Hark shifted his weight, ready. I felt the velvet pouch burning against my ribs like a coal made of secrets.

"You're standing in a church," the senior chaplain said, voice heavy with authority. "Spilling blood here would be... unfortunate."

"Then maybe nobody should bleed," I said.

Vale studied me, trying to read through the veil. "You're writing a story you can't finish," he said quietly.

"I'm finishing one you started."

His hand moved toward his sidearm.

And then everything went to shit.

.　　.　　.

The lights went out.

Not all of them—just enough to create confusion. Zeno's work, hacking the transport's power distribution. Emergency lighting kicked in, bathing everything in red.

"Go!" Bone Mask's voice shouted from somewhere in the chaos.

We ran.

The guards raised their rifles but hesitated—too many civilians, too much risk of hitting innocent priests. That hesitation cost them. We were past them, down the ramp, into the dock before they could get authorization to fire.

"Stop them!" Vale shouted. "Lock down Dock H!"

But Zeno was faster. The dock doors didn't close. The security barriers didn't activate. We ran through the crowd of pilgrims and tourists, our robes making us look like scared clergy fleeing danger instead of thieves fleeing justice.

Behind us, Vale gave chase, but he was in uniform, obvious, and the crowd slowed him down. By the time he cleared the congregation, we'd already ducked into a maintenance corridor.

"Robes off," Hark said.

We stripped fast, dumping the holographic vestments into a disposal chute. Underneath, we wore civilian clothes—just another group of station workers. The veils went into pockets. Hark slung the duffel over his shoulder like it contained laundry instead of stolen intelligence.

"Service passage, Gate G," Zeno said. "Thirty seconds before they realize you left through maintenance."

We walked. Not running. Running drew attention. We were just workers, heading home, nothing to see.

Gate G opened for us. The Verge air hit my face like freedom—recycled, thin, tasting like oil and old prayers, but ours. We were out.

"Where's the car?" Trixx asked.

"Maintenance Bay Seven," I said.

We ran now. Really ran. Feet pounding on metal grating, breath coming hard. Behind us, we heard Vale's voice on the dock speakers, ordering a station-wide lockdown.

Too late.

The Caprice sat waiting, engines already warm. Zeno had prepped her, knowing we'd need to move fast. We piled in, Hark taking the back seat, Trixx shotgun, me behind the wheel where I belonged.

I punched the thrusters and we screamed out of the bay, leaving Axis Ward behind in a blur of speed and stolen secrets.

●   ●   ●

We didn't breathe easy until we were three sectors away, buried in the anonymous traffic of the Verge's shipping lanes. The cloak-mesh made us look like just another cargo hauler, and nobody paid attention to cargo haulers.

"We did it," Trixx said, laughing with relief and disbelief. "We actually fucking did it."

"Don't celebrate yet," Hark said. "Vale's gonna tear this sector apart looking for us."

"Let him look," I said. I pulled the velvet pouch from my jacket, felt the seed inside. "We got what we came for."

"And what exactly did we come for?" Trixx asked.

I thought about the flash I'd seen in the reliquary. Ky's name. Vale's signature. Proof that my brother's death wasn't an accident or justified action—it was murder, ordered and executed by a Fed who thought he was above consequences.

"Justice," I said quietly.

"Justice don't pay bills," Hark said. "Auntie does."

He was right. We needed to deliver the seed, collect our payment. But first...

"Zeno," I said into my comm. "You still got that encryption setup?"

"Yeah, why?"

"Because I need you to copy this seed before we give it to Auntie. Make a backup. Hidden. Something nobody can trace."

"That's... that's dangerous, Nova. If Auntie finds out—"

"She won't. Can you do it?"

A pause. Then: "Yeah. I can do it. Meet me at the shop."

. . .

Zeno's shop was in the depths of Nova Block, hidden behind a legitimate repair business that fixed hover bikes for kids who couldn't afford real mechanics. The back room was where the real work happened—rows of equipment, screens showing code cascading like digital rain, the smell of solder and ambition.

He took the seed from me with hands that shook slightly. Not from fear—from excitement. This was the kind of tech he lived for.

"This is gonna take a few hours," he said, connecting the seed to his equipment. "The encryption is military-grade, layered, probably got countermeasures I haven't even seen before. But I can crack it. Copy it. Make it look like we never touched it."

"How long?" I asked.

"Three hours. Maybe four. Go get some rest. I'll call when it's done."

We left him to his work. Back at my apartment, exhaustion hit me like a freight train. The adrenaline crash was brutal—hands shaking, heart still racing, mind replaying every moment of the heist looking for mistakes.

Trixx collapsed on my couch, didn't even make it to the bedroom. "That was too close," she said. "Vale almost had us."

"But he didn't."

"This time." She looked at me with tired eyes. "Next time we might not be so lucky."

"There won't be a next time," I said. "We deliver the seed, get paid, and leave. Just like we planned."

"You promise?"

"I promise."

But even as I said it, I knew I was lying. Because I'd seen Ky's name in that seed. I'd seen proof that Vale had killed him. And I couldn't just walk away from that. Not now. Not ever.

Hark must've seen it on my face because he shook his head slowly. "Don't do it, kid."

"Do what?"

"Whatever you're thinking. That look says revenge. Revenge says dead."

"Vale killed my brother."

"Yeah. And you got proof now. So what you gonna do? Go shoot him? Turn yourself into a cop killer? Give him exactly what he wants—an excuse to wipe out the whole Block looking for you?"

"Then what am I supposed to do?"

"Be smart. Use what you got. Don't waste it on anger." He stood, metal hand glinting in the low light. "I'm going to sleep. You should too. Clear head makes better decisions than tired rage."

He left. Trixx was already asleep on the couch, her breathing soft and even. I covered her with a blanket, kissed her forehead, and went to stand by the window.

Outside, Nova Block hummed and breathed and lived. Somewhere out there, Vale was planning his next move. Somewhere, Auntie was counting her money. Somewhere, Bone Mask was vanishing back into whatever shadows he'd crawled from.

And here I was, standing in my shitty apartment with proof of murder in my pocket and no idea what to do with it.

The comm buzzed. Zeno.

"It's done. Come get it."

+ + +

CHAPTER 7

Payday and Consequences

Zeno looked like he hadn't slept in days, which was probably true. His eyes were bloodshot, cybernetic implants glowing brighter than usual, fingers still twitching like he was typing code in his dreams. But he was grinning like a kid who'd just solved the hardest puzzle in the universe.

"I did it," he said, holding up two identical-looking chips. "Perfect copies. The encryption was insane—military-grade, quantum-locked, with countermeasures that tried to fry my equipment twice. But I cracked it."

I took one of the chips. It looked exactly like the seed I'd stolen from the chaplain transport, down to the faint hum it made against my palm.

"Which one's which?" I asked.

"This one's the original," Zeno said, pointing to the one in his hand. "That one's the copy. Functionally identical. Every file, every name, every dirty secret Vale's been hiding. It's all there."

"Can they trace the copy back to us?"

"Not unless they're gods. I used ghost protocols, routed the data through dead servers, encrypted it with keys that don't exist in any database. As far as the universe is concerned, this copy was never made."

"Good." I pocketed the copy, felt its weight like a promise. "The original goes to Auntie. The copy stays hidden until I decide what to do with it."

"And what are you gonna do with it?" Zeno asked carefully.

I thought about Ky. About seeing his name in the Black Book, Vale's signature authorizing his execution. About all the other names in there—people the Federation had killed, disappeared, erased from existence because they were inconvenient.

"I don't know yet," I said. "But I'll figure it out."

Zeno looked worried but didn't push. Smart kid. He knew when to ask questions and when to shut up.

"Auntie's waiting for you," he said. "She messaged me an hour ago. Wants the seed delivered today. She's getting impatient."

"Then let's not keep her waiting."

. . .

Bay Twelve felt different this time. More tense. More dangerous. Auntie's projection chair was already there when we arrived, but she wasn't alone. Two large men stood behind her throne—muscle with good suits and better weapons. Her security, I assumed. She'd never needed them before, which meant she was taking this seriously.

"Little bell," she said as I approached. Her smile was warm, but her eyes were calculating. "You've caused quite a stir."

"It's what I do best."

"Indeed." She gestured and one of her men stepped forward, holding a scanner. "Before we proceed, I need to verify the merchandise. You understand."

"Verify away."

I handed over the original seed. The man took it carefully, like it might explode, and placed it in a specialized reader. Lights flickered. Code scrolled across a holographic display. Auntie watched, patient, as her expert examined the data.

"It's authentic," the man said after a long moment. "Federation encryption, recent timestamp, contents match the expected profile. This is the Black Book."

"Excellent." Auntie's smile widened. She made a gesture and a panel opened in the floor. A black case rose up, sleek and expensive. "Your payment. Three hundred seventy-five thousand credits. Clean, untraceable, Rhys-signed."

I took the case, opened it. Inside were credit chips—flowers of glass, each one glowing with internal light. More money than most people saw in a lifetime. Enough to disappear, to start over, to build something real.

"Pleasure doing business," I said.

"The pleasure is mine." Auntie stood—a rare gesture. She walked over to me, small and soft and more dangerous than any weapon I'd ever held. "You've done well, Nova. Very well. You've given me leverage over Vale, over the Federation. That's worth more than money."

"Happy to help."

"Are you?" She tilted her head, studying me. "Because I see something in your eyes. Anger. Pain. The look of a man who's planning something stupid."

I didn't answer. Couldn't lie to her, not when she was reading me like a book.

"Whatever you're thinking," she said quietly, "don't. Vale is a problem, yes. But he's a manageable problem. Going after him directly will only make things worse. For you, for your crew, for everyone in the Verge."

"He killed my brother."

"Yes. And I'm sorry for that. Truly. But revenge won't bring him back. It'll only get you killed."

"Maybe I don't care."

"You should." She put a hand on my arm, gentle but firm. "Because you're too valuable to waste on a suicide mission. You have talent, Nova. You have a crew who loves you. You have a future if you're smart enough to take it."

She pulled back, returned to her throne. "The Verge needs people like you. People who can move between the shadows and the light. People who aren't afraid to steal from gods. Don't throw that away for pride."

"I'll think about it," I said.

"Do more than think." She waved a hand, dismissing us. "Now go. Spend your money wisely. Rest. And when you're ready for another job, come find me."

We left with our payment, but her words echoed in my head all the way back to the Caprice.

•   •   •

Back at my apartment, we divided the money. It took hours—counting credits, transferring funds to hidden accounts, making sure everything was clean and untraceable. By the time we finished, we were all millionaires.

Hark stared at his share like he didn't quite believe it was real. "This is enough to retire," he said quietly. "Buy a place on one of the agricultural stations. Spend my last years growing tomatoes instead of shooting people."

"You should," I said.

"Should. But won't." He looked at me. "Not while you're still here, doing stupid shit that's gonna get you killed."

"I can take care of myself."

"Yeah, that's what every dead kid says." He pocketed his credit chips. "I'm gonna go sleep for about a week. Try not to start any wars while I'm unconscious."

"No promises."

He left. Trixx and I were alone, sitting on my couch, surrounded by more money than we'd ever imagined having.

"We could leave," she said. "Right now. Pack a bag, take this money, and disappear. Vale would never find us. We could have a real life, Nova. A good life."

"I know."

"But you're not gonna do it, are you?"

I looked at her. At her beautiful face, glow-ink pulsing soft purple, eyes that saw right through every lie I'd ever told.

"Not yet," I admitted. "I need to finish this first."

"Finish what? What's left to finish?"

"Vale needs to pay for what he did."

"He will pay. The Black Book will destroy him. Auntie will leak it, Vale will get arrested or demoted or worse. Justice will happen. You don't have to do anything."

"It's not the same."

"Why? Because you won't get to pull the trigger yourself?" She stood up, frustrated. "This is about revenge, Nova. Not justice. Revenge. And revenge gets people killed."

"Then maybe I deserve to die."

"Don't you fucking dare." She was in my face now, anger and fear mixing in her voice. "Don't you dare make me fall in love with you and then throw your life away like it doesn't matter. Like I don't matter."

"Trixx—"

"No. Listen to me. Ky is dead. That's horrible. That's unfair. But killing Vale won't bring him back. It'll just make you a murderer too. And then what? You go to prison? You die? What happens to me? To Hark? To everyone who cares about you?"

I didn't have an answer.

She grabbed my face, forced me to look at her. "Promise me you won't do anything stupid. Promise me you'll at least think about leaving with me. Promise me I'm not wasting my love on a dead man."

The word sat in my throat. Heavy. Complicated. She deserved better than a lie, but the truth would break her heart.

"I'm gonna try," I said. "That's all I got."

She searched my eyes for a long moment. Then something in her face shifted—not acceptance, but maybe understanding. The understanding of someone who loved a man she couldn't save from himself.

We ended up in bed, clothes scattered across the floor, her skin glowing bright in the darkness. We made love rough and urgent, like people who knew time was running out. When we finished, we lay tangled together, sweating and breathing hard.

"I love you," she whispered.

"I love you too."

"Then prove it. Choose me. Choose us. Choose life."

I wanted to. God, I wanted to. But every time I closed my eyes, I saw Ky's face. Heard his laugh. Remembered the way he'd followed me around when we were kids, looking up to his big brother like I was some kind of hero.

I'd failed him. I hadn't protected him. And now he was dead because of it.

How could I just walk away from that?

.   .   .

The next morning, the mesh exploded with news. Operation Exodus had officially begun. Vale had gotten authorization from Echelon Prime to conduct a "security sweep" of the Verge—a fancy way of saying he was going to kick down doors, arrest anyone who looked at him wrong, and make life hell for everyone who lived in Nova Block.

The official justification was "preventing terrorist activity." The real reason was finding me.

Hark called first. "Turn on the mesh. Channel Seven."

I did. Vale's face filled the screen—perfect uniform, perfect hair, perfect smile that didn't reach his eyes. He was giving a press conference in one of Echelon's fancy briefing rooms, surrounded by Federation flags and the kind of authority that came from never having to worry about rent.

"—increasing evidence of organized crime activity in the Verge sectors," he was saying. "Smuggling, theft, violence against Federation personnel. We have identified several key individuals who pose a significant threat to station security."

My picture appeared on the screen. Old ID photo from when I was eighteen, before I'd grown into my face. The caption read: KASH "NOVA" DELEON - WANTED FOR THEFT, ASSAULT, TERRORISM.

Terrorism. That was new.

"Mr. DeLeon is considered armed and dangerous," Vale continued. "Anyone with information regarding his whereabouts should contact Federation Security immediately. A reward of one hundred thousand credits has been posted for information leading to his capture."

The screen switched to other photos. Trixx. Hark. Zeno. Even Auntie Rhys, though they listed her as a "person of interest" rather than a suspect.

"Operation Exodus will restore order to these sectors," Vale said. "We will not tolerate criminal elements endangering honest citizens. The Federation stands for safety, for justice, for the rule of law. And we will enforce that law, no matter how difficult the task."

The broadcast ended. I sat there, staring at the blank screen, my face still burning in my memory.

"He's coming for us," Trixx said quietly. She'd been watching over my shoulder. "He's not even hiding it anymore."

"Good," I said. "Let him come."

"Nova—"

"I'm tired of running. Tired of hiding. Tired of letting him dictate how we live our lives." I stood up, grabbed my jacket. "He wants a war? Fine. We'll give him one."

"This is insane. He's got the entire Federation behind him. We're just—"

"Just what? Criminals? Terrorists? That's what he calls us, but we're just people trying to survive in a system that wants us dead. Fuck him. Fuck the Federation. Fuck everyone who thinks they can push us around because we're from the Verge."

I pulled out the copied seed, held it up. "This has everything. Every name, every crime, every dirty secret. We leak this, Vale loses everything. His career, his reputation, maybe even his freedom."

"And if we leak it, we lose our leverage," Trixx said. "Auntie will know we made a copy. She'll come after us too."

"Then we run. Like you wanted. We burn it all down and disappear."

"That's not a plan, Nova. That's suicide with extra steps."

"You got a better idea?"

She was quiet for a long moment. Then: "Yes. We wait. We let Auntie handle Vale. She's got the original Black Book. She's got power, resources, connections. She can destroy him without us risking everything."

"And what if she doesn't? What if she just uses it for leverage, keeps Vale around because he's useful?"

"Then we still have the copy. We still have options. But we don't burn our only lifeline just because you're angry."

She was right. I hated that she was right, but she was.

"Fine," I said. "We wait. But not forever. If Auntie doesn't handle Vale, we will."

"Deal."

•   •   •

Three days passed. Three days of watching the mesh, watching Vale's goons tear through the Verge, arresting people on bullshit charges, making examples of anyone who'd ever looked at them sideways.

Mama Leena called, scared. They'd been to her building, asking questions about Ky, about me. She'd told them nothing, but they'd threatened her, told her obstruction of justice was a crime.

I sent her more money. Enough to relocate if she needed to, enough to hire a lawyer if they arrested her. It wasn't enough— nothing was enough—but it was something.

Zeno went underground, literally. He moved his operation to the lower levels, the forgotten maintenance tunnels where the Federation didn't patrol because the air was bad and the gangs were worse. He was safe there, but isolated.

Hark bought a gun. Not his usual piece—something bigger, military-grade, the kind of weapon you bought when you were expecting war. He didn't say anything about it, just showed up at my door one day with the gun case and a look that said *get ready.*

And Trixx... Trixx tried to hold us together. Cooked meals even though I wasn't hungry. Made me laugh even when nothing was funny. Made love to me every night like she was trying to memorize my body before it became a memory.

On the fourth day, Auntie sent a message.

Come to Bay Twelve. Alone. Important.

I went. Told Trixx I'd be back soon, told Hark to watch her while I was gone. Took the Caprice through the back routes, watching for tails, making sure nobody followed.

Bay Twelve was different this time. The projection chair was gone. Instead, Auntie stood in person—first time I'd seen her physically present. She was smaller than I'd expected, older, wearing the same velvet but looking tired in a way holograms couldn't show.

"Thank you for coming," she said. No smile this time. Just weariness. "We need to talk about Vale."

"What about him?"

"He's escalating. Operation Exodus is worse than I anticipated. He's not just looking for you—he's using you as an excuse to purge the entire Verge. Arrests, deportations, executions. He's building concentration camps in the outer sectors, calling them 'processing centers.'"

"And you're telling me this why?"

"Because I made a mistake." She looked me in the eyes. "I thought the Black Book would be enough. That threatening to leak it would make him back down. But he doesn't care. He's willing to risk exposure if it means cleansing the Verge of 'undesirables.'"

"So leak it. Burn him."

"I can't. Not yet. If I leak it now, it'll make him a martyr. The Federation will cover for him, say the data was fabricated, use it as proof that the Verge needs to be controlled even harder."

"Then what the fuck are we supposed to do?"

She reached into her pocket, pulled out a small device. A comm unit, encrypted. "I have a contact. Someone inside Federation Intelligence. They can get the Black Book into the right hands— hands that will actually use it to prosecute Vale rather than protect him. But they need time. Two weeks."

"Two weeks? People are dying now."

"I know. But if we move too fast, Vale wins. Trust me. I've been doing this longer than you've been alive."

I took the comm unit. "Two weeks. Then what?"

"Then Vale falls. And the Verge gets a chance to breathe." She put a hand on my shoulder. "Stay alive until then. Stay hidden. Don't give him an excuse to kill you."

"I'll try."

"Do better than try."

•   •   •

I made it halfway back to Nova Block before they found me.

Two Federation interceptors, coming in fast from both sides. They'd been waiting, watching, knew I'd meet with Auntie.

"Nova," Zeno's voice crackled in my ear. "You got company. Two heavies, military-grade. They're boxing you in."

"I see them."

"Can you outrun them?"

I looked at the Caprice's readouts. We were fast, but those interceptors were faster. Military engines, military shields, military everything.

"Not a chance," I said.

"Then what are you gonna do?"

I thought about Trixx. About Hark. About Zeno and Mama Leena and everyone I'd dragged into this mess. Thought about Ky, dead because I hadn't been smart enough or fast enough or good enough to protect him.

Thought about the Black Book, sitting in my pocket like a loaded gun.

"Something stupid," I said.

And I punched the thrusters, heading straight for the nearest interceptor instead of away from it.

✦ ✦ ✦

CHAPTER 8

Chicken Run

The interceptor's pilot saw me coming and panicked. I could tell because he broke left hard, shields flaring bright blue as he tried to dodge. But I wasn't actually trying to hit him—that would've been suicide, and I wasn't quite that stupid yet.

I was trying to get past him.

The Caprice screamed through the gap between the interceptors, so close I could see the Fed insignia on their hulls. Laser fire lit up the space behind me, red tracers cutting through the void like angry fireflies. They missed. Barely.

"Nova, what the fuck!" Zeno's voice crackled in my ear, half-panicked, half-impressed. "You just flew between two military interceptors!"

"I know!" I yanked the stick hard right, diving toward the underside of Nova Block, using the station's mass as cover. The Caprice's engine whined, pushing limits it wasn't designed for. "Tell me something useful!"

"They're splitting up! One's going high, one's going low. They're trying to box you in again."

"Let them try."

I killed the engine, let momentum carry me forward while I sparked up a Black Death with shaking hands. The cigarette tasted like adrenaline and bad decisions. Through the canopy, I could see the Verge spinning slowly below me—home, prison, graveyard, all rolled into one rusted-out space station.

Trixx was gonna kill me for this. If Vale didn't kill me first.

The proximity alarm screamed. I punched the engine back to life and rolled left, feeling the Caprice groan under the strain. A plasma bolt sizzled past where I'd been a second ago, close enough that I could see my shields flicker and dim.

"Shields at sixty percent," the car's AI announced in that calm, female voice that sounded way too chill for a firefight. "Multiple hostile locks detected. Recommend evasive action."

"No shit," I muttered.

I dove again, this time heading for the shipping lanes—the crowded space between sectors where cargo haulers moved slow and stupid. It was risky. If I clipped one of those big-ass freighters, the Caprice would crumple like paper. But the interceptors were faster than me, better armed than me, and probably had better pilots than me.

My only advantage was that I was crazy and they weren't.

The shipping lane opened up ahead—a river of metal and lights, dozens of ships moving in coordinated patterns that took years to learn. I punched through the traffic like a bullet, weaving between haulers that were ten times my size, feeling the Caprice shake every time I got too close to their engine wash.

"Nova, you're gonna get yourself killed!" Zeno yelled.

"Not today," I said, though I wasn't sure I believed it.

One of the interceptors tried to follow me into the lanes. I watched in my rear display as he threaded through the first few ships, careful and precise. But then a hauler changed course—some computer glitch or human error—and the interceptor had to pull up hard to avoid a collision. By the time he recovered, I was three lanes over and accelerating.

The second interceptor was smarter. He went around the traffic, burning thrusters to circle wide and cut me off on the other side. Military tactics. Textbook shit. Probably would've worked if I was trying to run in a straight line.

But I wasn't.

I killed the engine again, flipped the Caprice end over end using attitude thrusters, and fired up the reverse engines. The car screamed—metal groaning, bolts rattling, every warning light on the dash lighting up like a Christmas tree. For a second, I thought I'd pushed too hard, that the whole thing would come apart.

But it held.

And now I was flying backward at sixty percent thrust, watching the interceptor come at me head-on.

"Say hello," I whispered, and opened fire.

The Caprice's guns weren't military-grade. They were street-legal plasma repeaters, the kind you bought to look tough, not to actually fight. But at this range, with the interceptor coming straight at me, they didn't need to be good. They just needed to be loud.

Blue plasma bolts hammered into the interceptor's shields. They held—of course they held—but the pilot got spooked. He broke off, diving under me, and I flipped the Caprice right-side-up and burned hard toward the nearest docking arm.

"Where you going?" Zeno asked.

"Gamma Section," I said. "The maze."

"Oh, that's smart. That's actually smart."

Gamma Section was the old part of the station, built before engineers figured out that straight lines and logical layouts were good ideas. It was a nightmare of narrow corridors, dead-end tunnels, and maintenance shafts that hadn't been mapped in decades. People got lost in there and died before they found their way out.

But I'd grown up here. I knew every shortcut, every hidden passage, every place where the metal was thin enough to punch through if you were desperate.

I hit the entrance to Gamma doing speeds that would've gotten me arrested if the Feds weren't already trying to kill me. The Caprice barely fit through the opening, scraping paint off both sides. Behind me, the interceptors had to slow down, had to be careful in the tight space.

Good.

The maze opened up ahead—a twisting path of metal corridors lit by flickering emergency lights. I flew by instinct, muscle memory, the stick feeling like an extension of my hands. Left, right, up, down, through gaps that looked too small until I was already through them.

The interceptors tried to follow. I heard them on the open channels, their pilots cursing and calling for backup, saying they had a "rogue element in Gamma Section, request additional units."

"They're calling for backup," Zeno said. "You got maybe five minutes before this place is swarming with Feds."

"Then I better move fast."

I pushed deeper into the maze, into sections so old the lights didn't work anymore. My headlights cut through the darkness, illuminating walls covered in graffiti and rust. This was the forgotten part of the station, the place where the poor and the desperate lived in hab-units that barely had air.

My comm crackled. Different voice this time. Calm, professional, the kind of voice that gave orders and expected them to be followed.

"Mr. DeLeon." Vale. Of course it was Vale. "You're making this harder than it needs to be."

I didn't answer. Just kept flying, kept dodging, kept trying to think of a way out that didn't end with me in a Federation cell or a Federation grave.

"I know you're listening," Vale continued. "Your friend Zeno is very good at encryption, but not good enough. I've been monitoring your channels since you left Bay Twelve."

Shit.

"I want to make you an offer," Vale said. "Turn yourself in. Right now. Land your vehicle and surrender. In exchange, I'll guarantee the safety of your crew. Miss Trixx, Mr. Harkness, young Zeno—they'll all walk away from this. You have my word."

"Your word ain't worth shit," I said before I could stop myself.

Vale laughed. It was a cold sound, like ice cracking. "Perhaps. But it's worth more than what you'll get by running. You can't hide forever, Mr. DeLeon. This station is mine. Every sector, every corridor, every breath of recycled air. And now that Operation Exodus is in full effect, I have the authority to search anywhere, arrest anyone, use any means necessary to maintain order."

"You mean kill anyone who ain't pure enough for your Echelon friends."

"I mean restore civilization to a sector that has forgotten what civilization means." His voice hardened. "You killed one of my officers. Stole Federation property. Conspired with known criminals. These are capital offenses. I should execute you on sight. But I'm offering you mercy. Surrender. Protect your crew. Be a man for once instead of a child playing at revolution."

I thought about Ky. About Vale's signature on the execution order, cold and official and final.

"Go fuck yourself," I said.

"So be it."

The comm cut out. And then the whole section shook.

"They're breaching the hull!" Zeno screamed. "They're cutting through from outside! Nova, get out of there!"

I looked back. Through the narrow corridor behind me, I could see cutting torches—bright blue flames eating through metal, opening the section to vacuum. They were going to vent the whole area, kill everyone inside just to get to me.

"How many people in this section?" I asked.

"Maybe fifty. Sixty. Families. Kids. Nova, you gotta move!"

I couldn't. If I left, those people died. Vale would seal the breach after I was gone, let them suffocate while he chased me to the next section.

"Nova!"

"I hear you!" I spun the Caprice around, heading back toward the breach. "Tell those people to seal their hab-units and pray their doors hold!"

"What are you doing?"

"Something stupid," I said again.

The cutting torch was almost through. I could see the blade of light getting wider, could feel the air getting thinner as pressure dropped. In a few seconds, the hull would breach completely and everything that wasn't bolted down would get sucked into space.

Including me.

I hit the cargo release, dumped everything that wasn't essential—spare parts, tools, the bottle of Remy I'd been saving. The Caprice got lighter, faster. I needed every advantage I could get.

The hull breached.

Air exploded outward, pulling me toward the opening. The Caprice's engine screamed, fighting the suction, barely winning. Through the gap in the hull, I could see the interceptor outside, its pilot probably grinning, thinking he had me.

I fired everything I had.

Plasma bolts, missiles, even the electromagnetic pulse gun Zeno had installed for emergencies. All of it, point-blank range, right into the interceptor's face.

His shields held for maybe two seconds. Then they collapsed.

The missiles hit first—two small warheads that weren't designed to kill, just to disable. They punched through the interceptor's armor and exploded inside the engine compartment. The interceptor shuddered, sparked, started to drift.

The EMP hit next. It fried every electronic system in range, including half my own gear. The Caprice's engine stuttered and died. The lights cut out. The dash went dark.

And we started falling.

No, not falling. Drifting. Toward the hull breach, toward space, toward death by vacuum.

I yanked manual controls, pulled the emergency lever that most people didn't even know existed. Mechanical linkages groaned to life—cables and gears and pre-digital tech from before everything needed a computer to work. The attitude thrusters sputtered, coughed, then caught.

The Caprice lurched sideways, away from the breach. We scraped against the corridor wall, losing paint and pride but not momentum. I threaded us through a maintenance shaft, into a different section, then another, putting distance between us and the venting air.

Behind me, emergency crews were already sealing the breach, saving the people I'd nearly gotten killed.

"Nova?" Zeno's voice was shaky. "You alive?"

"Maybe," I said. My hands were shaking. My whole body was shaking. "Engine's dead. Half my systems are fried. And I think I'm about to puke."

"Where are you?"

I checked the manual compass, the kind that used magnets instead of satellites. "Delta Section. Lower levels. Near the old market."

"Okay. Okay, I can work with that. There's a garage there— Mama Kess's place. She owes me a favor. Get there and lay low. I'll talk to her, get you hidden until the heat dies down."

"And the other interceptor?"

"Still flying. But he lost you in the maze. Federation's spreading out, searching every section. You got maybe an hour before they lock down Delta and start going door to door."

"Then I better hurry."

I nursed the Caprice through the corridors on manual controls, going slow, staying quiet. The old market appeared ahead—a sprawling bazaar of shops and stalls selling everything from food to weapons to fake IDs. It was crowded even now, even with Operation Exodus in full swing. People still needed to eat. Still needed to live.

Still needed hope.

Mama Kess's garage was at the edge of the market, marked by a faded sign that said "REPAIRS" in three languages. I parked the

Caprice in the alley beside it, killed the remaining systems, and sat there in the dark, breathing hard.

I'd survived. Somehow. Against two military interceptors and Vale's entire fucking operation.

But I couldn't keep running forever. Sooner or later, they'd find me. They'd find Trixx, Hark, Zeno, everyone I cared about.

And then what?

I pulled out the copied seed, held it in my palm. The Black Book. Everything Vale had ever done, every crime, every murder, every dirty secret. Enough to destroy him.

Or enough to get me killed trying.

My comm buzzed. Trixx's voice, scared and angry and beautiful.

"Nova? Baby? Zeno said you're alive. Said you're hiding in Delta. Is that true?"

"Yeah," I said. My voice sounded tired even to me. "I'm alive."

"Thank God. Stay there. I'm coming to get you."

"No. It's too dangerous. Vale's got the whole station locked down."

"I don't care. You're not doing this alone anymore. I'm coming. Hark's coming. We're your crew, remember? We don't leave family behind."

I wanted to argue. Wanted to tell her to run, to take the money and disappear while she still could. But I was too tired to lie anymore.

"Okay," I said. "But be careful."

"Always am," she said, and the lie made me smile.

I leaned back in the seat, closed my eyes, and let the exhaustion wash over me. Outside, I could hear voices—people talking, haggling, living their lives like the world wasn't falling apart.

Maybe it wasn't. Maybe it was just my world that was ending.

The Caprice's emergency lights flickered on, dim and red, painting everything the color of blood.

．　．　．

Two hours later, Trixx and Hark found me in Mama Kess's garage. The old woman had been good to her word—she'd hidden the Caprice under a tarp, locked the doors, and told the Federation search teams that she'd seen me heading toward the upper levels.

Trixx pulled me into a hug so tight I couldn't breathe. "You stupid, stupid man," she whispered. "You beautiful, reckless, stupid man."

"I know," I said.

Hark looked at the Caprice, at the damage, at the scorch marks and dents. "You flew through hell and came back," he said. "Not bad for a kid from the Verge."

"Not back yet," I said. "Vale's still out there. Still hunting us."

"Then we hunt him first," Hark said simply. He pulled out his new gun—the big military-grade one—and checked the charge. "You got the Black Book copy. We got skills. We got rage. And we got each other. That's enough."

"Is it?"

"Has to be." He looked at me with those cold eyes, one real and one glass. "Because running's over. Hiding's over. It's time to fight back."

Trixx pulled back, looked at me. Her glow-ink was pulsing fast, anxious. "Tell me we're not doing this. Tell me we're not going to war with the Federation."

I thought about Ky. About all the people Vale had killed. About the families being rounded up in Operation Exodus, shipped to processing centers that were really just concentration camps with better names.

I thought about the Black Book in my pocket, heavy as a gun.

"I'm sorry," I said. "But I can't promise that."

She closed her eyes. When she opened them again, they were hard. Determined. The look of someone who'd made a choice and would live with it, even if it killed her.

"Then we do it together," she said. "No more running solo. No more playing hero. If you're going to get yourself killed, I'm going to be right there with you."

"Me too," Hark said. "For better or worse."

"That's wedding vows," I said.

"Close enough," Hark said, and almost smiled.

My comm buzzed. Zeno's voice, excited and scared at the same time.

"Yo, you need to see this. Turn on Channel Seven. Right now."

I pulled up the mesh on my wrist display. Channel Seven was showing a live feed from Echelon Prime—some kind of press conference. Vale was standing at a podium, surrounded by Federation flags and serious-looking officers.

But he wasn't talking about Operation Exodus.

He was talking about Auntie Rhys.

"—arrested earlier today on charges of smuggling, conspiracy, and terrorism," Vale was saying. His face was calm, professional, the face of a man who'd won. "Ms. Rhys is believed to be the mastermind behind several recent criminal operations in the Verge sectors, including the theft of classified Federation materials. She is currently being held in Echelon Maximum Security pending trial."

The camera cut to Auntie being led away in chains. She looked small, tired, but not defeated. As the Feds walked her past the cameras, she looked directly at the lens.

Looked at me.

And mouthed two words: *Two weeks.*

The feed cut out.

"Fuck," I said.

"What does that mean?" Trixx asked. "Two weeks for what?"

I remembered what Auntie had said. About her contact in Federation Intelligence. About needing time to get the Black Book to the right people.

Two weeks until Vale fell.

If we could survive that long.

"It means we wait," I said. "Two weeks. We hide, we survive, and we wait for Auntie's plan to work."

"And if it doesn't work?" Hark asked.

I looked at the Caprice, at my crew, at the copy of the Black Book still sitting in my pocket like a loaded gun.

"Then we burn it all down ourselves," I said.

Outside, sirens wailed. Federation search teams, getting closer, tightening the net. In two weeks, either Vale would be destroyed or we would be.

There was no middle ground anymore.

No safe choices.

No way out except through.

"Come on," I said, grabbing my gear. "We need to move. Zeno's got a safehouse in the lower levels. We'll lay low there, figure out our next move."

"And then?" Trixx asked.

I looked at her, at Hark, at the life we'd built in the cracks and shadows of this dying station.

"Then we see if Auntie was right," I said. "If the Black Book can really bring down Vale. Or if we're all just dead people who haven't stopped breathing yet."

We left Mama Kess's garage through the back exit, moving through alleys and maintenance tunnels, ghosts in the machine. Above us, the Federation hunted. Around us, the Verge suffered. And ahead of us, two weeks stretched like an eternity.

Two weeks until everything changed.

Two weeks until war.

I sparked another Black Death, let the smoke fill my lungs, and kept walking into the darkness.

✦ ✦ ✦

INTERLUDE

The Lieutenant's Burden

Lieutenant Marcus Vale poured himself two fingers of whiskey—real whiskey, Earth-imported, not the synthetic garbage they served in the Verge—and studied the holographic display floating above his desk.

Forty-three arrests today. Twelve deportations. Three "resisting arrest" incidents that had resolved themselves permanently. The numbers were good. The numbers were always good when he ran operations personally.

His office in Federation High Command was immaculate. White walls, white furniture, white light. Clean. Pure. The way things should be. On the wall behind his desk hung his commendations— fifteen years of service, decorated twice for valor, promoted ahead of schedule because his superiors recognized what he was: a man who got results.

A man willing to do the work others found distasteful.

He pulled up the file on Kash DeLeon. The hybrid's face filled the screen—those blue-edged eyes that marked him as mixed, that copper hair wrapped in braids like some kind of tribal affectation. Half-human, half-Xytherian. An impossibility that should never have been allowed to exist.

Vale didn't hate hybrids. Hate was an emotion, and emotions were inefficient. What he felt was something colder, more practical:

the same clinical disgust a surgeon might feel toward a tumor. You didn't hate cancer. You simply removed it before it spread.

The door chimed. "Enter," he said without looking up.

Captain Torres walked in—a good officer, loyal, but soft. Too soft for what needed to be done. "Sir, the DeLeon subject escaped the intercept in Gamma Section. Two pilots injured, one vessel destroyed."

"I'm aware."

"Command is asking about the hull breach. Civilian casualties—"

"Were acceptable." Vale finally looked up. Torres flinched. They always flinched. "Seventeen residents of Sub-Level Eight. All documented hybrid sympathizers. Their removal from the population was... expedient."

"Sir, some of them were children."

"Some of them were future problems." Vale turned back to his display, pulling up the casualty report. Names, ages, genetic profiles. He scrolled through them with the same attention he might give a grocery list. "The Verge breeds resistance the way stagnant water breeds disease. You can't treat the symptoms. You have to drain the swamp."

Torres was silent. Vale could feel his discomfort, his moral objection, his weakness. Men like Torres were useful—they followed orders, maintained appearances, provided plausible deniability. But they would never understand the necessity of what Vale did.

They hadn't grown up in the border colonies, watching their father's farm fail because Xytherian imports undercut human labor. They hadn't seen their mother waste away from a disease the alien doctors could have cured but wouldn't—not for humans, not for the colonizers who'd "stolen" their trading routes. They hadn't buried a sister who'd made the mistake of loving a hybrid, who'd died giving birth to something that wasn't quite human and wasn't quite anything else.

Vale had buried her himself. Had looked at the thing that killed her—blue-edged eyes already open, already wrong—and felt nothing but cold certainty.

This was the future if left unchecked. Humanity diluted. Humanity weakened. Humanity bred out of existence by species that had been traveling the stars while humans were still living in caves.

"Operation Exodus is proceeding on schedule," Vale said, dismissing the casualty report. "Processing centers are at sixty percent capacity. By month's end, the Verge will be clean."

"And DeLeon?"

"A temporary embarrassment." Vale smiled—the expression that made subordinates nervous, that made suspects confess, that made his superiors overlook certain irregularities in his methods. "He thinks he's started a revolution. He's started a countdown. Every hour he runs, I learn more about his network. Every ally he contacts becomes a name on my list. He's not evading capture. He's mapping his own extinction."

Torres nodded, still uncomfortable, still obedient. "The Council is concerned about the footage leak. Public opinion—"

"Is manageable. The footage shows me executing a criminal who resisted arrest. The context is unfortunate, but context can be manufactured." He pulled up another file—media contacts, influencers, opinion-shapers who owed him favors or feared his files. "By next week, Nova DeLeon will be remembered as a terrorist who attacked Federation officers. His brother will be a tragic casualty of his violence. And I will be the hero who restored order."

"And if the hybrid coalition gains traction? The protests—"

"Will be contained. People protest when they feel safe enough to complain. Remove that safety, and they remember their priorities."

Vale finished his whiskey, savored the burn. "Fear is a more reliable tool than hope, Captain. Hope requires imagination. Fear only requires examples."

He stood, straightening his uniform with practiced precision. Every crease aligned. Every medal in place. The uniform of a man who believed in something larger than himself.

"Schedule a press conference for tomorrow," he said. "I want to announce the expansion of Operation Exodus to the outer sectors. And Captain? Find me the hybrid's woman. The purple one. She's the key to breaking him."

Torres hesitated. "Sir, targeting romantic partners—"

"Is efficient. DeLeon's weakness is sentiment. He killed Vex over his brother. He'll surrender for his lover." Vale walked to the window, looked out at the station spinning slowly against the stars. Millions of people out there. Millions of potential problems. "That's the difference between us and them, Captain. They act on emotion. We act on principle. That's why we win."

Torres saluted and left. Vale remained at the window, watching the void.

Somewhere out there, Nova DeLeon was running. Planning. Believing he could change things. It was almost admirable—the way insects were admirable, building their tiny civilizations in the cracks of human infrastructure. Busy. Purposeful. Ultimately irrelevant.

The Federation had survived for three centuries. It would survive this. It would survive everything, because men like Vale were willing to do what was necessary. To make the hard choices. To remove the tumors before they spread.

He thought about the hybrid child he'd seen executed that morning. A boy, maybe eight years old, caught stealing food from a Federation supply depot. The mother had screamed. The boy had cried. And Vale had felt nothing—not cruelty, not satisfaction, just the quiet certainty of a man performing routine maintenance.

You didn't hate the rust you scraped off a ship's hull. You simply removed it.

He poured another whiskey and returned to his reports. Tomorrow there would be more arrests. More deportations. More problems solved with the simple application of force and will.

The work was never done. But Lieutenant Marcus Vale was a patient man.

And patience, like purity, always won in the end.

✦ ✦ ✦

CHAPTER 9

Rats in the Walls

Zeno's safehouse was in Sub-Level Nine, which was a polite way of saying "the asshole of the station." Down here, the air recyclers barely worked, the lights flickered more than they stayed on, and the walls sweated condensation that smelled like rust and despair. Nobody came down here unless they had to. Not even the Feds.

Which made it perfect for hiding.

"Home sweet fucking home," Zeno said, keying open a door that looked like every other door in the corridor—dented, graffitied, forgotten. Inside was a single room, maybe twenty feet square, with a mattress on the floor, a jury-rigged computer setup that probably violated every electrical code ever written, and enough empty noodle containers to build a fort.

"You live here?" Trixx asked, trying to hide the disgust in her voice and failing.

"Sometimes," Zeno said defensively. "When I need to disappear. It ain't pretty, but it's off-grid. No official records. Power's tapped from the main line so there's no usage signature. And the walls are thick enough to block most scanning equipment."

"Most?" Hark asked.

"Look, you want guarantees, go buy insurance. You want to hide from the Federation, this is as good as it gets."

I looked around the room. There was one small window—if you could call it that—showing the exterior hull and the void beyond. Through it, I could see the distant lights of other stations, other habitats, places where people lived normal lives without worrying about getting disappeared by their own government.

Must be nice.

"How long we staying?" I asked.

Zeno shrugged. "Long as you need to. I got food for maybe a week if we ration. Water's recycled from the main system—tastes like ass but it won't kill you. And entertainment..." He gestured to his computer setup. "I got the entire mesh archived. Movies, shows, porn, news feeds, everything. We won't be bored."

"Just slowly suffocating in a metal box," Trixx muttered.

"Better than suffocating in a Federation cell," Hark said. He dropped his gear in the corner, pulled out his gun, and started field-stripping it. Old habits from his military days. Clean your weapon, secure your perimeter, prepare for the worst.

I sat on the mattress. It smelled like old sweat and defeat. "We need a plan."

"The plan is we wait," Trixx said. "Two weeks. Like Auntie said."

"And if her plan doesn't work?"

"Then we use your copy of the Black Book. Leak it ourselves. Burn Vale and run."

"Run where?" I asked. "Vale's got Operation Exodus going. Every sector's being searched. Every ship leaving the station is being inspected. Even if we make it out, where the fuck do we go?"

Nobody had an answer for that.

Zeno broke the silence. "I might have something. A contact on Freeport Station—you know, the independent colony out past the

Drift. They don't cooperate with the Federation. Don't extradite. It's basically a pirate haven, but they've got legitimate business too. We could disappear there."

"How much?" Hark asked.

"What?"

"How much to buy passage and new identities?"

Zeno thought about it. "Maybe two hundred thousand? Per person? New biometrics, clean backgrounds, the whole package."

I did the math. Four of us. Eight hundred thousand credits. We had about a million and a quarter from the jobs, but that money was supposed to be our future. Our way out. Spending most of it just to run...

"We'll think about it," I said.

"Don't think too long," Zeno said. "Every day we wait, Vale tightens the noose."

•   •   •

The first day in the safehouse was the hardest. We were all jumpy, paranoid, listening to every sound in the corridor outside. Every footstep could be Feds. Every voice could be a search team. Every creak of metal could be them cutting through the door.

But nothing happened.

Day two was worse. The boredom set in. There's only so many times you can check your weapons, count your money, or stare at the same four walls before you start losing your mind.

Trixx tried to keep busy. She did exercises—push-ups, sit-ups, the kind of prison workout Hark had taught her. She cleaned her guns until they gleamed. She even tried cooking with the shitty rations Zeno had stashed, making something that was supposed to be noodles with synthetic meat but tasted like cardboard soaked in salt.

We ate it anyway.

Hark was quiet. He sat in the corner, smoking herb and Nova Dust mixed together, staring at nothing. Sometimes he'd tell stories about his time in Titan Penitentiary—the fights, the gangs, the way you had to always watch your back or end up dead. Other times he'd just sit there, lost in memories I couldn't see.

Zeno worked on his computers, fingers flying across holographic keyboards, doing... something. I never understood half of what he did. Code, hacks, information gathering. He was plugged into the mesh 24/7, monitoring news feeds, tracking Federation movements, watching for any sign that Auntie's plan was working.

And me? I drank.

There was a bottle of cheap whiskey in Zeno's stash—some synthetic shit that tasted like paint thinner but got you drunk fast. I sat by that little window, smoking Black Deaths and working through the bottle, watching the station rotate slowly against the stars.

"You're gonna kill yourself like that," Trixx said on the third day. She sat next to me, took the bottle from my hands, took a pull herself. Made a face. "Jesus. That's horrible."

"That's the point."

She handed it back. "You wanna talk about it?"

"About what?"

"Whatever's eating you. And don't say nothing, because I know you. You got that look. Like you're planning something stupid."

I took another drink. "I keep thinking about Ky. About how he died. Vale ordered it, but Vex pulled the trigger. And I killed Vex, so that should make me feel better, right? That should be enough revenge."

"But it's not."

"No. It's not. Because Vex was just a tool. Vale's the one who wanted my brother dead. Vale's the one who saw Ky as just another mongrel to be eliminated. And until Vale pays, nothing's settled."

"Nova..."

"I know what you're gonna say. Revenge won't bring him back. It'll just get me killed. I've heard it from Auntie, from Hark, from you. And you're all right. But I can't let it go. Every time I close my eyes, I see Ky. Floating in space. Cold and alone and dead because some racist Fed decided hybrids weren't worth keeping alive."

Trixx was quiet for a long time. Then she said, "My mom was killed in a Federation raid."

I looked at her. "You never told me that."

"Never talk about it. What's the point? She's dead, the Feds who killed her are probably still out there living their lives, and nothing I do will change it." She took the bottle again, drank deep. "She was a smuggler. Small-time shit, nothing that should've gotten her killed. But they came in hot, no warnings, just started shooting. She was caught in the crossfire. Died bleeding out on the deck while I hid in a cargo container and listened to her scream."

"Trixx—"

"I was twelve. After that, I bounced around the Verge, did whatever I had to do to survive. Stole, fought, sold myself when I had no other choice. I was so angry, Nova. So full of rage that I couldn't think straight. I wanted to kill every Fed I saw. Wanted to burn down Echelon and watch them all choke on the smoke."

"What changed?"

"Nothing. I'm still angry. Still want to see them pay. But I realized something: the Federation doesn't care if I'm angry. They don't care if I want revenge. They'll just kill me and find another reason to justify it. The only way to beat them is to survive. To live well despite everything they've done. To build something they can't take away."

She looked at me with those beautiful eyes. "That's what I want with you. A life. A future. Something real. Not revenge. Not justice. Just... us."

I wanted to tell her yes. Wanted to promise I'd let it go, that we'd take the money and run, that we'd build that life she was talking about.

But I couldn't lie to her. Not about this.

"Two weeks," I said. "If Auntie's plan works and Vale goes down, I'll let it go. I'll leave with you and never look back. But if it doesn't work..."

"Then you'll do something stupid," she finished.

"Yeah."

She leaned her head on my shoulder. "Then I guess I got two weeks to change your mind."

We sat there together, passing the bottle back and forth, watching the stars turn slowly outside the window.

◦　　◦　　◦

Day five, Zeno pulled up a news feed that made us all stop what we were doing.

"You need to see this," he said.

The screen showed footage from the Verge—Nova Block Six-Nine, my neighborhood. Federation troops were moving through the streets in full tactical gear, kicking in doors, dragging people out of their homes. Most of them were hybrids like me. Some were just poor. All of them were terrified.

"Operation Exodus, Day Five," the news anchor said in that fake-concerned voice they used. "Federation Security forces continue their sweep of Verge sectors, arresting individuals suspected of criminal activity and gang affiliation. So far, over three thousand suspects have been detained and transferred to processing centers for evaluation."

"Processing centers," Hark said bitterly. "That's what they're calling concentration camps now?"

The footage continued. I saw Mama Leena's building. Saw Feds going through her door. My heart stopped.

"Can you check on her?" I asked Zeno. "See if she's okay?"

Zeno's fingers flew. "She's... not in the arrest database. But she's not answering her comm either."

"Fuck." I stood up, started pacing. "We gotta get her out. We gotta—"

"We can't," Hark said quietly. "We go out there, we're dead. And then we can't help anyone."

"So we just leave her? Let Vale grab her because she knew Ky? Because she helped me?"

"We don't know if he grabbed her. Maybe she went underground. Maybe she's fine. But running out there on a maybe will get us all killed for sure."

I wanted to argue. Wanted to grab my gun and storm out there, consequences be damned. But Hark was right. I knew he was right.

Didn't make it easier.

Trixx put a hand on my arm. "We'll check on her when it's safe. When the heat dies down. I promise."

I nodded, not trusting myself to speak.

The news feed kept playing. More arrests. More scared faces. More people being loaded into transport ships, heading to places where questions weren't asked and answers didn't matter.

"Three thousand people," Zeno said. "In five days. At this rate..."

He didn't finish. Didn't need to. We all knew the math. If Vale kept going at this pace, the Verge would be empty in a month. Everyone who didn't fit his vision of purity would be gone. Disappeared. Erased.

"This is genocide," Trixx whispered. "Slow, bureaucratic genocide."

"It's ethnic cleansing," Hark said. "Been doing it for centuries. Different excuses, same result. The powerful decide the powerless don't deserve to exist, and the universe looks away."

"Not this time," I said. "The Black Book has proof. Names, dates, orders. Vale's signature on execution warrants. When that gets out—"

"If it gets out," Hark corrected. "Auntie's in custody. Her contact might be compromised. The whole plan could be dead."

"Then we use my copy."

"And become targets even bigger than we already are? Nova, think about this. We leak that data, Vale knows we have it. Knows we copied it. He'll hunt us to the ends of the universe."

"He's already hunting us!"

"Now he's hunting criminals. If we leak the Black Book, he'll be hunting threats to Federation security. Big difference. First one, he wants us arrested. Second one, he wants us dead."

We sat in angry silence. Outside, the universe kept turning. Inside, we were trapped in a metal box, waiting for a plan that might never work, watching people die while we hid like rats in the walls.

*   *   *

Day seven, Trixx and I had sex for the first time since going underground.

It wasn't planned. We were just lying on the mattress, trying to sleep, and suddenly her hands were on me and mine were on her and we were kissing like drowning people looking for air.

Zeno and Hark made themselves scarce—Zeno went to check the corridor, Hark went to "inspect the perimeter," which was code for giving us privacy in a room with no doors.

We made love desperate and quiet, trying not to make noise, trying to remember what it felt like to be alive instead of just existing. Her skin glowed purple in the darkness, beautiful and alien and perfect. I traced the lines of glow-ink with my fingers, memorizing every curve, every mark, like I might never get another chance.

After, we lay tangled together, sweating in the recycled air.

"I love you," she whispered. "Even when you're stupid. Even when you're self-destructive. Even when you're planning to get yourself killed. I love you."

"I love you too," I said. And meant it. "If we get out of this—"

"When we get out of this."

"When we get out of this, I'm gonna marry you. Make it official. Give you my real name and everything."

She laughed. "Your real name? You mean Kash? That's not exactly romantic."

"It's all I got."

"It's enough." She kissed me. "But let's survive first. Then we can talk about weddings."

"Deal."

We stayed like that until Zeno knocked on the wall—the signal that he was coming back. By the time he returned, we were dressed and sitting on opposite sides of the room like nothing had happened.

But something had changed. Some promise had been made. Some line had been crossed.

We were in this together now. All the way. For better or worse.

Till death do us part.

•   •   •

Day nine, the power went out.

Not just in our room. The whole sub-level. One second the lights were on, the next we were sitting in complete darkness, the only illumination coming from Zeno's computer screens running on battery backup.

"What the fuck?" Zeno said, fingers already flying over his keyboards. "The main grid just went down. All of Sub-Levels Eight through Twelve. That's not a malfunction. That's deliberate."

"Vale?" I asked.

"Has to be. He's shutting down power to flush out anyone hiding in the lower levels. Without power, there's no heat, no air circulation, no water recycling. We got maybe twelve hours before the air goes bad."

"Options?" Hark asked. He already had his gun out, checking the charge by feel in the darkness.

"We move," Zeno said. "There's another safehouse on Sub-Level Four. It's got independent power, separate air. But we gotta cross through five levels of station to get there, and with Operation Exodus still running, the corridors are probably crawling with Feds."

"We got gear to avoid scanners?" I asked.

"Some. EM scramblers, thermal blockers. Enough for maybe two people to move invisible. The rest of us would have to go loud if we get spotted."

"Then we split up," Hark said. "Two go quiet, two go loud if needed. Meet at the new safehouse."

"I don't like splitting up," Trixx said.

"Me neither," I said. "But we don't have a choice. We stay here, we die. We move together, we're too obvious. We split up, we got a chance."

Zeno was already packing his gear—computers, hard drives, the essential shit he couldn't leave behind. "I'll go quiet. I know the routes, know how to move unseen."

"I'll go with you," Hark said. "I'm old. I'm quiet. And I can shoot anyone who looks at us wrong."

That left me and Trixx as the loud option. Made sense. We were younger, faster, better in a fight if it came to that.

"Okay," I said. "We give you two a thirty-minute head start. You get to Sub-Level Four and secure the safehouse. We follow after, different route. If we get spotted, we lead them away from you. If things go sideways, we meet at... where's a good fallback?"

"The old church in Gamma Section," Trixx said. "Sacred ground. Even Vale's goons won't search there."

"Sacred ground doesn't mean shit to the Federation," Hark said.

"It means something to the people who live there. And they'll protect us if we need it."

"Fine. Old church in Gamma. But let's hope it doesn't come to that."

We geared up in the darkness—weapons, ammunition, what little money we could carry. Zeno distributed the EM scramblers and thermal blockers. They were small devices, clipped to belts, that made you look like background noise to most scanning equipment.

"Don't trust them completely," Zeno warned. "They work on automated systems and drone scanners. Actual human eyes will still see you fine."

"Better than nothing," Hark said.

They left first, slipping out the door like ghosts, barely making a sound. I watched them disappear into the darkness of the corridor, wondering if I'd ever see them again.

Trixx checked her gun—a sleek plasma pistol that fit in her hand like it was made for her. "You ready?"

"No," I said honestly. "But let's go anyway."

•　•　•

The station at night—or what passed for night in the lower levels—was different. Darker. More dangerous. The emergency lights cast weird shadows that moved when you didn't expect them. The air was thinner, harder to breathe, tasting like metal and fear.

We moved through corridors that were supposed to be empty but weren't. People were still here, still living in the darkness, burning candles and huddling together for warmth. They watched us pass with hollow eyes, saying nothing, asking nothing.

"Vale's killing them," Trixx whispered. "Slow and cruel. Cutting off power, resources, hope. Making the Verge so miserable that people will beg to be taken to his processing centers."

"Can't let that happen."

"How are we gonna stop it?"

I didn't have an answer.

We made it to Sub-Level Six before things went wrong.

The corridor ahead was blocked—not by Feds, but by a gang. Local boys, maybe sixteen or seventeen years old, wearing mismatched armor and carrying weapons that looked more dangerous to them than to anyone else.

"Hold up," the leader said. He was tall, skinny, with a face full of scars and eyes that had seen too much too young. "This is our territory. You wanna pass, you gotta pay."

"We don't got time for this," I said.

"Then make time." He raised his gun—some ancient projectile weapon that probably jammed more than it fired. "Toll is one thousand credits. Per person."

"Or what?"

"Or we take it from your bodies."

I looked at Trixx. She looked at me. We were thinking the same thing: we could take these kids. Easy. But that would mean shooting, and shooting would bring the Feds.

"Fine," I said. Pulled out two credit chips, tossed them. "Two thousand. Now move."

The leader caught the chips, checked them, smiled. "Pleasure doing business. You didn't see us, we didn't see you. That's how it works down here now."

He stepped aside. We passed through, feeling their eyes on our backs the whole way.

"This is what Vale wants," Trixx said when we were clear. "Turn us against each other. Make us rob and kill our own people just to survive. That way he doesn't have to do it himself. We'll destroy ourselves."

"We're not destroyed yet."

"Give it time."

We kept moving. Sub-Level Five. Sub-Level Four. Getting closer. The air was getting better, warmer, which meant the power was still working on these levels. We passed checkpoints—Federation drones doing automated patrols—but Zeno's scramblers worked. The drones scanned right through us like we were ghosts.

The new safehouse was in an abandoned medical clinic, the kind of place that used to treat people too poor to afford real doctors. Now it was empty, stripped of everything valuable, just walls and memories.

Zeno and Hark were already there, setting up equipment, checking sight lines.

"Made it," I said.

"Barely," Hark said. "You were followed for about three blocks by a Fed patrol. They didn't see you, but they came close."

"How close?"

"Close enough that I had my rifle aimed at their squad leader's head, ready to drop him if he spotted you."

"Didn't know you had our backs like that."

"Always," Hark said. "That's what family does."

We secured the new safehouse—blocked the windows, set up early warning systems, prepared escape routes. By the time we finished, we were all exhausted, running on adrenaline and fear.

"How much time left?" I asked.

"On Auntie's two-week plan?" Zeno checked his computer. "Five more days. Five more days until whatever she set in motion either works or doesn't."

"And if it doesn't?"

"Then we find out how good you are at burning the universe down," Hark said.

I thought about the Black Book. About all those secrets. About Vale's signature on Ky's execution order.

Five more days.

Five more days to decide if I was gonna be smart or stupid.

If I was gonna choose life or revenge.

If I was gonna be the man Trixx loved or the ghost Ky needed.

Outside, the station groaned and shifted, metal crying against metal. Somewhere up in the Verge, people were being arrested, disappeared, erased. Somewhere in Echelon, Vale was sleeping peacefully in his clean bed with his clean conscience, dreaming of a universe without mongrels and hybrids and anyone who didn't fit his vision of perfection.

Five more days.

And then one way or another, someone was gonna die.

I just hoped it wasn't me.

✦ ✦ ✦

CHAPTER 10

Processing

Day ten started with screaming.

Not close. Maybe three or four corridors away. But sound carried in the station's guts, especially when someone was terrified enough to forget that screaming just brought more trouble.

I was up before the others, smoking by the small window in our new safehouse, watching the sun—or what passed for a sun out here—rise over the curve of the station. The screaming cut through the quiet like a knife.

Hark was awake instantly, gun in hand, old soldier instincts kicking in. "How many?"

"Can't tell," I said. "But it's bad."

Zeno was already at his computers, pulling up surveillance feeds from cameras he'd hacked into. "Federation raid. Sub-Level Three, residential sector. They're hitting multiple hab-units simultaneously. Tactical teams, full armor. This isn't a search. This is a sweep."

On the screen, I could see them—Feds in black gear with white helmets, moving through corridors like a plague, kicking down doors, dragging people out. Most of the people weren't resisting. They just looked confused, scared, clutching children or bags with whatever they could grab in thirty seconds.

"Processing run," Hark said quietly. "That's what we called them in the war. Round up everyone in a sector, sort them later. Efficient. Brutal. Effective."

"Where are they taking them?" Trixx asked. She'd woken up, pulled on clothes, was standing behind me with her hand on my shoulder.

Zeno tapped keys, following the data streams. "Transport ships docked at Bay Seven-Alpha. They're loading people directly from the raid. No booking, no charges, no lawyers. Just... gone."

"How many people?"

"This raid? Maybe two hundred. Families, mostly. Some individuals. But there's more." He pulled up a map of the station. Red dots covered huge sections of the Verge. "Operation Exodus is hitting everywhere today. Day ten of the operation. Coordinated sweeps across fifteen sectors. Estimated five thousand people will be processed today alone."

"Jesus," Trixx whispered.

"Eight thousand total so far," Zeno continued. "Vale's moving faster now. He's got the Federation Council's full authorization. No oversight, no limits, no accountability. He can arrest anyone for any reason and ship them to processing centers with no trial, no appeal, nothing."

I watched the screens. Watched a woman being dragged from her home, a baby in her arms, crying for someone to help. Watched an old man get shoved to the ground when he moved too slow. Watched a kid, maybe ten years old, punch a Fed in the leg and get stunned unconscious for his trouble.

This is what they do, I thought. This is what they've always done. Take what they want. Hurt who they want. And call it law and order.

"This is wrong," I said.

"It's genocide," Hark said flatly. "Systematic removal of undesirables. They dress it up with legal language, call it security operations, but it's the same shit humans have been doing to each other for millennia. Pick a group, dehumanize them, then make them disappear."

"We have to do something."

"Like what?" Zeno asked. "We're four people. They're an army."

"So we just watch? We just let Vale ship thousands of people to death camps?"

"They're not death camps," Trixx said, but her voice was weak. "They're processing centers. They evaluate people, relocate them to other stations—"

"You believe that?" I turned to look at her. "You really think Vale's running refugee relocation programs?"

She was quiet.

"I looked into it," Zeno said. "Hacked the transport manifests, tried to track where the ships are going. You know what I found?"

"What?"

"Nothing. The ships disappear. No arrival logs at other stations, no documentation of where these people end up. It's like they just vanish into space."

The implication hung in the air like poison.

"He's killing them," Hark said. "Maybe not immediately. Maybe he's putting them to work first, extracting value before disposal. But yeah, they're not being relocated. They're being eliminated."

"We need proof," Trixx said. "We need evidence before we—"

"We have evidence!" I pulled out the copied Black Book seed, held it up. "This has everything. Vale's orders, his plans, his crimes. We leak this, the whole universe sees what he's doing."

"And we become targets," Trixx said. "Nova, we talked about this. We wait for Auntie's plan. Four more days. Just four more days and—"

"How many people die in four days? A thousand? Two thousand? How many is acceptable before we're allowed to act?"

She didn't have an answer.

My comm buzzed. Unknown number. I almost didn't answer, but something made me.

"Yeah?"

"Kash DeLeon?" A woman's voice, older, scared. "This is Dr. Sarah Chen. I'm calling from the medical center on Nova Block Six-Nine. Your friend Mama Leena is here."

My heart stopped. "Is she okay?"

"She's... she was injured during a raid. Federation forces damaged her hab-unit, she got caught in the crossfire. She's stable now, but she's asking for you. She says it's urgent."

"I'm coming."

"Wait—the Feds are still in the area. It's not safe—"

I cut the connection. Started grabbing gear.

"Nova, don't," Trixx said. "It could be a trap."

"I don't care."

"You should care! They could be using her to draw you out!"

"Then they'll get what they want." I checked my gun, loaded extra charge packs. "Mama Leena helped me after Ky died. She's the only family I got left besides you three. I'm not leaving her."

"Then we go together," Hark said. He was already armed, already moving toward the door. "Crew sticks together."

"Hark—"

"Don't argue. I'm old, I'm mean, and I've seen enough people die alone. We bring her back here, get her safe, then we can fight about what to do next."

Trixx looked at me, then at Hark, then sighed. "Fine. But we do this smart. In and out, no heroics, no picking fights. We get Mama Leena and we ghost."

"Agreed," I said.

Zeno pulled up a route on his screens. "Medical center is ten blocks from here. Federation's doing sweeps, but they're moving in patterns. If you time it right, you can slip through the gaps. I'll monitor their movements, guide you through."

"What about you?" I asked.

"Someone needs to stay and watch the equipment. Plus, I'm not much good in a fight." He handed me a small device. "Encrypted comm. Direct line to me. If shit goes sideways, I'll do what I can."

We left the safehouse armed for war—Hark with his military rifle, Trixx with dual plasma pistols, me with my trusty Glock and a shotgun strapped to my back. If the Feds wanted a fight, we'd give them one.

* * *

Nova Block Six-Nine looked like a battlefield. Burn marks on the walls where plasma fire had hit. Debris scattered across corridors.

Doors kicked in, belongings scattered, signs of hurried departures everywhere.

And it was quiet. Too quiet. The Block used to be alive—music playing, people talking, kids running around. Now it was a ghost town. Everyone who could leave had left. Everyone else was hiding.

"Three blocks out," Zeno's voice crackled in my ear. "Fed patrol just passed through. You got maybe five minutes clear."

We moved fast, sticking to the shadows, weapons ready. I saw faces in windows—people watching us, saying nothing, hoping we'd pass by without bringing trouble to their doors.

I didn't blame them. These days, just being seen with the wrong people could get you shipped to processing.

The medical center was still standing, though it had seen better days. The front entrance was damaged, probably from the same raid that hurt Mama Leena. We went in through a side door, staying low.

Inside smelled like antiseptic and fear. The waiting room was full of people—injured from raids, sick from bad air in the lower levels, old folks who'd been ignored too long. A nurse with tired eyes looked up as we entered.

"We're here for Mama Leena," I said.

She nodded toward a back room. "She's in there. But make it quick. Feds are doing rounds, checking patient lists. If they find her here, they'll take her to processing."

"Why would they take her? She's just an old woman."

The nurse gave me a look that said I was stupid. "They're taking everyone. Old, young, sick, healthy. Doesn't matter. If you're from the Verge and you're not pure human, you're on the list."

We pushed through to the back room. Mama Leena was on a bed, bandaged around her ribs, breathing shallow. She looked older than I remembered, frailer, like the raid had stolen years from her.

"Kash," she said when she saw me. Her voice was weak. "You came."

"Of course I came." I pulled up a chair, took her hand. It felt like paper in mine, thin and fragile. "What happened?"

"Feds kicked down my door. Said they were searching for contraband, for weapons. I told them I'm just an old woman, I got nothing. But they didn't care. They started tearing my place apart, breaking things. When I tried to stop them, one of them hit me with his rifle. Cracked my ribs. Would've killed me if Dr. Chen hadn't been making rounds."

"I'm sorry," I said. Guilt was eating me alive. "This is my fault. They came for you because of me."

"Don't be stupid. They came for me because I'm a hybrid and Vale's cleaning house." She coughed, winced in pain. "But you're right that you're in danger. That's why I called. I have something for you."

She reached under her blanket, pulled out a data chip. "After Ky died, I went through his things. Found this hidden in his room. Never looked at it—didn't feel right. But maybe you should have it now."

I took the chip. It was small, unmarked, could've been anything. "What is it?"

"Don't know. But Ky was careful. If he hid something, it was important."

"Mama Leena—"

"Shh." She squeezed my hand. "I'm old, Kash. Old and tired and maybe dying. But you're young. You got your whole life ahead of you. Don't waste it on revenge. Don't become like them."

"They killed Ky."

"I know. And that's a pain you'll carry forever. But killing Vale won't bring him back. It'll just create more orphans, more grieving mothers. The cycle has to end somewhere."

She was right. I knew she was right. But knowing didn't make the rage go away. Didn't fill the hole where my brother used to be.

Zeno's voice crackled in my ear. "Nova, we got a problem. Fed patrol changed course. They're heading your way. ETA three minutes."

"We gotta go," Hark said from the doorway. He'd been watching the corridor.

"Come with us," I said to Mama Leena. "We got a safehouse. We can protect you."

"I'm too old to run," she said. "And too hurt to move. You go. Take that chip. And promise me you'll think about what I said."

"Mama—"

"Promise me."

"I promise." The lie tasted like ash in my mouth.

She smiled. "Good boy. Now go. Before you get caught being a hero."

We left her there, and it felt like abandoning family. But she was right—we couldn't carry her, couldn't protect her if the Feds found us together. The best thing we could do was disappear.

We made it to the corridor before we heard the boots.

Heavy, synchronized, military precision. A full squad, maybe ten men, coming from the direction we needed to go.

"Back way," Trixx said.

We reversed course, heading deeper into the medical center. But there were more boots behind us now. They were boxing us in, same tactic they'd used in the space chase.

"They knew we'd come," Hark said. "Someone talked, or they monitored the call. Either way, we're made."

"Options?" I asked.

"Fight or hide."

"Roof," Trixx said. "We go up, cross to the next building, disappear into the blocks."

"Roofs are exposed. They'll have drones."

"You got a better idea?"

I didn't.

We found stairs, started climbing. Three floors up, the medical center opened onto a small rooftop garden—one of those community projects where people tried to grow real plants in space because it reminded them of planets they'd never see again.

Through the garden, we could see the neighboring buildings. Close enough to jump if you were crazy. Far enough that you'd die if you missed.

"Zeno," I said into the comm. "We're on the roof of the medical center. Need an exit strategy."

"Working on it. Building to your north has an access shaft that leads to the maintenance tunnels. From there you can reach the safehouse."

"How far north?"

"Twenty feet. One jump."

Trixx looked at the gap. "That's not twenty feet. That's thirty, at least."

"I'm rounding down to make you feel better."

"Not helping."

The door to the roof burst open. Federation troops poured out, weapons raised, lights cutting through the smoke from someone's fire on a lower level.

"Kash DeLeon!" the lead officer shouted. "You're under arrest for terrorism, murder, and conspiracy against the Federation! Surrender now and you won't be harmed!"

"They're lying," Hark said quietly. "They'll shoot you the second you give up."

I looked at Trixx. At Hark. At the gap between buildings.

"How good are you at jumping?" I asked.

"Terrible," Trixx said.

"Me too." I sparked a Black Death, took a drag, flicked it at the Feds. "Guess we're about to get better."

And I ran.

Full sprint across the roof, heading for the edge, feeling Trixx and Hark beside me. Behind us, the Feds were shouting, warning us to stop, threatening to shoot.

Then they did shoot.

Plasma bolts sizzled past my head, close enough to feel the heat. One hit the rooftop in front of me, melting a hole I almost fell into. But I kept running, kept pushing, because stopping meant dying.

The edge came up fast. Too fast. No time to think, no time to reconsider.

I jumped.

For a second, I was flying. Wind in my face, void below me, nothing but faith and momentum keeping me alive. Time stretched. I could see everything—the station spinning slowly, the stars beyond, Trixx beside me, face set in determination, Hark on her other side, old but still strong.

Then gravity remembered I existed and pulled me down.

I hit the other roof hard, rolled, felt something in my shoulder pop. Pain shot through me but I was alive, I was across, I'd made it.

Trixx landed next to me, graceful as always, barely stumbling. She was already helping me up, checking me for injuries.

"You okay?"

"No," I said. "But I'm alive."

Hark landed last, hit the roof like a sack of meat, and didn't get up right away.

"Hark!" Trixx rushed to him.

He was breathing, moving, but slow. "I'm fine. Just old. And gravity's a bitch."

Across the gap, the Feds had stopped at the edge. A few of them were aiming rifles, calculating if they could make the shot. One of them raised a comm to his mouth—calling for drones, probably, or air support.

"Move," I said.

We found the access shaft Zeno had mentioned, climbed down into the maintenance tunnels, and ran like hell. Behind us, I could hear the Feds coordinating, spreading out, searching.

But these were our tunnels. Our station. Our home.

And down here, we knew every shortcut, every dead end, every place to hide.

We lost them in the maze of pipes and cables, doubled back twice, then split up and reconvened at a junction point Zeno had marked. By the time we made it back to the safehouse, we were exhausted, bleeding, and pissed off.

But we were alive.

And that counted for something.

. . .

Back at the safehouse, Zeno was waiting with medical supplies and bad news.

"They're escalating," he said, showing us the feeds. "After you escaped, Vale gave a speech. Called you terrorists. Said you attacked a medical center, endangered patients. He's using it as justification to declare martial law on the entire Verge. Full military lockdown. No one in or out without authorization."

"Fuck," I said.

"Gets worse. He's accelerating the processing timeline. The raids tonight are bigger, more aggressive. They're not just taking hybrids anymore. They're taking anyone who looks at them wrong. Anyone who might be sympathetic. Anyone who doesn't cheer loud enough when Vale's face shows up on the mesh."

On the screen, I could see it happening. Federation troops moving through sectors like locusts, loading transport ships with people who'd never be seen again.

"How many?" Trixx asked.

"By the end of tonight? Ten thousand. Maybe more."

"In one night?"

"He's cleaning house fast. Probably worried that Auntie's plan is coming together, wants to consolidate power before it drops. Or maybe he just doesn't care anymore about looking legitimate."

I pulled out the data chip Mama Leena had given me. "Zeno, can you check this? See what's on it?"

He took it, plugged it into his system. Lights flickered. Code scrolled.

His face went pale. "Holy shit."

"What?"

"It's... it's surveillance footage. From the day Ky died. He was wearing a recording device, something small, hidden. It captured everything."

My heart stopped. My hands started shaking. "Show me."

He pulled up the video. The image was shaky, taken from a chest-mounted camera. I could see through Ky's eyes as he walked through a corridor, heading to meet someone.

Then the corridor opened up. And Vale was there.

Not Vale's subordinates. Not some patrol officer. Vale himself, in full uniform, standing with Vex and two other Feds.

"Kash DeLeon's brother," Vale was saying. His voice was clear, calm. "We need to send a message. The hybrids need to understand that there are consequences for stepping out of line."

"You want me to kill him?" Vex asked. He sounded uncertain. "He's just a kid."

"He's a symbol. And symbols are powerful. Kill him. Make it public. Let his brother see what happens when mongrels forget their place."

Ky's voice, young and scared: "I didn't do anything. I'm not part of Kash's crew. I'm just trying to—"

Vale pulled a gun. Not a plasma weapon. An old-fashioned projectile pistol, the kind that left evidence, that made noise.

He handed it to Vex. "Do it. Now."

The video cut out before the shot, but we all knew what came next.

Silence filled the safehouse. Heavy, angry silence that pressed down on my chest like a weight.

I couldn't breathe. Couldn't think. All I could see was Vale's face on that screen. Calm and cold and certain. The face of a man who thought he was above consequences.

The face of the man who'd ordered my baby brother executed like he was nothing.

"He did it himself," I said quietly. My voice sounded far away, like it belonged to someone else. "Vale was there. He ordered it directly. He wanted Ky dead to send me a message."

"That's premeditated murder," Hark said. "On camera. With audio. That's not just evidence. That's a fucking conviction."

"We leak this," Zeno said, "Vale's done. Not just fired. Prison. Maybe execution."

I looked at the frozen image on screen—Vale's face, that mask of righteous certainty.

"How long until Auntie's plan kicks in?" I asked.

"Four days."

"Four days while Vale ships ten thousand people to death camps." I stood up, checked my gun. The rage was back, hot and bright and pure. "No. No more waiting. We leak everything. The Black Book. This footage. All of it. Tonight."

"Nova—" Trixx started.

"Don't. Don't tell me to wait. Don't tell me to be patient. I've been patient. I've been smart. And people are dying. Ky died. Mama Leena's dying. How many more before we're allowed to act?"

"If we leak this, we burn every bridge," Hark said. "Auntie's plan fails. Vale comes for us with everything he's got. And we're four people with some guns against an army."

"Then we better make it count." I looked at Zeno. "Can you leak it anonymously? Make it untraceable?"

"Yeah. But the second it hits the mesh, every intelligence service in the sector will be trying to find the source. They'll trace it eventually."

"How long do we have?"

"Maybe twelve hours. Maybe less if they're good."

"Then we make those twelve hours hell for Vale. We leak the data, then we disappear. Head to your contact on Freeport Station. Start over."

"And if Vale catches us before we make it?"

I didn't answer. Didn't need to. We both knew what that meant.

Trixx was looking at me like she'd never seen me before. "This is it, isn't it? No more waiting. No more planning. We're really doing this."

"We're really doing this."

She kissed me, hard and desperate, like she was trying to memorize what I tasted like.

Zeno's fingers were already flying across keyboards, uploading the footage, preparing the Black Book data for release. "This is gonna break the mesh. Every news service, every intelligence agency, every person with a screen is gonna see this. Vale's face next to Ky's murder. His signature on execution orders for thousands of people."

"Good," I said. "Let the universe see who he really is."

The upload bar crawled across the screen. Slow, agonizing, but inevitable.

"Five minutes until it drops," Zeno said. "After that, we're committed. No taking it back."

I thought about Mama Leena's words. About Trixx begging me to choose life over revenge. About Hark's warnings and Auntie's plan.

But I also thought about Ky. About his scared voice on that video. About ten thousand people on transport ships heading nowhere good. About all the people Vale had killed because they weren't pure enough for his perfect universe.

Fuck patience. Fuck waiting. Fuck playing it safe.

Some things were worth dying for.

"Do it," I said.

Zeno hit enter.

And somewhere in the digital void, the truth started spreading.

✦ ✦ ✦

CHAPTER 11

The Fall

The mesh went fucking insane.

Within five minutes of Zeno hitting upload, every news channel in the sector was breaking into regular programming. Within ten minutes, the footage of Vale executing Ky was trending on forty different platforms. Within twenty minutes, riots started in the Verge.

We watched it unfold on Zeno's screens, sitting in our safehouse while the universe caught fire.

"Holy shit," Zeno kept saying. "Holy shit, it's everywhere. Every major outlet. Independent journalists. Even Federation-controlled media can't ignore it. The footage is too damning."

On screen, Vale's face filled a hundred different feeds. That moment frozen in time—gun in hand, cold expression, ordering a kid's death because his brother wasn't "pure" enough. The audio played on loop: *"Kill him. Make it public. Let his brother see what happens when mongrels forget their place."*

"Public sentiment is turning," Zeno said, pulling up social metrics. "Echelon citizens are calling for his resignation. Federation officers are distancing themselves. Even the Council is putting out statements about 'investigating these serious allegations.'"

"Fuck their investigations," I said. "That footage is proof. Vale murdered Ky in cold blood."

"Doesn't matter to them. They'll stall, they'll spin, they'll try to bury it under bureaucracy. But the people..." He pulled up another feed. "The people are pissed."

The screen showed crowds gathering in the Verge. Thousands of people, filling the corridors and plazas, chanting. At first I couldn't make out the words, but then Zeno turned up the audio.

"Justice for Ky! Justice for the Verge! Vale must fall! Vale must fall!"

My brother's name. Being chanted by people who'd never met him, who only knew him as a victim, as a symbol of everything wrong with the Federation's treatment of hybrids and the poor.

I wanted to feel triumphant. Vindicated. But all I felt was hollow.

"Ky would've hated this," I said quietly. "He didn't want to be famous. Just wanted to live."

"Now he's a martyr," Hark said. "Sometimes the dead do more than the living ever could."

Another feed showed Federation troops forming barricades, trying to contain the crowds. But there were too many people, and they were too angry. Years of oppression, of raids, of Operation Exodus—it had all been building, and now it was exploding.

"It's not just the Verge," Trixx said, pointing to another screen. "Look. Echelon Prime. They're protesting too."

She was right. Even in the rich sectors, people were gathering. Not as many, not as angry, but still there. Holding signs that said things like "Justice for All" and "Vale Broke the Law" and "Hybrids Are People Too."

This is what I wanted, I thought. This is what I fought for. So why does it feel like I'm drowning?

"Federation is scrambling," Zeno said. "Emergency Council session called. Vale's being summoned to testify. They're suspending Operation Exodus pending investigation."

"How long before they trace the leak to us?" I asked.

"Hard to say. I routed it through seventeen different proxies, used ghost protocols, made it look like it came from inside Federation Intelligence. But they're good. They'll figure it out eventually." He checked his systems. "We probably have eight to ten hours before they narrow it down to this sector. Maybe six hours before they pinpoint the building."

"Then we move now," Hark said. "Pack what we can carry, burn what we can't, and ghost before they find us."

"Move where?" Trixx asked. "Every port is locked down. Every checkpoint is scanning for us. We're the most wanted people in the sector right now."

"Zeno's contact on Freeport," I said. "We still have that option?"

Zeno was typing, checking something. "Yeah, but there's a problem. With the leak, Federation's put the entire station on high alert. Military checkpoints everywhere. Biometric scans. DNA verification. We'd need to be ghosts to get through, and my scramblers aren't that good."

"So we're trapped."

"For now. But the riots are spreading. If they get big enough, Federation will have to pull resources from checkpoints to deal with crowd control. That's our window."

"How big do the riots need to be?" Trixx asked.

Zeno pulled up a tactical map. "Station-wide. Multiple sectors. Overwhelming numbers. If they're dealing with fifty thousand people in the streets, they can't spare the manpower to guard every exit."

"Fifty thousand people," I said. The number felt unreal. "That's a revolution."

"That's what you started," Hark said, looking at me with something that might've been respect or might've been concern. "You leaked that footage, you lit the match. Now the whole station's burning."

Yeah. Now the whole station's burning. And people are gonna die because I couldn't wait four more days.

My comm buzzed. Unknown number again. I almost didn't answer, but curiosity got the better of me.

"Yeah?"

"Mr. DeLeon." It was Vale. His voice was tight, controlled, but I could hear the rage underneath. "Congratulations. You've successfully started a riot. I hope you're proud."

"Prouder than you'll ever know."

"You think you've won. You think that footage will destroy me. But you don't understand how power works. The Council will investigate, yes. They'll make noise, appease the masses. But in the end, I'm too valuable to lose. I keep the Verge in line. I maintain order. They need me."

"The whole universe just watched you murder a kid."

"The whole universe watches atrocities every day and does nothing. This will be no different. In a week, people will forget. In a month, it'll be old news. But you... you'll still be hunted. Still be running. Still be dying slowly every day until I catch you."

"You sound scared."

"I sound like a man who's about to burn your entire world down." His voice went cold. "You wanted to play revolutionary? Fine. Let's see how you handle the consequences. Operation Exodus is suspended, you say? Well, I'm about to show you what real escalation looks like."

The line went dead.

"That sounded bad," Trixx said.

"Zeno, what's he doing?" I asked. "Pull up his location, his communications, anything."

Zeno's fingers flew. "He's... he's at Federation High Command. Broadcasting to all military units. Oh fuck. Oh fuck, he's declaring martial law. Full martial law. Not just the Verge—the entire station. He's calling the riots an armed insurrection."

"Can he do that?"

"He just did. Look."

The screens changed. Vale's face appeared, standing at a podium in full military dress uniform, medals gleaming, face calm and authoritative.

"Citizens of the station," he began. "I come before you in a time of crisis. Forces seeking to destabilize our society have spread dangerous lies and incited violence across multiple sectors. In response to this threat, I am invoking Emergency Protocol Seven, granting Federation Security full military authority to restore order by any means necessary."

"Any means necessary," Hark repeated. "That's code for lethal force authorized."

Vale continued: "The footage you have seen is a fabrication. A sophisticated fake created by criminal elements to undermine legitimate law enforcement. The individual known as 'Ky DeLeon' was a criminal suspect who resisted arrest. His death, while tragic, was justified under Federation law."

"Bullshit!" I shouted at the screen.

"These criminals—Kash DeLeon, known as 'Nova,' and his associates—will be brought to justice. Anyone harboring them, assisting them, or failing to report their location will be charged as accomplices to terrorism. The penalty is death."

The screen split. One side showed Vale's face. The other showed my face, Trixx's face, Hark's face, Zeno's face. Our bounties had increased. Five million credits. Each. Dead or alive.

"Effective immediately," Vale said, "a curfew is in effect. Anyone found in public spaces without proper authorization will be detained. Resistance will be met with appropriate force. We will restore order. We will protect the innocent. And we will eliminate the threat posed by these terrorists."

The broadcast ended.

"We're fucked," Zeno said quietly.

"How bad?" I asked.

"Five million credits each? Every bounty hunter, mercenary, and desperate person on this station is gonna be looking for us. And with martial law, Vale can shoot anyone he claims is harboring us without trial."

"The riots—"

"Won't matter. He's got authorization for lethal force. He can massacre protesters and call it restoring order."

I looked at the screens showing the crowds in the Verge. All those people, chanting my brother's name, demanding justice. They were about to get slaughtered because of what I did.

The weight of it hit me like a physical thing. I'd started this. I'd lit the match. And now people were gonna burn.

"We have to stop this," I said.

"How?" Trixx asked. "We're four people. He's got an army."

"We got the truth. That footage is real. The Black Book is real. People know it. They saw it with their own eyes."

"And Vale's calling it fake news. Claiming it's fabricated. Half the people will believe him just because it's easier than accepting that their government murders children."

"Then we need more proof. Something he can't deny."

"Like what?"

I thought about it. The footage showed Vale ordering Ky's death. The Black Book showed his signature on thousands of execution orders. But both could be claimed as fakes, as manipulations, as criminal conspiracies.

We needed something direct. Something undeniable.

We needed Vale himself.

"We need a confession," I said.

"You want to make Vale confess?" Hark asked. "How? Walk up and ask nicely?"

"We ambush him. Capture him. Beat the truth out of him on camera. Show the universe who he really is."

"That's suicide."

"You got a better idea?"

Nobody did.

"Vale's at Federation High Command," Zeno said. "That's the most secure building on the station. Military guards, surveillance, automated defenses. We'd never get in."

"Then we get him to come out."

"How?"

I thought about what Vale wanted. What would make him leave safety and come to us.

"Me," I said. "He wants me dead more than anything. We offer a trade. Me for the protesters. Tell him I'll surrender if he stands down, ends martial law, stops the crackdown."

"He'll never agree to that," Trixx said.

"He will. Because he's arrogant. Because he thinks he's already won. And because having me in custody gives him legitimacy. He can parade me around, make me the villain, use my arrest to justify everything he's done."

"And when he comes to collect you?"

"We take him. Force him to confess. Broadcast it live so he can't claim it's edited."

"That's not a plan," Hark said. "That's ten different ways to die."

"You're right. It's terrible. But it's all we got." I looked at my crew. At the people who'd become my family when I had nothing left. "I'm not asking you to come with me. This is my fight. My brother. My revenge. You've done enough."

"Shut the fuck up," Trixx said. "We're crew. We don't leave each other. If you're doing this stupid-ass suicide mission, we're doing it with you."

"Trixx—"

"I said shut up. I love you, you stupid man. I'm not letting you die alone."

Hark stood up, checked his rifle. "I'm in. Always wanted to kidnap a Federation officer. Now's my chance."

Zeno was quiet for a moment, then nodded. "Fuck it. Can't spend my bounty if I'm dead anyway. Let's go out big."

I looked at them—my family, my crew, the people who'd stuck with me through everything. We were about to do something incredibly stupid. We'd probably die.

But at least we'd die together.

"Okay," I said. "Let's kidnap a fucking fascist."

. . .

The plan was simple, which meant it was probably gonna fail.

Zeno sent a message to Vale's office, routed through encrypted channels, claiming to be me. The message was short: "Sick of running. Willing to trade. Me for the protesters. Meet at the old church in Gamma Section. Alone. One hour. If you bring troops, I disappear and the next leak is worse."

We didn't expect him to come alone. But we hoped he'd come with a small team—small enough that we could handle it.

The old church was perfect for an ambush. One entrance, good sight lines, places to hide. It used to be a real church before people stopped believing in gods who let them suffer. Now it was just a shell, used by squatters and addicts looking for somewhere quiet to die.

We got there first. Set up positions. Hark on the high ground with his rifle. Trixx at the entrance with her pistols. Zeno in the back with his tech, ready to broadcast whatever happened. And me in the center, bait on a hook, waiting for the shark to bite.

"Backup's in place," Trixx said through comms. "I got word to the protest leaders. They're watching the broadcast. If this works, if Vale says anything incriminating on camera, they'll move."

"How many?"

"Couple hundred, staged three blocks away. They want justice as bad as we do. They just need proof."

That was the real plan. Not kidnapping—humiliation. Get Vale to confess on live broadcast, let the people see who he really was, and let them decide what happened next.

"He's coming," Zeno said through comms. "Three vehicles. Looks like... twelve soldiers, maybe fifteen. Plus Vale."

"Fifteen to four," Hark said. "I've had worse odds."

"When?"

"Titan Penitentiary, '34. We were outnumbered twenty to one and still took the yard. These Federation boys are soft. They'll break."

I hoped he was right.

The vehicles stopped outside. I heard boots on stone, weapons clicking, orders being given in sharp military tones. Then the door opened and Vale walked in.

He looked different without the uniform polish of his broadcasts. Tired. Angry. Older. But still dangerous. He had his gun out, scanning the room, looking for threats.

"DeLeon," he said when he saw me. "I'm surprised. I didn't think you had the courage to surrender."

"I don't. But I got the courage to end this."

"End this?" He laughed, sharp and bitter. "You started a riot that's killed fourteen people so far. You leaked classified intelligence. You've branded yourself a terrorist. There's no ending that doesn't involve your death."

Fourteen people. The number hit me like a punch. Fourteen people dead because I couldn't wait four more days.

"Maybe," I said, pushing the guilt down. "But I'm taking you with me."

"Is that so?" He gestured and his soldiers entered, fanning out, weapons trained on me. "Fifteen against one. I like those odds."

"Who said I was alone?"

Hark's rifle cracked. One of the soldiers dropped, clean headshot, dead before he hit the ground.

Chaos erupted. Soldiers scattered, looking for cover, trying to find the shooter. Trixx opened fire from the entrance, plasma bolts taking down two more. Zeno triggered the doors, slamming them shut, trapping everyone inside.

"Ambush!" someone shouted. "It's an ambush!"

Vale dove behind a pillar, screaming orders. "Take them alive! I want them alive!"

But his soldiers weren't listening. They were firing wildly, hitting walls and pews and nothing important. These weren't combat veterans. These were city cops in military gear, playing soldier, and now that the shooting started they were panicking.

I pulled my gun and started working. Short controlled bursts, aiming for legs and arms, trying not to kill if I could help it. These weren't the real enemy. They were just kids following orders.

But Vale... Vale was fair game.

I rushed his pillar, using the chaos as cover. He saw me coming, tried to bring his gun around, but I was faster. I hit him hard, full body tackle, and we went down together in a tangle of limbs and anger.

He was stronger than he looked. He got an arm free, smashed his gun into my face. My vision went white, blood pouring from my nose, but I held on. Got my hands around his throat, started squeezing.

"Confess," I hissed. "Tell them what you did. Tell them you killed Ky."

"Fuck... you..."

"Zeno!" I shouted. "Play the footage!"

On every screen in the station, the video started playing. Ky walking down the corridor. Vale waiting with Vex. *"Kill him. Make it public. Let his brother see what happens when mongrels forget their place."*

Vale's face went white as he heard his own words echo through the church, broadcast to millions.

"That's you," I said, loosening my grip just enough for him to breathe. "That's your voice. That's your order. Everyone's watching. Everyone knows."

His soldiers had stopped fighting. They were staring at the screens, at their commander's face next to a murdered kid's.

"You can deny it," I said. "You can claim it's fake. Or you can tell the truth for once in your miserable life. Maybe the people will give you a trial instead of a lynching. Your choice."

Something broke behind his eyes. The arrogance, the certainty, the belief that he was untouchable—all of it cracking under the weight of his own words played back to him.

"I killed your brother," he gasped. The words came out broken, defeated. "Because he was... he was inferior. Because he was a half-breed mongrel who didn't deserve to breathe the same air as pure humans. And I'd do it again... I'd kill everyone like you... until this station is clean."

There it was. Not just a confession extracted under duress—a declaration. His true self, exposed for the universe to see.

Vale's face went pale as the full weight of what he'd said landed. "No," he whispered. "No, you can't—"

The doors burst open. But it wasn't more Federation troops.

It was the protesters.

Hundreds of them, flooding into the church, carrying improvised weapons, wearing makeshift armor. They'd seen the broadcast. Seen Vale confess. And they'd come for justice.

"Vale must fall!" someone started chanting. Others picked it up. "Vale must fall! Vale must fall!"

Vale's soldiers looked at each other, then at the crowd, then at Vale. One by one, they lowered their weapons. They weren't dying for a murderer. Not for this.

Vale tried to run. But the crowd was everywhere, blocking every exit, pressing in with the weight of years of oppression and anger.

"You're under arrest," I said, standing over him. "For the murder of Ky DeLeon. For crimes against humanity. For genocide. And for being a racist piece of shit who thought he was above the law."

"You can't arrest me. You're not law enforcement."

"Nah. But they are." I pointed to the crowd. "The people. We're arresting you in the name of the Verge. In the name of everyone you've killed. In the name of justice you tried to deny."

"This isn't justice! This is mob rule!"

"Welcome to the revolution, motherfucker."

The crowd surged forward. For a moment, I thought they might tear him apart right there. But Trixx fired a shot into the ceiling, the plasma bolt leaving a scorch mark that got everyone's attention.

"We're not killers!" she shouted. "We're not like him! We arrest him properly. We put him on trial. We show the universe that we're better than the Federation."

The crowd hesitated, torn between rage and righteousness.

"She's right," someone said. An older woman, someone I recognized from Nova Block. "We do this right. We make it legal. So nobody can say we were wrong."

"But we don't trust Federation courts," someone else said. "They'll protect him."

"Then we hold our own trial," I said. "Right here. Right now. With the whole universe watching. Let everyone see the truth. Let them judge for themselves."

The crowd agreed. They dragged Vale to the front of the church, bound him with zip-ties, set up lights and cameras so everything would be documented.

Zeno was grinning. "This is crazy. This is the craziest thing I've ever seen. We're putting a Federation officer on trial in an abandoned church with mob justice and live streaming it."

"Is it working?" I asked.

"Streaming to forty million viewers and climbing. This is the biggest broadcast in the sector. Everyone's watching."

Good. Let them watch. Let them see what happens when the oppressed finally fight back.

The trial took three hours. People came forward, one by one, telling their stories. How Vale's orders had killed their loved ones. How Operation Exodus had destroyed their lives. How the Federation had treated them like animals for years, and Vale was the worst of them.

Vale said nothing. Just sat there, hands bound, face a mask of contempt.

When it was my turn, I told them about Ky. About how he died. About the footage showing Vale's direct involvement.

"The evidence is clear," I said to the cameras, to the universe watching. "Lieutenant Vale ordered the execution of an innocent kid because of his heritage. He orchestrated genocide under the guise of security operations. He murdered thousands and called it law enforcement. And he did it all because he believed some lives matter less than others."

The crowd voted. Unanimous. Guilty on all charges.

"What's the sentence?" someone asked.

I looked at Vale. At this man who'd taken so much from me, from everyone in the Verge. Part of me wanted him dead. Wanted to put a bullet in his head and end it.

But that wasn't justice. That was revenge. And I'd promised Mama Leena I'd think about the difference.

"Life in prison," I said. "In Titan Penitentiary. Let him rot in the same hell he sent so many others to."

"That's too good for him," someone shouted.

"Maybe. But we're not him. We're better. We have to be."

The crowd accepted it. Some reluctantly, but they accepted it.

Vale finally spoke. "You think this changes anything? The Federation will come for you. They'll crush this little rebellion. They'll execute you all for treason."

"Maybe," I said. "But they'll have to explain to forty million people why they're protecting a murderer. Good luck with that."

*   *   *

We left the church with Vale in custody, surrounded by protesters who'd become revolutionaries, broadcast to a universe that was watching history happen in real time.

We'd done it. We'd actually fucking done it.

But the victory felt hollow. Felt temporary.

"What now?" Trixx asked.

"Now?" I lit a Black Death, let the smoke fill my lungs. The taste was bitter. Everything was bitter. "Now we see if this revolution sticks. Or if we just painted bigger targets on our backs."

My comm buzzed. An encrypted message from someone identifying themselves as "Auntie's Contact."

The message was short: "You didn't wait for my timeline. But you achieved the same result. Vale is finished. The Council is in chaos. Operations Exodus is permanently suspended. You've won. Now disappear before the Federation decides you're too dangerous to let live."

"We won," I said quietly. The words felt strange in my mouth.

"We won," Trixx repeated, like she couldn't quite believe it.

Hark clapped me on the shoulder. "Not bad for a kid from the Verge."

Zeno was already packing up his gear. "We should move. Federation might be in chaos, but they'll reorganize eventually. And when they do, we're still criminals. Still worth five million each."

He was right. We'd won the battle, but the war was just beginning. Fourteen people were dead because I'd started riots. Vale was arrested but the Federation was still standing. And we were still fugitives with the biggest bounties in the sector.

Still. For now. For this moment.

We'd won.

And my brother's name would be remembered not as a victim, but as the spark that started a revolution.

I just hoped the cost wouldn't be too high.

✦ ✦ ✦

CHAPTER 12

Victory's Price

We didn't go back to the safehouse. Too risky. Even with Vale in custody and the revolution spreading, we were still wanted criminals with five million credit bounties on our heads. Every merc and desperate fool on the station would be looking for us.

Instead, we went to ground in a place nobody would think to look—Echelon Prime. The rich sectors. The place where Feds lived and people like us were supposed to be invisible.

Zeno knew a guy who knew a guy. Some rich kid playing revolutionary, letting protesters crash in his penthouse while his parents were off-station. The apartment was insane—floor-to-ceiling windows showing the void, furniture that probably cost more than everything I'd ever owned, air that didn't taste like recycled ass.

"Welcome to how the other half lives," Zeno said, dropping his gear on a couch that looked too clean to sit on. "They got real food here. Like, actual vegetables grown in dirt. Not synthetic shit."

Hark was already checking the perimeter, old habits. "Windows are vulnerable. No cover. If someone comes for us, we're trapped."

"Nobody's coming," I said, though I didn't quite believe it. "The whole station's in chaos. Federation's too busy dealing with protests to hunt us right now."

"For now," Hark said. "But chaos doesn't last forever. Eventually they'll restore order, and when they do, we're back to being public enemy number one."

He was right. We'd won a battle, but the war wasn't over.

Trixx found the bathroom and nearly cried. "They have a shower. A real shower with water pressure and everything. I'm not leaving this apartment."

"Take your time," I said. "We're not going anywhere tonight."

She disappeared into the bathroom. A minute later I heard water running, heard her make a sound that was half moan, half sob. We'd been living in safehouses and hiding spots for so long, I'd forgotten what comfort felt like.

What it felt like to not be running.

Zeno was already plugged into the apartment's mesh system, fingers flying across holographic screens. "The trial's still trending. Forty-three million views now. Federation's releasing statements calling it illegal, saying Vale's confession was coerced. But nobody's buying it. Public opinion is overwhelmingly against them."

"What about the protesters?" I asked.

"Still in the streets. Bigger crowds than before. They're not just demanding Vale's punishment anymore. They're demanding systemic change. End to hybrid discrimination, equal rights, representation in the Council. This is real revolution shit."

"Will it work?"

"Maybe. The Federation's scared. They've never dealt with organized resistance on this scale. If the movement stays strong, stays unified, they might actually have to give concessions."

"And if it doesn't stay unified?"

Zeno shrugged. "Then the Feds wait for it to fracture, pick off the leaders, and go back to business as usual. That's how these things usually end."

I sparked a Black Death, stared out the window at the station slowly rotating against the stars. Somewhere out there, Ky was still floating. Still cold. Still dead.

But at least now people knew his name. Knew his story. Vale had tried to make him disappear, tried to erase him like he never existed.

We'd made sure that didn't happen.

That should've felt like enough. But it didn't.

"You did good, kid," Hark said, joining me at the window. He lit up his own smoke—herb mixed with something that smelled expensive. "Ky would be proud."

"Would he? I started a revolution. Got people killed. Almost got us all killed."

"You got justice. That's more than most people ever get. More than I ever got for the friends I lost."

"Doesn't feel like enough."

"Never does." He took a long drag, let smoke curl around his face. "But it's what we got. And sometimes that has to be enough, or we drive ourselves crazy chasing perfect justice that doesn't exist."

The bathroom door opened. Trixx came out wrapped in a towel, her purple skin glowing clean for the first time in days, her hair damp and loose around her shoulders. She looked like a different person—softer, younger, like the weight of the world had lifted just a little.

"Your turn," she said to me. "And trust me, you need it. You smell like smoke and blood and revolution."

"That's my natural scent."

"It's terrible. Go shower."

I went. The bathroom was ridiculous—marble everything, gold fixtures, a shower big enough for three people. I stripped off my clothes, looked at myself in the mirror. I looked like shit. Bruises from the fight with Vale, cuts from broken glass, exhaustion etched into every line of my face.

I looked like someone who'd been at war.

I guess I had been.

The shower was everything Trixx promised. Hot water, actual pressure, soap that smelled like something other than industrial cleaner. I stood under the spray for what felt like hours, watching dirt and blood and the last two weeks circle the drain.

Watching everything I'd done wash away, even though I knew it never really would.

When I came out, Zeno and Hark had made themselves scarce. The lights were dimmed. Trixx was sitting on the massive bed, still in her towel, looking at me with an expression I couldn't quite read.

"Come here," she said.

I went. Sat next to her on sheets that probably cost more than my car.

"We won," she said quietly. "Vale's finished. Ky's been avenged. Operation Exodus is over. We actually won."

"Yeah."

"So why do you look so sad?"

I didn't know how to answer that. How to explain that victory felt hollow when your brother was still dead. That justice didn't bring anyone back. That I'd gotten what I wanted but it didn't fill the hole inside me.

"I thought it would feel different," I said finally. "I thought when Vale fell, when everyone knew what he did, I'd feel... I don't know. Complete. Like I'd finished something."

"But you don't."

"No. I just feel tired. And empty. And like maybe Mama Leena was right—revenge doesn't fix anything. It just creates more pain."

Trixx took my hand, laced her fingers through mine. "You're wrong. It did fix something. Not for you, maybe. But for everyone else. For all the people who've been suffering under Vale's regime. For all the hybrids who thought they didn't matter. You showed them they do matter. That their lives are worth fighting for."

"Cost a lot of people to prove that point."

"Everything worth doing costs something. You can't make change without breaking things first."

She shifted closer, her towel slipping a little, showing the curve of her shoulder. Her glow-ink pulsed soft purple in the dim light, beautiful and hypnotic.

"I'm proud of you," she said. "Even when you were reckless. Even when you scared me. Even when I thought you were gonna get yourself killed. I'm proud of what you did."

"I couldn't have done it without you. Without the crew."

"I know. That's what makes it mean something. You didn't do this alone. You brought us with you. Made us part of something bigger than just surviving."

She kissed me. Soft at first, gentle, like she was asking permission. I kissed back, pulling her close, feeling her warmth against me.

The kiss deepened. Her hands were in my hair, my hands were on her waist, and suddenly we were falling back onto the bed, tangled together, all the fear and tension and adrenaline from the last two weeks finding a different outlet.

"I love you," I whispered against her lips.

"I love you too," she said. "And I'm gonna show you how much."

She pushed me onto my back, straddled me, the towel falling away completely. Her body was incredible—purple skin smooth and perfect, glow-ink tracing patterns that pulsed brighter as she got more aroused.

We made love slow, then fast, then slow again. Her on top, me on top, tangled together in expensive sheets that probably cost more than everything I owned. She said my name like a prayer. I said hers like an answer.

When we finished, she collapsed against my chest, breathing hard, glow-ink slowly fading back to its resting pulse.

"That was..." I didn't have words.

"Yeah," she agreed. "It was."

We lay there for a while, still tangled together, neither of us wanting to move. Eventually I rolled off her, pulled her against my side. She fit perfectly, her head on my chest, one leg thrown over mine.

"What happens now?" she asked quietly.

"What do you mean?"

"Vale's gone. The revolution's started. We're still wanted criminals, but we won. So what do we do? Where do we go?"

I thought about it. About Zeno's contact on Freeport Station. About starting over somewhere new, somewhere the Federation couldn't reach us.

But also about the people in the streets. The revolution we'd started. The work that still needed doing.

"We disappear," I said. "Use the money, buy passage to Freeport, get new identities. Start fresh."

"And leave everyone here? Leave the revolution we started?"

"We're not leaders, Trixx. We're criminals who got lucky. The revolution doesn't need us anymore. It needs organizers, politicians, people who know how to build something that lasts."

"And we just run away?"

"We survive. That's what you wanted, right? A life together? A future?"

She was quiet for a long time. "Yeah. That's what I wanted. Still want it. But it feels wrong to leave when there's still so much work to do."

"We've done our part. More than our part. Now it's someone else's turn."

"You really believe that?"

"I'm trying to." The words felt heavier than they should. Like I was trying to convince myself as much as her.

She kissed my chest, right over my heart. "Okay. We disappear. Start over. Build something new. But promise me something."

"What?"

"Promise me you won't look back. Won't second-guess this. Won't spend the rest of your life wondering if we should've stayed and fought."

I thought about the Verge. About Vale's empire crumbling. About everything we'd burned to get here.

"I won't," I said. The truth, for once. Some things you couldn't go back to even if you wanted to.

We fell asleep like that, wrapped around each other, safe for the first time in weeks. Outside, the revolution continued. Inside, we dreamed of futures that might actually be possible.

. . .

I woke up to Zeno shaking my shoulder. Trixx was still asleep next to me, naked and beautiful in the morning light filtering through the windows.

"What?" I mumbled.

"We got a problem," Zeno said quietly. "Federation's reorganizing faster than expected. They're issuing new warrants, consolidating power, using the chaos to crack down harder. And they're specifically looking for us."

"I thought we had time."

"We did. But Vale's got friends in high places. Even in custody, even disgraced, he's still dangerous. And he's putting pressure on the Council to hunt us down."

"How much time do we have?"

"To get off-station? Maybe a day. Two if we're lucky. After that, every port will be locked down tight."

I looked at Trixx, still sleeping peacefully. Thought about the conversation we'd had last night. About disappearing, starting over, building a life.

About leaving behind the revolution we'd started.

"Contact your guy on Freeport," I said. "Tell him we're coming. We need transport, new identities, the full package. Whatever it costs."

"It's gonna cost most of your money."

"Don't care. Just make it happen."

Zeno nodded, left us alone. I lay back down, pulled Trixx close. She stirred, mumbled something, pressed against me.

"Morning," she said sleepily.

"Morning."

"What time is it?"

"Time to go. Zeno says we got maybe a day before the Federation locks everything down."

She was awake immediately. "Where are we going?"

"Freeport. New identities. New life. Everything we talked about."

"Everything we talked about," she repeated. Smiled. "Okay. Let's do it. Let's disappear and never look back."

"You sure?"

"I'm sure. I've got you. I've got the crew. That's all I need."

We got dressed, packed what little we had. Zeno was already coordinating with his contact, arranging transport, buying the documents we'd need.

Hark was by the window, smoking, watching the station. "Revolution's still going strong," he said. "People are organizing, forming committees, demanding a seat at the table. This might actually stick."

"Good," I said. "They deserve it."

"You gonna miss it? Being the guy who started all this?"

"No. I'm gonna be the guy who survived it. That's enough." Even as I said it, I wasn't sure I believed it.

He smiled, rare and genuine. "Smart kid. Maybe you'll make it after all."

. . .

We left Echelon Prime the same way we'd come in—quietly, carefully, like ghosts. The station was different now. More alive. People in the streets talking about the revolution, organizing, planning. The Verge wasn't just surviving anymore. It was fighting back.

And we were leaving it all behind.

Part of me wondered if that made us cowards. But the bigger part—the part that was tired of running and fighting and losing people—just wanted to live.

Zeno's contact met us at a private dock—some smuggler with more money than sense, willing to risk Federation heat for the right price. The ship was small but fast, designed for running blockades and dodging patrols.

"This is it," the smuggler said. "Last transport off-station before the lockdown. You're lucky I owe Zeno a favor."

"How much?" I asked.

"Eight hundred thousand. For all four of you. New identities, passage to Freeport, and enough bribes to get through Federation checkpoints without questions."

Nearly everything we had. But what was money compared to freedom?

"Deal," I said.

We loaded up. Took one last look at the station—at the Verge, at Nova Block Six-Nine, at everything that had been home for my whole life.

"Ready?" Trixx asked.

"No," I said honestly. "But let's go anyway."

The ship lifted off, pulling away from the station, heading for the jump point that would take us to Freeport. As we accelerated, I watched the station shrink in the viewport, watched it become just another light among millions.

Somewhere down there, Ky was still floating. Still cold. Still dead.

But his name would live on. His death had meant something. Had changed something.

That had to be enough.

"What are you thinking?" Trixx asked, squeezing my hand.

"That maybe Mama Leena was right. Maybe revenge doesn't fix anything. But justice... justice can change the world."

"And what about us? What are we gonna do with our new lives?"

I pulled her close, kissed her forehead. "Whatever we want. That's the whole point of freedom, right? We get to choose."

"I choose you," she said.

"I choose you too."

Behind us, the station faded to a pinpoint of light, then disappeared entirely as we jumped. The revolution would continue without us. The fight would go on.

But we were done fighting.

We were going to live.

And maybe, just maybe, we'd finally be happy.

✦ ✦ ✦

CHAPTER 13

Freeport

Freeport Station looked like someone had taken every mistake humanity ever made and put it in orbit.

The place was massive—bigger than our home station, sprawling and chaotic, built without plan or oversight. Sections grafted onto sections, illegal construction everywhere, no Federation flags, no laws worth a damn. It was beautiful in the way a scar is beautiful— proof that you survived something that should've killed you.

"Welcome to paradise," the smuggler said as we approached the main dock. His name was Kross, and he had the kind of face that had seen every con and run half of them. "Freeport's got three rules: don't steal from anyone who can kill you, don't fuck with the families, and mind your own business. Break those rules, you're on your own."

"What about the Federation?" Trixx asked. "They have any presence here?"

Kross laughed. "Feds got an embassy in the diplomatic sector, but they don't enforce shit. Freeport's independent—no extradition treaties, no cooperation, nothing. It's why every criminal, revolutionary, and asshole in the sector ends up here eventually."

"Sounds like home," Hark muttered.

We docked at Bay Forty-Seven, deep in the civilian sector where no one asked questions if you didn't volunteer answers. The air here smelled different—recycled through too many lungs, flavored with a hundred different cultures cooking food that probably violated health codes on any civilized station.

I loved it immediately.

Kross led us through customs, which was really just a bored clerk in a booth who stamped our new identities without looking up. According to our papers, I was Marcus Chen, independent trader. Trixx was Violet Chen, my wife. Hark was our "security consultant" James Park. Zeno was our "technical specialist" Leo Martinez.

"Remember your names," Kross said as we cleared customs. "Use them in public, think in them in private. The second you slip up and use your real names, someone's gonna notice. And on Freeport, information is currency."

"What about the money?" I asked. We'd paid him eight hundred thousand, nearly everything we had.

"Already deposited in your accounts under your new names. Clean, untraceable, spread across three banks so it doesn't attract attention." He handed me a credit chip. "This has fifty thousand on it. Walking-around money. Don't spend it all in one place, and for fuck's sake, don't act like tourists."

"We're not tourists," I said.

"No, you're refugees with five million credit bounties on your real heads. Even worse. Stay smart, stay quiet, and you might survive long enough to enjoy your new lives."

He left us at a transit hub, disappearing into the crowd like he'd never existed.

"Now what?" Zeno asked. He looked nervous, out of place without his computers and his safehouses. We all did. We were used to knowing the territory, knowing which blocks were safe and which would get you killed. Here, everything was foreign.

"Now we find a place to live," Trixx said. "Somewhere cheap but not too cheap. We need to blend in, look like regular people doing regular shit."

"I don't know how to be regular people," I admitted.

"Then we learn," Hark said. "Fast."

•   •   •

We found an apartment in the Market District—three rooms, shared bathroom down the hall, windows that looked out on a street full of vendors selling everything from food to weapons to fake IDs. The rent was five hundred credits a month, which felt like highway robbery until the landlord explained that was cheap for Freeport.

"You're lucky," she said. She was an older woman, human, with the kind of eyes that had seen every scam. "Had a vacancy because the last tenant got himself killed in a gambling dispute. His blood's still on the floor if you look under the rug."

"We'll take it," I said.

She handed over the keys. "Rent's due first of every month. Miss a payment, I change the locks. No exceptions, no sob stories. This is Freeport—everyone's got problems."

The apartment was small but functional. One room for me and Trixx, one for Hark, one for Zeno to set up his computers. The furniture was shit—mismatched, stained, probably older than me. But it was ours. Or at least, it was Marcus Chen's.

Not Nova's. Nova didn't exist anymore. Nova was back on the station we'd fled, floating in space with my brother's ghost.

"Home sweet home," Trixx said, dropping her bag on the bed. The mattress sagged under the weight. "This is depressing."

"This is freedom," I said. "No Feds hunting us. No Operation Exodus. No revolution. Just... life."

"You make it sound boring."

"Maybe boring is good."

She looked at me like I'd grown a second head. "You? Boring? Baby, I give you a week before you're climbing the walls."

"I can do boring. Watch me."

"I will."

* * *

The first week was strange.

We woke up without checking for Federation raids. Ate breakfast at street vendors who didn't know our names. Walked through markets where people haggled instead of ran.

Normal felt wrong. Like wearing someone else's skin.

"You're twitching," Trixx said one morning at a noodle stand. "Every time someone walks behind you, you reach for a gun that's not there."

"Force of habit."

"We're safe here."

"For now."

She was right. I knew she was right. But trouble always found us eventually.

Hark found security work. Zeno set up shop as a tech consultant. Both seemed almost happy.

Me? I didn't know what to do with myself. Who was I without the fight? Without Ky's death driving me forward?

"You need a job," Trixx said on day five.

There were transport companies that needed pilots. I applied to TransFreight Solutions using my new identity. They hired me the same day.

The job was simple: pick up cargo at one dock, deliver it to another dock, don't ask questions about what's in the containers. The pay was shit compared to what we used to make running jobs, but it was legal. Mostly.

And it was boring as hell.

"How's the straight life?" Hark asked one night. We were at a bar called The Rusty Bolt, drinking cheap beer and watching a fight break out over a card game.

"Weird," I admitted. "I keep waiting for someone to shoot at me. When they don't, I feel disappointed."

"That's the adrenaline addiction talking. You got hooked on danger, now normal life feels empty."

"Is that what happened to you? After the war?"

"Yeah. Took me years to adjust. Even now, I still miss it sometimes. The clarity of combat. The simple math of survival. Real life's messy. No clear enemies, no obvious victories."

"How do you deal with it?"

"I found new battles to fight. Smaller ones. Personal ones. Like keeping your stupid ass alive." He drained his beer. "You'll find your thing. Just gotta give it time."

Time. That was the problem. I had too much of it now. No urgency, no immediate threats, no reason to move fast and think faster.

And the empty hours gave me too much space to think. About Ky. About the fourteen people who died in riots I'd started. About whether running away made me smart or just a coward.

My comm buzzed. Unknown number. I almost didn't answer, but paranoia got the better of me.

"Yeah?"

"Mr. Chen?" A woman's voice, professional, cold. "This is Kira Voss from the Merchant Guild. I'm calling about a business opportunity."

"I'm not interested."

"You should be. I represent clients who are willing to pay substantial sums for your... particular skill set. Skills that involve high-speed transport, discretion, and a certain disregard for conventional regulations."

"I'm a legitimate cargo pilot now. Try someone else."

"Marcus Chen is a legitimate cargo pilot. But Nova... Nova is something else entirely."

My blood went cold. "I don't know what you're talking about."

"Of course you don't. But if Nova were interested in a job that pays fifty thousand credits for one night's work, he might want to meet me at The Broken Chain tomorrow at midnight. Come alone. Or don't come at all."

She hung up.

"Fuck," I said quietly.

"What?" Hark asked.

"Someone knows who we are."

•   •   •

I didn't tell Trixx about the call. Didn't want her worrying, didn't want the lecture about how we were supposed to be living clean now. Instead, I told her I was picking up a late shift, kissed her goodnight, and headed to The Broken Chain.

The lie tasted like ash. Like every other lie I'd told to protect people who ended up hurt anyway.

The bar was in the Deep Docks—the part of Freeport where the criminals were honest about being criminals. No pretense, no facades, just people doing illegal shit and not apologizing for it.

Kira Voss was sitting in a corner booth, wearing a suit that probably cost more than our apartment. She was human, maybe forty, with the kind of confidence that came from having power and knowing how to use it.

"Nova," she said as I sat down. "Or should I call you Marcus?"

"Depends on whether you're planning to blackmail me."

"I don't blackmail. I negotiate. There's a difference."

"Talk."

She slid a tablet across the table. On it was a photo of a ship—sleek, fast, Federation military design. "That's the Artemis Dawn. Federation intelligence vessel, currently docked at the embassy sector. My client wants certain data files that are stored in its secured archives."

"Your client wants me to rob a Fed ship? On Freeport?"

"Not rob. Acquire. There's a difference."

"Not from where I'm sitting."

"The job pays fifty thousand credits. Clean, untraceable. And more importantly, it ensures your real identity remains... confidential."

There it was. The blackmail disguised as a job offer.

"How many people know?" I asked.

"Just me. And I'm very good at keeping secrets, as long as I'm properly compensated."

"And if I say no?"

"Then by tomorrow morning, every bounty hunter on this station will know that the revolutionary who took down Lt. Vale is living in the Market District under the name Marcus Chen. I imagine that would be unfortunate for you and your crew."

I wanted to punch her. Wanted to put a gun to her head and make her delete whatever information she had. But that would just confirm her suspicions and make things worse.

"What's in the files?" I asked.

"That's not your concern. You get in, download the data to this chip—" she placed a small drive on the table "—and get out. Simple."

"Nothing's ever simple."

"Then consider it complicated but lucrative." She stood up, straightened her suit. "You have twenty-four hours to decide. If you're in, be at Dock Ninety-Three tomorrow night at midnight. If you're not, well... it was nice knowing Marcus Chen."

She left. I sat there, staring at the data chip, feeling the weight of every choice I'd ever made pressing down on me.

I'd come to Freeport to escape. To start over. To be someone other than the criminal, the revolutionary, the fuck-up who kept making things worse.

But maybe Trixx was right. Maybe I wasn't built for boring.

Maybe I was just built for trouble.

Or maybe trouble was just built to find me, no matter how far I ran.

· · ·

I got back to the apartment around 2 AM. Trixx was still awake, sitting by the window, smoking one of my Black Deaths.

"You smell like a bar," she said without looking at me.

"Went out for a drink."

"With who?"

"Myself."

She turned. Her glow-ink was pulsing slow, sad purple. "You're lying. And you're bad at it."

"Trixx—"

"Don't. Just don't. Whatever stupid thing you're about to do, don't do it." She stood up, came over to me. "We left that life behind. We agreed. No more jobs, no more risks, no more playing with fire."

"Someone knows who we are."

Her face went pale. "What?"

"Someone contacted me. Knows our real identities. Wants me to do a job or they leak it to every bounty hunter on the station."

"Fuck. Fuck! Nova, we need to run. Get off-station before—"

"We can't keep running. Every station we go to, someone will eventually figure it out. We're too high-profile now. Too famous."

"So what do we do?"

"We do the job. Get leverage on whoever's blackmailing us. Then we make sure they can't talk."

"That's your plan? Do crime to stop people from knowing you did crime?"

"You got a better idea?"

She didn't. We both knew she didn't. But the silence hung there between us, heavy with all the promises we'd made about leaving that life behind.

"I'm coming with you," she said finally.

"No."

"Yes. You're not doing this alone. We're crew, remember? We don't leave each other."

"Trixx—"

"I said I'm coming. You can argue, but I'll just follow you anyway. So save us both the time and say yes."

I looked at her. At this woman who'd stuck with me through everything, who'd risked her life for mine more times than I could count, who loved me despite every reason not to.

Who'd believed me when I said we could start over. Who'd trusted me when I promised we could leave the violence behind.

And here I was, dragging her back into it. Again.

"Okay," I said. "We do it together."

"Always," she said, and kissed me like it might be the last time.

Like maybe she knew what I knew—that we'd never really escaped. That we were still the same people, just wearing different names. That trouble would always find us because we were made of it.

And maybe that was okay.

Maybe that was just who we were.

✦ ✦ ✦

INTERLUDE

What She Carries

Freeport Station, Day Three

Trixx couldn't sleep.

Nova was breathing slow and deep beside her, finally peaceful for the first time since they'd arrived. The apartment was quiet—Hark's snores rumbling through the thin walls, Zeno's keyboard clicking softly in the other room, the hum of Freeport's recycled air. Normal sounds. Safe sounds.

She hated them.

She slipped out of bed, careful not to wake him, and padded barefoot to the window. The Market District sprawled below, still alive even at three in the morning—vendors hawking bootleg tech, pleasure workers calling from doorways, a fight breaking out in an alley that nobody bothered to stop. Chaos and life and noise.

It should have felt like freedom. Instead it felt like a cage with prettier bars.

She pressed her palm against the cold glass and watched her glow-ink pulse—slow, steady, the purple light reflecting back at her like an accusation.

You're not Violet Chen, the light seemed to say. *You're Trixxie Malone from the Rings. Daughter of Marcus Malone, who taught you to shoot when you were eight and died when you were twelve.*

Daughter of Keera Malone, who sold you to a pleasure house when you were fourteen because she couldn't afford to feed you anymore.

She'd escaped that house at sixteen. Killed a man to do it—her first, but not her last. Then she'd drifted through the Outer Colonies, working jobs she didn't talk about, building skills she wished she didn't need.

Until Nova.

She'd met him at a card game in some shithole bar on the far side of the station. He'd been cocky, reckless, running his mouth about a job that was obviously going to get him killed. She'd told him so. He'd laughed and asked if she wanted to help him not die.

Six months later, she was here. Running from the Federation. Hiding under a fake name. Watching the man she loved destroy himself trying to avenge a brother he couldn't save.

And she'd do it all again. That was the fucked up part. If Nova called her right now and said *I need to go back, I need to fight,* she'd grab her gun and follow him into hell.

Because that's what love was, in the Verge. Not flowers and promises. Not safety and stability. Love was following someone into the dark and trusting them not to get you killed.

Or trusting yourself to survive when they did.

She thought about her father. About the way he'd held her hands around the grip of that first pistol, adjusting her stance, teaching her to breathe. *"Squeeze, don't pull. Let the shot surprise you."* She thought about the look on his face when the gang members came for him—not scared, just... tired. Like he'd always known this was how it ended.

She thought about her mother. About the day she'd walked Trixx to that pleasure house and said *"Be good. Make money. Survive."* No tears. No apologies. Just practical cruelty from a woman who'd given up on softness a long time ago.

Trixx had survived. She'd learned to be hard because soft girls didn't make it out of places like that. She'd learned to use her body as a weapon and a tool, to read men's weaknesses before they even knew what they wanted, to smile while she calculated exactly how to destroy someone.

Then Nova had looked at her like she was a person instead of a product. Like she mattered. Like she was worth something beyond what her body could do.

And the hard shell she'd built started to crack.

That's what scared her most. Not the Federation. Not the bounties. Not even the five million credits that made them the most wanted criminals in the sector.

What scared her was this: she'd finally found something worth living for, and she could feel it slipping away.

Nova thought this was over. Vale arrested, revolution started, time to disappear and build a normal life. But Trixx had seen his face when the news feeds showed more black sites, more prisoners, more people suffering. She'd seen the way his hands twitched toward guns that weren't there.

He wasn't done fighting. He'd never be done fighting. And one day, that fight was going to kill him—and probably her too, because she wasn't letting him die alone.

So what do you do? she asked herself. *What do you do when you love someone who's always running toward the fire?*

She didn't have an answer. She wasn't sure there was one.

Behind her, Nova stirred. "Trixx? You okay?"

She wiped her eyes—when had she started crying?—and turned with a smile she'd practiced a thousand times. "Yeah, baby. Just couldn't sleep. Go back to bed."

"Come with me."

"In a minute."

He was already drifting off again, trusting her to come back, trusting her to be there when he woke up. That trust was the most precious thing she owned.

And the most terrifying.

She looked out the window one more time. Somewhere out there, people were still suffering. Still fighting. Still dying for the same cause Nova had almost died for.

This isn't over, she thought. *This is just the intermission.*

When the next act started, she'd be ready. She'd follow him into hell and fight her way back out. Because that's what love was.

That's what love cost.

She went back to bed, curled against his warmth, and pretended to sleep until morning.

✦ ✦ ✦

CHAPTER 14

The Artemis Job

Planning a heist against the Federation while pretending to be law-abiding citizens was a special kind of stupid. But we'd been stupid before and survived. Mostly.

"You're not telling Hark and Zeno," Trixx said as we walked through the Market District the next morning. She was wearing civilian clothes—a simple dress that hid glow-ink—trying to look like a normal person doing normal shopping. "They think we're retired."

"We are retired. This is just... one last job."

"That's what everyone says. Then there's another last job. And another. Until there's a final job that actually is final because you're dead."

"Poetic."

"I'm serious, Nova. We involve them, we drag them back into the life. They're doing good here. Hark's got his security work. Zeno's making honest money. We can't—"

My comm buzzed. Zeno's face appeared on the screen, grinning.

"Yo, heard you got a job offer from Kira Voss. The Merchant Guild fixer. When were you gonna tell me?"

I looked at Trixx. She looked at the sky like she was asking God for patience.

"How the fuck did you find out?" I asked.

"Please. I monitor every communication in and out of our building. Paranoia keeps us alive, remember? Plus, Voss isn't exactly subtle. She's been asking questions about you for three days. Did background checks, pulled your employment records, even tried to hack your banking info before I blocked her."

"You blocked her?"

"Yeah, but she's good. Give her another week and she'll crack my defenses. Whoever trained her knows their shit."

Trixx grabbed my comm. "Zeno, we're handling this. You and Hark stay out of it."

"Too late. Already told Hark. He's very disappointed you tried to handle it alone, by the way. Says family doesn't hide shit from family, and you should know better."

"Zeno—"

"Meet us at The Rusty Bolt in twenty minutes. We're gonna plan this properly or not at all."

He hung up.

"I fucking hate that kid sometimes," Trixx muttered.

"You love that kid."

"That doesn't mean I don't hate him."

* * *

The Rusty Bolt was empty at midday—just us, the bartender who didn't care, and a drunk sleeping in the corner. Hark and Zeno were already there, looking at a holographic layout Zeno had pulled up.

"Federation intelligence vessel," Zeno said as we sat down. "Artemis Dawn. Docked at Embassy Sector, Bay Seven. Guards, sensors, the full military package. She's been here for two weeks, doing 'diplomatic liaison' work, which is code for spying on everyone and pretending it's legal."

"How'd you get that schematic?" I asked.

"Hacked the Freeport port authority. Wasn't even that hard. Their security is shit." He zoomed in on the ship's interior. "The archives Voss wants are here—" he pointed to a section near the engineering deck "—in a secured vault. Biometric locks, encrypted access, probably armed guards."

"So it's impossible," Trixx said.

"Not impossible. Just very difficult and likely to get us killed."

"That's your definition of possible?"

Zeno shrugged. "I've worked with worse odds."

Hark lit up a smoke, stared at the schematic with the kind of focus that made people nervous. "Embassy sector's neutral ground. Freeport respects that, which means no local security interference. But it also means if the Feds catch us, Freeport won't help. We're on our own."

"We're always on our own," I said.

"Yeah, but usually we got exit strategies. Here, we get caught, we're probably getting executed. The Federation's not exactly forgiving about people who rob their intelligence ships."

"Then we don't get caught."

"Genius plan. Why didn't I think of that?"

"Because you're old and your brain's slow."

"Fuck you."

"Fuck you too."

Trixx slammed her hand on the table. "Can we focus? We got twenty-four hours to figure this out or Voss burns us. So either we find a way in, or we run. Again."

"We're not running," I said.

"Then start planning."

Zeno pulled up more data. "The ship changes guard shifts at midnight. That's our window—fifteen minutes when they're transitioning, coordination's sloppy, people are tired. We hit them then."

"How do we get on board?" Hark asked.

"Maintenance access. Every ship's got external ports for station techs to run diagnostics. I can fake credentials, make it look like scheduled maintenance. You two go in as techs—" he pointed at me and Trixx "—while Hark and I provide support from outside."

"What kind of support?" Hark asked.

"The kind where I hack their security systems and you shoot anyone who looks at them wrong."

"That's my kind of support."

"What about the vault?" I asked. "Biometric locks aren't exactly easy to crack."

"They are if you have the right fingerprints." Zeno grinned. "The ship's captain is Commander Sarah Trent. She visits The Broken Chain every Friday night, gets drunk, sometimes takes people home. This Friday's in two days. We're gonna make friends with her."

"Make friends how?"

"Trixx is gonna seduce her, get a DNA sample, and I'm gonna print a fake biometric reader glove. Easy."

Trixx stared at him. "You want me to fuck a Fed to steal her DNA?"

"I mean, you don't have to fuck her. Just get close enough to grab a hair or some saliva. But fucking her would be more thorough."

"I'm not fucking a Fed."

"Your call. But it's either that or we find another way in, which doesn't exist."

She looked at me. "This is your fault."

"How is this my fault?"

"Everything is your fault. Always."

"That's fair."

•   •   •

Friday night came too fast. Trixx spent the day getting ready—hair done, makeup perfect, wearing a dress that was basically illegal in most jurisdictions. Her glow-ink was fully visible, pulsing bright purple, making her look like every fantasy and bad decision rolled into one.

"I look like a prostitute," she said, checking herself in the mirror.

"You look beautiful," I said honestly.

"I look like bait."

"Beautiful bait."

"That doesn't make it better."

"You don't have to do this. We can find another way."

She turned, looked at me with those eyes that saw through every lie I'd ever told. "There is no other way. You know it. I know it. So let's stop pretending this isn't happening and just... get it done."

"I love you."

"I know. That's why I'm doing this stupid shit."

We headed to The Broken Chain separately. Me and Hark took a booth in the back, nursing drinks and trying to look inconspicuous. Zeno was outside in a van, monitoring communications and ready to guide Trixx through the play.

Commander Trent showed up at 9 PM, still in uniform but with her jacket unbuttoned, looking for the kind of fun that would make her regret her choices in the morning. She was maybe thirty-five, fit, attractive in that military way where everything was precise and controlled.

Trixx made her move at 9:30. Walked up to the bar where Trent was sitting, ordered a drink, made conversation. From where I was sitting, I couldn't hear what they were saying, but I could see Trent getting interested. Leaning closer. Laughing at something Trixx said. Touching her arm.

"She's good," Hark muttered. "Natural liar. Must be why she likes you."

"You're hilarious."

"I know."

By 10 PM, they were sitting in a booth together. By 10:30, they were kissing. By 11, Trent was paying the tab and leading Trixx toward the door.

"She's leaving with the target," Zeno said in my earbud. "DNA acquisition likely. Stand by."

They left together, heading to what was probably Trent's quarters. I tried not to think about what was happening. Tried not to imagine Trixx with someone else, even if it was for the job.

But I did think about it. Couldn't stop thinking about it. About Trixx touching her, kissing her, doing whatever needed to be done to get what we needed.

It was just a job. Just work. Nothing personal.

But it felt personal.

"You good?" Hark asked.

"No."

"You're gonna have to be. Can't do this job if you're emotional about your girl fucking a Fed."

"She's not fucking her. She's just... acquiring samples."

"That's what we're calling it?"

"Shut up."

"You know she's only doing this for you, right? She hates this shit. But she's doing it anyway because you got blackmailed into a job you shouldn't have taken alone in the first place."

"I know."

"So maybe think about that before you get all jealous and possessive."

He was right. Of course he was right. But knowing it didn't make the jealousy go away.

Thirty minutes later, my comm buzzed. Text from Trixx: *Got it. Heading back. Don't be weird.*

She showed up twenty minutes later, looking slightly disheveled but triumphant. Handed Zeno a small vial with hair and what was probably saliva.

"Happy?" she said.

"Very," Zeno said, already running analysis. "This is perfect. Give me twelve hours and I'll have a working biometric glove."

Trixx sat down next to me. "I need a drink. Several drinks. And then a shower. And then maybe therapy."

"You okay?" I asked.

"I'm fine. She was nice, actually. Lonely. Talked about how hard it is being a Fed on Freeport, how everyone hates her. I almost felt bad."

"She's still a Fed."

"I know. That's the only reason I could go through with it." She flagged down the bartender. "Whiskey. Double. Actually, just leave the bottle."

She didn't look at me. Didn't touch me. Just drank, staring at nothing, processing whatever had happened in that room.

And I couldn't ask. Couldn't make it about me and my jealousy when she'd just done something she hated for our survival.

So I just sat there with her. Drank with her. Let the silence say what words couldn't.

* * *

The next night, we were ready. Zeno had built the biometric glove, tested it twice, confirmed it would fool the vault's sensors. Hark had acquired weapons—nothing military-grade, just small plasma pistols we could hide under maintenance uniforms.

"Remember," Zeno said as we geared up. "You got fifteen minutes once you're inside. Any longer and the guards will notice the diagnostic is taking too long. Get in, get the data, get out."

"What if something goes wrong?" Trixx asked.

"Then improvise. You're good at that."

"That's not reassuring."

"It's all I got."

We took a transport to the Embassy Sector, showing our fake maintenance credentials at the checkpoint. The guard barely looked at us—just scanned the IDs, saw they checked out, waved us through.

"Too easy," Hark muttered. "Something's wrong."

"Or security's just lazy," I said.

"Security's never lazy on military vessels."

He was right to be paranoid. But we were committed now. No turning back.

The Artemis Dawn was beautiful in that dangerous way military ships are—sleek, armed, designed to kill efficiently. We approached the maintenance hatch, used the access codes Zeno had provided. The hatch opened with a pneumatic hiss.

"You're in," Zeno said in our earbuds. "Heading to engineering deck. Take the corridor left, then down two levels. Vault's at the end."

We moved through the ship like ghosts. The corridors were empty—most of the crew was off-duty, the skeleton watch focused on external threats, not internal ones. Stupid. They'd gotten comfortable on Freeport, forgot that neutral ground didn't mean safe ground.

The vault was exactly where Zeno said it would be. A heavy door, biometric scanner, probably armed guards on the other side.

"Now what?" Trixx whispered.

"Now I do my thing." I pulled out the glove Zeno had made, pressed it against the scanner. For a second, nothing happened. Then the light turned green and the door clicked open.

"We're in."

No guards. Just a small room full of data servers, humming quietly, storing secrets the Federation didn't want anyone to know.

"Find the archive," Zeno said. "Should be labeled BLACKSITE-7. Download everything to the chip."

I plugged in the chip Voss had given me, started the download. Progress bar crawled across the screen—5%, 10%, 15%.

"This is taking too long," Trixx said, watching the door.

"Can't make it go faster."

"Someone's coming," Hark said through the comm. "Two guards, heading your way. ETA two minutes."

"We're at thirty percent."

"Speed it up."

"I'm trying!"

The download kept crawling. 40%. 50%. Voices in the corridor, getting closer. Footsteps. The guards were early, must've noticed something wrong.

"Nova—" Trixx pulled her gun.

"Wait."

70%. 80%. The door handle started turning.

"Get down!" Trixx shoved me behind a server rack just as the door opened. Two Federation guards entered, weapons drawn, scanning the room.

"Intruders!" one of them shouted into his comm. "Archive breach! Repeat, archive breach!"

Trixx fired first. Her plasma bolt took one guard in the chest, dropped him clean. The second guard returned fire, his shot missing by inches, melting a hole in the server behind my head.

I pulled my gun, fired blind. Got lucky—hit him in the shoulder, spun him around. Trixx finished him with a headshot.

"Download complete," the terminal announced cheerfully.

I grabbed the chip, yanked it free. "We gotta move!"

Alarms started screaming. Lights turned red. Lockdown protocols activating, doors slamming shut throughout the ship.

"Fuck!" Zeno yelled. "They've sealed the ship! You're trapped!"

"There's always a way out," I said, running. Trixx was right behind me, firing at guards who were pouring into the corridors now, responding to the breach.

"Maintenance shaft," Hark said. "Deck three, section B. Emergency exit. But you gotta override the locks from inside."

"On it!" I skidded around a corner, nearly ran into three more guards. Dropped, rolled, came up firing. Got one in the leg, another in the chest. The third tackled me, and we went down hard.

He was bigger, stronger, trained. But I was desperate. I got my gun under his chin and pulled the trigger. His head snapped back. Blood on my face. No time to process.

"This way!" Trixx dragged me up. We ran through the ship, guards shouting behind us, plasma fire lighting up the corridors.

Found the maintenance shaft. The door was locked, red light blinking.

"Zeno, we need this door open!"

"Working on it! Their security's better than I thought!"

"Work faster!"

Gunfire behind us. Close. Too close. I turned, fired suppressing shots, buying time. Trixx was next to me, doing the same. We were about to get swarmed.

The door clicked green.

"Go!" I shoved Trixx through. She fell into the shaft, grabbed a ladder, started climbing down. I followed, pulling the door shut just as guards rounded the corner.

They fired at the door. It held. Barely.

We climbed down fast, hands burning on the ladder, until we reached the external hatch. Hark was waiting outside with a stolen transport.

"Move your asses!" he shouted.

We jumped. Fell three meters, hit the transport's deck hard. Hark punched the thrusters and we were gone, accelerating away from the Artemis Dawn while alarms howled and lights flashed.

Behind us, the ship was lighting up—searchlights, defensive weapons, communications going crazy as they realized we'd escaped.

"Did you get it?" Zeno asked.

I checked the chip. Data intact. "Yeah. We got it."

"Then get to the rendezvous. Now. Before they lock down the whole sector."

We made it to Zeno's van with seconds to spare. Behind us, Federation security was spreading out, searching, setting up checkpoints. But we were gone, disappeared into Freeport's maze of streets and sectors.

"That was too close," Trixx said, breathing hard, adrenaline making glow-ink pulse like a strobe.

"But we made it," I said.

"This time."

Back at the safehouse, Zeno plugged in the chip, started analyzing what we'd stolen.

His face went pale.

"What?" I asked. "What's on there?"

"It's... it's not just data. It's names. Locations. The Federation's entire network of black sites. Places where they disappear people. Where they send the processed."

"From Operation Exodus?"

"Yeah. And before. Going back years. There's thousands of names here, Nova. Thousands of people who were supposed to be dead or relocated but were actually—"

He pulled up a file. Video footage from one of the black sites.

I wished I hadn't looked.

People in cages. Medical equipment. Bodies on tables being carved up, harvested, discarded. Screaming that no one would ever hear. Children. Old people. Hybrids. Anyone the Federation deemed undesirable, processed like meat.

My stomach turned. I'd seen violence. I'd killed people. But this... this was systematic. Industrial. Evil distilled into bureaucracy and efficiency.

"They're not processing people," Hark said quietly. "They're harvesting them. Organs, genetic material, anything valuable. The ones who survive become slaves. The ones who don't... they get recycled."

Trixx turned away, hand over her mouth, looking sick.

"Voss wanted us to steal this?" I said. "Why? What's her game?"

"I don't know," Zeno said. "But whoever she's working for, they just got the keys to the Federation's darkest secrets."

My comm buzzed. Voss.

"Good work, Nova. The chip, please. You know where to meet me."

"What are you gonna do with this?"

"That's not your concern. Just deliver the chip and we're square. Your secret stays secret."

"And if I don't?"

"Then I leak your identity and you spend the rest of your very short life running from bounty hunters. Your choice."

She hung up.

I looked at my crew. At the data showing thousands of people being tortured, murdered, harvested. At proof of genocide on a scale that made Operation Exodus look small.

This was bigger than Vale. Bigger than one station. This was the whole rotten system laid bare.

"We can't give this to her," Trixx said. "Whatever she's planning, it's bad."

"But if we don't, she burns us."

"Then we burn her first," Hark said simply. "Find out who she's working for. Take them down before they can use this information."

"Or," Zeno said slowly, "we leak it ourselves. Give it to the media. Let the whole universe see what the Federation's really doing."

I thought about the last time we'd leaked data. About Vale's arrest. About how we'd barely escaped with our lives.

About how fourteen people had died in the riots we'd started.

"That worked so well last time," I said.

"Last time we exposed one officer. This time we're exposing the entire system. This is bigger than Vale. This is everything."

He was right. We all knew he was right.

But were we ready for what came next? For the war that would follow? For making enemies of not just the Federation, but whoever Voss worked for?

"If we leak this," I said, "we're not just fighting the Federation. We're fighting whoever Voss works for too. We'll have enemies on all sides."

"When don't we?" Trixx said.

I looked at the chip. At the weight of all those lives, all those secrets, all that evil distilled into a few terabytes of data.

I thought about Ky. About the fourteen people who died. About whether I was helping or just making things worse.

But then I looked at the video again. At the people in cages. At the children being harvested.

Some things you couldn't walk away from.

Some things demanded a response, no matter the cost.

"Fuck it," I said. "Let's burn the whole thing down."

✦ ✦ ✦

CHAPTER 15

Point of No Return

The decision hung in the air like smoke from Hark's cigarette—thick, choking, impossible to ignore.

"Let's burn the whole thing down," I'd said. Like it was simple. Like we weren't about to make enemies of the most powerful people in the fucking universe.

Zeno was already moving, fingers flying across his screens. "If we're doing this, we need to do it right. Can't just dump the data somewhere and hope it spreads. We need multiple distribution points, encrypted channels, backups in case they try to suppress it."

"How long?" I asked.

"To set up properly? Six hours. Maybe eight."

"We don't have eight hours," Trixx said. "Voss expects us at the rendezvous in three. When we don't show, she's gonna know something's wrong."

"Then we move fast." Hark stubbed out his smoke, his metal eye whirring as it focused. "Zeno handles the tech. We handle Voss."

"Handle how?" I asked.

"We meet her. Tell her the deal's changed."

"You mean we tell her to go fuck herself."

"Politely, yeah."

My comm buzzed. Voss. Right on schedule.

"Status update, Nova. Are we still on for the exchange?"

I looked at my crew. At Trixx with her hand on her gun. At Hark cracking his metal knuckles. At Zeno surrounded by holographic screens showing the Federation's darkest secrets.

"Yeah," I said. "We're on. Same place, same time."

"Good. Don't be late."

She hung up.

"You're actually meeting her?" Zeno asked.

"Can't have her sending bounty hunters after us while you're trying to leak the data. We'll keep her busy, buy you time."

"She's dangerous, Nova. Whoever she works for, they got serious resources."

"So do we. We got each other."

"That's corny as fuck," Trixx said.

"Doesn't make it less true."

* * *

The rendezvous was at a warehouse in the Deep Docks—neutral ground, supposedly. The kind of place where deals went down and bodies got disappeared if things went wrong.

We showed up thirty minutes early, scouted the location. Single entrance, multiple exits if you knew where to look. Shipping containers stacked high, creating a maze of metal. Good for ambushes. Bad for quick escapes.

"I don't like this," Hark muttered, hand resting on his gun.

"You don't like anything."

"That's because everything is trying to kill us."

Voss arrived exactly on time, walking through the warehouse entrance like she owned the place. She was alone—at least, appeared to be. But I'd learned that alone didn't mean unarmed or unprepared.

She was dressed casual today. Expensive casual. The kind of clothes that whispered money without screaming it. Her face was calm, professional, betraying nothing.

"Nova," she said, stopping ten feet away. "You brought friends."

"Yeah, well. Trust is in short supply these days."

"Wise. Do you have the chip?"

I pulled it from my pocket, held it up. "Right here. But we need to talk first."

Her eyes narrowed slightly. "Talk about what? We had a deal."

"Deals change. We looked at what's on this chip. Saw what the Federation's really doing in those black sites. Saw the names, the numbers, the footage."

"And?"

"And we got questions. Like what the fuck you want with this information. Who you're working for. What's your angle."

"My angle is none of your business. Just give me the chip and walk away."

"Can't do that."

The temperature in the room dropped about twenty degrees. Voss's calm facade cracked just a little, showing something cold and dangerous underneath.

"Excuse me?"

"You heard me. We're not giving you the chip. Not until we know what you're planning to do with it."

"I could expose your real identities right now. One call and every bounty hunter on this station knows who you really are."

"You could," I agreed. "But then you don't get the data. And something tells me your bosses would be real disappointed if you fucked this up."

Voss stared at me for a long moment. Then she smiled. Not a friendly smile. The kind of smile sharks give right before they bite.

"You're making a mistake."

"Probably. But we're used to that."

"You have no idea what you're interfering with. The forces you're provoking. This information—it's not just about exposing the Federation. It's leverage. Power. Whoever controls it controls the narrative."

"Exactly," Trixx said. "And we're not letting you control shit."

"So what's your plan? Leak it yourselves? Become heroes of the revolution?" Voss laughed, sharp and bitter. "You think that worked out so well last time? Vale's in prison, sure. But the system's still intact. The Federation's still in power. All you did was give them a martyr and make yourselves targets."

She wasn't wrong. The thought cut deeper than I wanted to admit.

"Better than helping you weaponize it," I said.

"I'm trying to save lives, you idiot. The people I work for—they want to use this information to broker peace. To negotiate terms that actually protect hybrids and refugees. Give the Federation something to trade so they stop the genocides."

"Bullshit," Hark said flatly. "If your bosses wanted peace, they wouldn't need blackmail material. They'd come to the table honestly."

"There is no honest in politics. There's only leverage and timing."

"Then fuck politics," I said. "We're putting this information where everyone can see it. Let the people decide what to do with it."

Voss's hand moved toward her jacket. Faster than I expected. But not faster than Trixx.

Trixx had her gun out and aimed before Voss cleared her holster. "Don't."

Voss froze. "You're really willing to shoot me?"

"I've shot Feds for less."

"I'm not Federation."

"No. You're worse. You're the kind of person who profits from everyone else's suffering. So yeah, I'll shoot you. Happily."

Voss slowly raised her hands. "You're making enemies you can't afford."

"Add them to the list," I said. "We're leaving now. Don't follow us. Don't come looking for us. And when you talk to your bosses, tell them the data's going public whether they like it or not."

"They'll kill you for this."

"Everyone wants to kill us. Get in line."

We backed out slowly, guns trained on Voss the whole time. She didn't move, just watched us with those cold eyes, calculating, planning her next move.

Outside, Hark sparked up immediately. "That went well."

"Define well," Trixx said.

"Nobody died. That's well enough for me."

My comm buzzed. Zeno.

"Tell me you got good news," I said.

"Depends on your definition of good. The distribution network's ready. I can push the data to fifteen different media outlets, fifty independent journalists, and about two hundred activist networks simultaneously. Once it's out, it's out. Can't be suppressed."

"That's good news."

"The bad news is I'm picking up weird traffic. Someone's been scanning for our location. High-level military encryption. Not Federation—something else."

"Voss's people?"

"Probably. They know you didn't give her the chip. They're gonna come looking."

"How long do we have?"

"Hour. Maybe two if we're lucky."

"Do it," I said. "Release everything. Now."

"Nova, once I do this, there's no taking it back. We'll be targets for the rest of our lives."

"We're already targets. At least this way we choose what we're dying for."

Silence on the line. Then: "Alright. Uploading now. Data dump goes live in five minutes."

The world was about to change. Again.

And I couldn't shake Voss's words. About leverage versus exposure. About making the Federation into a cornered animal.

Maybe she was right. Maybe we were about to make things worse.

But maybe some truths had to come out, no matter the cost.

. . .

We made it back to the safehouse with thirty minutes to spare. Zeno had the feeds up on every screen—news outlets, social media, activist channels. Waiting for the bomb to drop.

"You sure about this?" Trixx asked, sitting next to me on the couch. Her hand found mine, squeezed tight.

"No. But I'm sure about not giving it to Voss. Everything else is just damage control."

"We could run. Right now. Before the data drops. Disappear before everyone knows we did this."

"Better than being dead."

"Maybe. But I'm tired of hiding. Tired of running. Tired of letting other people decide what information the universe gets to see."

Hark poured drinks. Straight whiskey, the expensive shit we'd stolen from the penthouse. "To making historically bad decisions."

"To family," I corrected.

"That's the same thing."

We drank. The whiskey burned, warm and harsh and perfect.

Zeno's computer chimed. "Data's live. It's spreading."

The screens lit up. Headlines appearing in real-time:

BREAKING: FEDERATION BLACK SITE NETWORK EXPOSED

LEAKED DOCUMENTS REVEAL MASSIVE GENOCIDE OPERATION

THOUSANDS MISSING: WHERE ARE THE PROCESSED?

View counters started climbing. Ten thousand. Fifty thousand. A hundred thousand. The numbers accelerating, exponential growth as the information spread across the mesh.

"Holy shit," Zeno whispered. "It's going viral. Every major outlet's picking it up."

Video footage from the black sites started playing on news channels. The harvesting chambers. The processing facilities. Bodies in rows. Names in databases. Evidence of systematic murder on a scale that made Operation Exodus look like a warm-up act.

My comm exploded. Messages flooding in from numbers I didn't recognize:

Is this real?

Who leaked this?

The Federation needs to answer for this

SHARE EVERYWHERE

Within twenty minutes, the data had been viewed five million times. Within an hour, twenty million. The story was too big to suppress, too well-documented to deny.

The Federation released a statement calling it propaganda. Fake news. Enemy disinformation designed to destabilize galactic peace.

Nobody was buying it.

Protests started within two hours. Not just on Freeport—everywhere. Stations across the Federation territories. Planetary colonies. Even on Earth, in the Federation capital itself. Millions of people demanding answers. Demanding justice. Demanding the end of the black site program.

"We did it," Trixx said, watching the screens in disbelief. "We actually fucking did it."

"No," Hark said quietly. "We started it. The people are doing it. We just gave them the ammunition."

My comm buzzed. Unknown number. I almost didn't answer. But something made me.

A voice I didn't recognize. Male. Cold. Professional.

"You've made a serious mistake, Mr. DeLeon."

"Who is this?"

"Someone who would have preferred to handle this quietly. Diplomatically. But you've forced our hand."

"Voss's boss?"

"Ms. Voss works for people who work for people who work for me. You've disrupted years of careful planning. Jeopardized negotiations that could have saved millions of lives."

"Bullshit. You wanted to use that information for leverage. Control. We just made sure everyone has access to the truth."

"The truth?" He laughed. "The truth is a weapon, Mr. DeLeon. And you just handed it to amateurs. Now the Federation's backed into a corner. Scared animals lash out. They'll double down on the violence. Crack down harder on dissent. More people will die because of what you've done."

"Or maybe they'll be held accountable for once."

"Accountability is a luxury of the weak. The strong make their own rules. You'll learn that lesson soon enough."

"Is that a threat?"

"It's a guarantee. You've been marked, Mr. DeLeon. You and your entire crew. There's nowhere you can hide that we won't find you. Nothing you can do that we won't see. Your revolution ends in blood. Probably your own."

The line went dead.

"Well," I said to the crew, "that was ominous."

"Who was it?" Trixx asked.

"Voss's boss. Or her boss's boss. Someone high up the food chain. Said we're marked. That we're all dead."

"So, Tuesday," Hark said, pouring another drink.

"Pretty much."

Zeno pulled up new data. "Shit. He might be right about the crackdown. I'm seeing mobilization orders across Federation space. Military deployments. Martial law declarations. They're preparing for something big."

"Let them prepare," I said. "The information's out. Can't put it back in the box."

"No, but they can kill everyone talking about it. Suppress the story through force. Make an example of anyone who spreads it."

"Then we make sure the story keeps spreading. Faster than they can suppress it."

"How?"

"I don't know yet. But we'll figure it out."

My comm buzzed again. Different number this time. I recognized it immediately.

Mama Leena.

"Baby, what did you do?" Her voice was shaking. Not from fear—from anger. "The whole station's going crazy. Federation's locking down sectors. Arresting anyone they think might be involved."

"We leaked the black site data. Had to, Mama. People needed to know."

"People needed to stay alive! Now the Feds are coming down hard. There's been shootings. Three protesters dead in Market District alone. They're using your leak as an excuse to crack down on everyone."

Guilt hit me like a punch to the gut. Three more deaths. Three more people who'd be alive if I'd made a different choice.

"We were trying to help—"

"I know. I know you were. But baby, sometimes help looks a lot like harm. You started something you can't control. And now people are paying the price."

"What do you want me to do?"

"Survive. That's all I ever wanted. For you and Ky to survive. But Ky's gone and you're..." She paused, voice breaking. "You're becoming something I don't recognize. A revolutionary. A martyr waiting to happen."

"I'm just trying to do what's right."

"Right for who? The people dying in the streets? The families being torn apart? Right and wrong aren't always clear, Nova. Sometimes they're the same damn thing."

She hung up.

I sat there with the comm in my hand, staring at nothing. Three people dead already. How many more by tomorrow? By next week?

Fourteen from the first leak. Three from this one. Seventeen people dead because of choices I'd made.

The screens showed the chaos spreading. Protests turning violent. Federation troops firing on civilians. The body count climbing. All because we'd released the truth.

Was the truth worth this?

"Maybe Voss was right," I said quietly. "Maybe we should have given her the data. Let her people handle it properly."

"Fuck that," Trixx said. "The violence isn't our fault. It's the Federation's. They created those black sites. They killed all those people. They're the ones shooting protesters. We just showed everyone what they've been hiding."

"But if we hadn't—"

"Then nothing would have changed. The genocide would have continued quietly. More people would die, but nobody would know. At least now they're fighting back."

"Small comfort to the people getting shot."

"There is no comfort in war, kid," Hark said. "Just choices. You picked a side. Now you live with it."

I sparked a Black Death with shaking hands. The smoke helped, a little. Enough to think clearly.

Mama Leena was right. Voss was right. Trixx was right. They were all right, somehow, and that made it worse.

"We need to leave Freeport," I said. "Tonight. Before Voss's people find us. Before the Federation traces the leak back to us."

"Where do we go?" Zeno asked.

"Anywhere. Nowhere. Somewhere they won't think to look."

"That's not a plan."

"It's all I got."

Trixx stood up, started packing. "Then it'll have to do. Hark, grab the weapons. Zeno, wipe all the systems. Nova, get the money. We're ghosts in thirty minutes."

We moved efficiently, practiced. This wasn't our first time running. Probably wouldn't be our last.

Twenty minutes later, we were packed and ready. The apartment looked like nobody had ever been there. All traces erased. All evidence wiped.

On the screens, the revolution continued. Millions of people demanding justice. Demanding change. Demanding an end to the Federation's reign of terror.

We'd started it. Now we had to survive it.

And live with the knowledge that we'd traded lives for truth. Seventeen deaths so far. How many more before this was over?

"Ready?" I asked my crew.

"Never," Trixx said. "But let's go anyway."

We slipped out into Freeport's maze of corridors and passages, disappearing into the crowds, just four more faces in a station of millions.

Behind us, the data continued spreading. The truth continued spreading. The fire we'd started continued burning.

And somewhere out there, Voss and her mysterious bosses were planning their revenge.

• • •

We made it to the transport docks without incident. Bought passage on a freight hauler heading to the Outer Reaches—some colony world nobody gave a shit about. New identities. New lives. The same old running.

As the ship prepared for departure, I watched Freeport through the viewport. Watched the protests. Watched the chaos. Watched the revolution we'd sparked consuming everything.

"You think we did the right thing?" I asked Trixx.

She leaned against me, her head on my shoulder. "I think we did the only thing. Right or wrong doesn't matter when you're out of options."

"That's not comforting."

"Nothing about this life is comforting. But at least we're in it together."

The ship's engines fired. We pulled away from Freeport, leaving another home behind, another life abandoned.

My comm buzzed one last time. Unknown number. Against my better judgment, I answered.

"Hello, Nova." Not Voss. Someone else. A woman's voice. Older. Refined. Dangerous in the way expensive things are dangerous.

"Who is this?"

"Someone who's been watching you for a long time. You've become quite the problem solver. First Vale. Now this. You have a talent for disrupting systems."

"Yeah, well. It's a gift."

"I'd like to offer you a job."

"Not interested."

"You haven't heard the offer yet."

"Don't need to. Every job offer I've taken lately has ended with people trying to kill me."

"This one's different. This one involves taking down the people who sent Voss after you. The real powers behind the black sites. The ones who've been pulling strings for decades."

I should have hung up. Should have blocked the number. Should have ignored it completely.

But I didn't.

"Keep talking," I said.

She laughed. "Good. I had a feeling you'd be interested. When you reach the Outer Reaches, look for a woman named Sylla Reed. She'll explain everything. Consider it an audition for something much bigger than stealing data chips."

"And if I don't?"

"Then you keep running. Keep hiding. Keep watching people die because of information you leaked. Your choice, Nova. But I think you're tired of running. I think you want to fight back for real this time."

The line went dead.

"Who was that?" Trixx asked.

"I don't know. But whoever she is, she knows too much about us."

"Another trap?"

"Probably."

"We going anyway?"

I looked at my crew. At Trixx with her glowing purple skin. At Hark with his metal eye. At Zeno with his cybernetic implants. All of us marked. All of us targeted. All of us too stubborn to quit.

All of us carrying the weight of seventeen deaths. Of choices that might have been right or wrong or both.

"Yeah," I said. "We're going anyway."

Because that's what we did. We walked into traps. Made bad decisions. Survived impossible odds.

We were Galactic Trap Lords. And our story was just getting started.

✦ ✦ ✦

CHAPTER 16

Hunters and Hunted

Three days into the journey to the Outer Reaches, I realized we'd fucked up.

The freight hauler *Meridian's Hope* was exactly what you'd expect from a ship carrying cargo nobody gave a shit about—slow, cramped, and smelling like recycled air mixed with industrial lubricant. We'd booked passage in the crew quarters, sharing a cabin the size of a closet, eating protein paste that tasted like regret.

But we were supposed to be safe. Anonymous. Just four more refugees running from the chaos we'd started.

Then Zeno's homemade scanner started screaming.

"Shit," he said, staring at the screen with the kind of expression that usually preceded explosions. "Shit shit shit."

"Eloquent," Hark muttered from his bunk. "Care to elaborate?"

"We're being followed. Two ships, maybe three. They've been matching our course for the last six hours. Just outside normal sensor range, but I rigged this scanner to see farther."

I was at his side in two steps. "Federation?"

"No. Signatures are wrong. These are private military contractors. Expensive ones. The kind rich people hire when they want someone disappeared quietly."

"Voss's people," Trixx said, already checking her weapons.

"Probably. Or her boss's people. Or whoever the fuck is pissed we leaked their genocide files." Zeno pulled up more data. "They're not making a move yet. Just following. Waiting."

"Waiting for what?"

"For us to get far enough from civilization that nobody hears us scream."

I sparked a Black Death with hands that weren't quite steady. We'd been stupid. Thought we could just run, just hide, just disappear into the black. But you don't steal information worth billions and expect people to forget about it.

Seventeen people dead from our last two leaks. And now we might add a whole ship's crew to that count.

"How long until they make their move?" Hark asked.

"If I was them? I'd wait until we're in the dead zone between systems. No stations nearby. No help coming. Just empty space where bodies float forever."

"How long until we hit that dead zone?"

Zeno checked the navigation. "Four hours. Maybe five."

"Then we got four hours to figure out how to not die," I said.

"Great plan. Very detailed."

"You got a better one?"

"Yeah. We convince the captain to change course. Head somewhere populated. Somewhere these mercs won't risk a public firefight."

I shook my head. "Captain won't change course. Freight haulers run on schedules. Miss a delivery window, they lose contracts. He's not risking his livelihood for four passengers he doesn't know."

"Then we make him risk it," Trixx said.

"How? Hold him at gunpoint? Great way to make sure he calls station security as soon as we're in range."

"No. We tell him the truth. That we're being hunted. That if those ships catch us, they'll kill everyone on board to cover their tracks. Make him understand that changing course is the only way everyone survives."

It wasn't a bad plan. But it relied on the captain giving a shit about passengers instead of profit. In my experience, profit usually won.

"Let's try it," I said. "But if he says no, we're taking the ship."

"Taking it how?" Hark asked. "This isn't a car, kid. You can't hotwire a freight hauler."

"Zeno can. Right?"

Zeno looked uncomfortable. "I mean... theoretically? I've never actually hijacked a ship this big. But the principles are the same. Override the nav computer, lock out the captain's controls, fly it manually."

"There you go. Easy."

"Nothing about that is easy."

"We'll figure it out. We always do."

•　•　•

The captain's name was Reeves. He was maybe fifty, weathered like old leather, with the kind of face that said he'd seen too much and trusted too little. His office was barely bigger than our cabin—just a desk, a chair, and walls covered in shipping manifests and navigation charts.

"Let me get this straight," he said after we explained. "You're wanted criminals. You pissed off some very powerful people. And now professional killers are following us, planning to murder everyone on my ship to get to you."

"That's about right, yeah," I said.

"And you want me to change course. Lose my delivery contract. Probably get blacklisted by the Merchant Guild. All to save your asses."

"And everyone else's asses. They'll kill your whole crew to eliminate witnesses."

Reeves leaned back in his chair, studying us with eyes that had seen every con and lie the universe had to offer. "Why should I believe you?"

Zeno pulled up the scanner data on a portable display. "This is the tracking signature. Two ships, PMC-class, following at optimal pursuit distance. They're not smugglers or pirates. Pirates would've hit us already. These guys are professionals. They're waiting for the perfect moment."

Reeves looked at the data. His expression didn't change, but something flickered in his eyes. Recognition. Or maybe fear.

"I know that signature," he said quietly. "Valkyrie Division. Corporate mercenaries. Top-tier. They don't fuck around."

"Then you know we're not lying," Trixx said.

"I know you're in deep shit. That doesn't mean I'm diving in with you." He stood up, started pacing. "You know what happens if I break contract? I lose everything. My ship gets seized. My crew gets blacklisted. We all end up in debt for the rest of our lives."

"Better than dead," I pointed out.

"Is it?" He stopped, looked at me with something like pity. "You're young. You think survival is winning. But sometimes survival is just losing slower. Sometimes the smart move is to cut your losses."

"You're going to give us to them?" Trixx's hand moved toward her gun.

"I'm considering my options."

"Don't." Hark's voice cut through the tension like a blade. "I was on Titan for fifteen years. Met a lot of men who made the smart play. The safe play. The play that kept them alive at someone else's expense." He locked eyes with Reeves. "Every single one of them died anyway. Because when you deal with people like Valkyrie Division, there's no safe play. Only victims."

Reeves stared at him for a long moment. Then he sat back down, heavy and tired.

"What do you want me to do?"

"Change course," I said. "Head for the nearest station with actual security. Somewhere Valkyrie can't touch us without consequences."

"That's Helios Station. It's eight hours away, opposite direction. We'll miss our delivery window by two days."

"But you'll live."

He laughed, bitter and sharp. "Live to be broke and blacklisted. Great trade."

"We'll pay you," I said. "For the contract you're losing. For the risk. All of it."

"With what? You're refugees. You probably got enough credits for a meal and a bunk."

I pulled out the credit chip. The one with what was left from all our jobs. About 300,000 credits—enough to buy a small ship or bribe a dozen officials.

"This enough?" I asked.

Reeves stared at the chip like it might explode. "That's... where the fuck did you get that much money?"

"Does it matter?"

"It matters if it's stolen. If it's traceable. If taking it puts me in more danger than I'm already in."

"It's clean," Zeno said. "Well, mostly clean. Untraceable, anyway. We've been washing it through dummy accounts for weeks."

"Mostly clean," Reeves repeated. "That's not exactly confidence-inspiring."

"It's 300k credits for eight hours of flying in the wrong direction," I said. "Best payment you'll get all year."

He picked up the chip, turned it over in his hands, weighing his options. Profit versus survival. Safety versus risk. The eternal calculation of people who lived on the edge.

"Alright," he said finally. "I'll change course. But if those mercs catch us anyway, I'm throwing you out the airlock and hoping they leave the rest of us alone."

"Fair enough."

. . .

We felt the course change immediately. The *Meridian's Hope* wasn't made for quick maneuvers. It groaned and shuddered as the engines redirected, swinging our trajectory toward Helios Station.

"They're gonna notice," Zeno said, watching his scanner. "They're gonna know we changed course and they're gonna move up their timetable."

"How long until they hit us?"

"Twenty minutes. Maybe less."

"Can we outrun them?"

"In this piece of shit? No chance. They're faster, more maneuverable, and probably armed with military-grade weapons. We're a cargo hauler with shields designed to stop micrometeors, not missiles."

"Then we can't run. We have to fight."

"Fight how?" Trixx asked. "We got pistols and attitude. They got ships and professional killers."

"We got Zeno and desperation. That's worth something."

Zeno was already pulling up the ship's systems. "Okay. Okay, I can work with this. The *Hope* isn't armed, but she's got industrial equipment. Cargo manipulators, tow cables, emergency thrusters. If I reroute power and override some safety protocols—"

"Can you weaponize her?" Hark interrupted.

"I can make her dangerous. That's not quite the same thing."

"It'll have to do."

The proximity alarm started screaming. On the viewscreen, two ships appeared—sleek black predators with no identification markings. They moved with military precision, flanking us on both sides.

Captain Reeves' voice crackled over the intercom. "All hands, we are under attack. Seal your compartments. Brace for incoming fire. This is not a drill."

"Incoming transmission," Zeno said.

A man's face appeared on the screen. Mid-thirties, handsome in that generic way military contractors always were, with eyes that had seen too much death and stopped caring about it.

"Attention *Meridian's Hope*. You are carrying wanted criminals. Surrender them immediately and you will not be harmed. Refuse and we will board by force. You have sixty seconds to decide."

The transmission cut off.

"Friendly guy," I said.

"They're positioning for a boarding action," Zeno reported. "Coming in from both sides. Classic pincer. They'll mag-lock to our hull, cut through, and flood the ship with troops."

"How many troops?"

"Each ship can probably carry ten to fifteen soldiers. So we're looking at twenty to thirty armed mercs versus four of us and whatever crew Reeves has that can fight."

"Crew's eight people," Hark said. "Mostly engineers and cargo handlers. Not fighters."

"So it's thirty to four. Great odds."

"I've had worse," Hark said again.

"When the fuck did you have worse?" I asked.

"I just told you. Titan, '34."

"You keep talking about that. We gonna hear the full story someday?"

"If we live through this."

The mercs weren't waiting for an answer. They came in fast, engines flaring bright blue as they burned hard toward us. The *Hope* shuddered as magnetic grapples locked onto our hull—heavy metallic thuds that echoed through the ship.

"They're attached," Zeno said. "Cutting torches activating. Hull breach in thirty seconds."

"Can you vent the sections they're cutting into?" I asked.

"Not without killing anyone in those sections. Including us, probably."

"Then we do this the hard way. Trixx, Hark—weapons up. We're going hunting."

We grabbed everything we had—guns, knives, one of Zeno's homemade EMP grenades, and a lot of bad attitude. The ship's corridors were narrow, industrial, designed for cargo not combat. But narrow worked in our favor. Made it hard to bring superior numbers to bear.

"They're through!" Zeno shouted. "Starboard side, Deck Two. Multiple contacts. They're spreading out fast."

Gunfire erupted somewhere forward. Screams. The sound of a crew that wasn't ready for war.

We ran toward the fight.

The first merc we found was executing a crew member in cold blood—some young kid who probably thought freight hauling was a safe job. The merc had his gun to the kid's head, about to pull the trigger.

Trixx shot him first. Center mass, clean kill. He dropped like his strings got cut.

The kid stared at us, terrified. "They're everywhere! They're killing everyone!"

"Get to the engine room," I told him. "Lock the door. Don't open it for anyone but us."

He ran.

We moved forward, clearing rooms one by one. The mercs were good—professional, coordinated, communicating through encrypted channels. But they were expecting scared civilians, not people who'd survived gang wars and Fed raids and revolutions.

We hit them hard. Hark took point with his rifle, picking off targets from distance. Trixx moved like a purple ghost, glow-ink making her look inhuman and beautiful and terrifying. I covered the flanks, watching corners, making sure nobody got behind us.

We dropped five mercs in the first two minutes. But there were so many more.

Five more deaths. Five more bodies. Add them to the count.

"They're adapting," Hark said, reloading. "Changing tactics. They know we're here now."

"Then we show them what that costs."

They came in a rush—six mercs moving in coordinated pairs, covering each other, using tactics we couldn't match. We dropped back, using the corridor as a choke point, making them come at us one at a time.

Hark's rifle cracked over and over. Trixx's pistols sang harmony. I fired controlled bursts, conserving ammo, picking shots carefully.

Bodies hit the floor. But they kept coming.

"We can't hold here!" Trixx shouted over the gunfire.

"We don't have to! We just need to buy Zeno time!"

"Time for what?"

"You'll see!"

I hoped. I really fucking hoped.

My comm crackled. Zeno's voice, strained and excited. "Okay, I did something incredibly stupid. When I say run, you run toward the airlock. The main one. Run fast and don't stop."

"What did you do?"

"Something that might kill us all but will definitely kill them."

"That's specific."

"Just trust me!"

The mercs rushed us again. This time we broke and ran, falling back toward the airlock like Zeno said. Behind us, the mercs gave chase, probably thinking we were retreating, thinking they had us.

"Now!" Zeno screamed.

I looked back just in time to see the cargo bay doors blow open.

Everything not bolted down exploded toward space. Crates, equipment, three mercs who'd been in the wrong place. And all the air—a hurricane of oxygen rushing out the massive hole Zeno had created.

The mercs behind us stumbled, got pulled backward by the suction. Some grabbed hold of walls. Others weren't fast enough.

Screaming. Brief and terrible and then silence as the void took them.

We made it to the airlock, sealed the door, watched through the porthole as the cargo bay became a vacuum and the mercs died hard.

"You blew a hole in the ship!" I shouted at Zeno through comms.

"Emergency vent! It'll seal automatically in sixty seconds! But I got rid of half their troops!"

"And our cargo!"

"You wanted a weapon! I gave you a weapon!"

He had a point.

The cargo bay sealed itself, emergency bulkheads slamming down, cutting off the void. But the damage was done. Half the mercs were dead or incapacitated. The other half were probably reconsidering their career choices.

At least a dozen dead now. Maybe more. I was losing count.

"Incoming transmission," Zeno said.

The same man from before. But his face wasn't calm anymore. He looked pissed. And scared.

"That was a mistake," he said. "You just killed my people. Now this isn't business. It's personal."

"Good," I said. "Personal means you'll make mistakes."

"I'm going to board your bridge. I'm going to execute your captain. And then I'm going to hunt you through this ship until I find you. And when I do, you're going to wish you'd surrendered."

"We're not really the surrendering type."

"You will be. When I'm done with you."

The transmission cut out.

"Well," Hark said, reloading for the third time. "He seems upset."

"We're going to the bridge," I said. "If he wants a fight, we'll give him one."

· · ·

The bridge was chaos. Captain Reeves was barricaded behind his console, armed with a shotgun he probably hadn't fired in years. Two of his crew were dead. The others were hiding.

Two more. Nineteen total now. Still counting.

"They're coming!" he shouted when he saw us. "They're cutting through the bridge door!"

"I know. Let them."

"Are you insane?"

"Probably. But we got a plan."

"What plan?"

"Kill them all and take their ships."

"That's not a plan! That's suicide!"

"Semantics."

The bridge door glowed red as cutting torches worked through from the other side. Ten seconds. Maybe less.

We took positions. Hark high. Trixx low. Me in the center. Three shooters. One door. A killing zone.

The door fell inward with a metallic crash.

The merc commander came through first—cocky, confident, gun raised.

We lit him up.

All three of us fired at once. He went down hard, armor absorbing some of the damage but not all of it. He hit the floor and didn't move.

His team poured through after him—angry, reckless, abandoning tactics for rage. It was what I'd counted on. Personal meant sloppy.

We dropped four in the first exchange. The rest fell back, realized they'd walked into an ambush, tried to retreat.

But Zeno had sealed the corridor behind them. Trapped them in the killing zone.

It was over in thirty seconds.

When the smoke cleared, we were standing and they weren't.

Maybe twenty-five deaths total. Maybe thirty. All because they'd been sent to kill us. All because we'd leaked information that powerful people wanted hidden.

I wasn't sure if that made it better or worse.

"Jesus Christ," Captain Reeves whispered, staring at the carnage.

"You're welcome," I said.

"Get off my ship. Right now. Take one of their ships and get the fuck off my ship."

"That was the plan."

• • •

The mercs' ships were beautiful. Military-grade corsairs, armed to the teeth, engines that could burn for weeks without refueling. Exactly what we needed.

We picked the one that looked less shot up, keyed in using the dead commander's access codes, and fired up the engines.

"This is stolen," Trixx said as we settled into the cockpit.

"Everything good we own is stolen," I pointed out.

"Fair."

The *Meridian's Hope* shrank behind us as we burned away, heading back toward Helios Station. Behind us, the remaining merc ship was dead in space, its crew floating in the cargo bay we'd vented.

"They're going to send more," Zeno said. "Voss's people. The Federation. Everyone we've pissed off."

"Let them," I said.

The words came easier than they should have. Twenty-five, maybe thirty people dead in the last hour. Added to the seventeen from before. Forty-seven deaths I was connected to.

At some point, you stopped being a person trying to do good and became something else. A weapon. A problem. A body count.

Maybe that was okay. Maybe that was what the universe needed.

Or maybe I was just getting good at lying to myself.

"We're done running," I said, pushing the thoughts down.

"What are we doing instead?"

"We're meeting Sylla Reed. Taking that job offer. Going on offense."

"We don't even know what the job is."

"Doesn't matter. It's better than waiting for the next assassin squad to find us."

Trixx looked at me, her purple skin glowing in the dim cockpit light. "You're really doing this. Picking a fight with the most powerful people in the universe."

"We already picked the fight. We just weren't fighting back yet."

She smiled. Sharp and dangerous and beautiful. "Good. I'm tired of running too."

Hark sparked a smoke, stared out at the stars. "So we're joining another revolution."

"Yeah."

"You know these things usually end bloody."

"They always end bloody," I said. "Question is whether we're the ones bleeding or the ones making them bleed."

"And if we're all bleeding?"

"Then at least we picked the fight worth dying for."

The stars stretched ahead of us—infinite, dangerous, full of enemies and possibilities.

We'd started a war. Now it was time to finish it.

Or die trying.

✦ ✦ ✦

CHAPTER 17

Between the Stars

The military corsair we'd stolen was too nice for us.

Everything worked. The engines purred instead of screamed. The shields held steady without flickering. The cockpit had actual seats instead of the cobbled-together shit I was used to. It even had a climate control system that kept the air at a comfortable temperature instead of alternating between freezing and cooking.

"I could get used to this," Trixx said, stretched out in the co-pilot seat with her boots on the console. Her glow-ink was dim now, relaxed, just a soft purple pulse at her throat and wrists.

"Don't," Hark warned from the back. He was cleaning his rifle, the methodical movements of a man who'd done it ten thousand times. "Nice things make you soft. Soft makes you dead."

"You're such a ray of sunshine," Trixx said.

"I'm realistic. There's a difference."

I was flying on autopilot, letting the ship's computer handle the boring parts while I smoked and thought about everything that had just happened. We'd killed maybe twenty professional mercenaries. Stolen a military-grade ship. Made enemies of people powerful enough to send Valkyrie Division after us.

And somehow we were still alive.

"Zeno, how long until we reach the Outer Reaches?" I asked.

He looked up from his makeshift tech station—three computers wired together in a way that probably violated every safety regulation. "Forty-eight hours at current speed. But I can push the engines harder, get us there in thirty-six."

"Don't push too hard. Don't want to burn out our new ride before we even get where we're going."

"Fair point. Forty-eight hours it is."

Forty-eight hours in a ship with nothing to do but think. That sounded like torture.

"I'm gonna sleep," Hark announced. "Wake me if someone tries to kill us."

"When," I corrected. "Wake you when someone tries to kill us."

"Pessimist."

"Realist."

He disappeared into one of the crew cabins. A minute later, Zeno followed, mumbling something about needing to rewire the communications array.

That left me and Trixx alone in the cockpit, surrounded by stars and silence and the hum of the engines.

"You okay?" she asked.

"Define okay."

"Not having a breakdown. Not contemplating suicide. Not spiraling into existential dread about the choices we've made."

"Then no, I'm not okay."

She laughed, soft and sad. "Me neither."

I sparked another Black Death, offered it to her. She took it, inhaled deep, passed it back. We shared the cigarette in comfortable silence, watching the stars slide by.

"We killed a lot of people today," she said finally.

"Yeah."

"Does it bother you?"

I thought about it. "Should it?"

"I don't know. Normal people would say yes. But we're not normal people."

"They were trying to kill us."

"I know. But that doesn't make them less dead."

I took another drag, held the smoke in my lungs. "Ky used to ask me that. After jobs that went bad. After fights where people died. He'd ask if it bothered me. If I felt guilty."

"What did you tell him?"

"I told him that guilt was a luxury. That we did what we had to do to survive. That the universe didn't care about our feelings, so why should we care about theirs."

"But did you believe that?"

"Sometimes. Other times I'd lie awake at night seeing their faces. Wondering who they were. If they had families. If anyone would miss them."

"And now?"

"Now I'm too tired to care. They made their choices. We made ours. Everyone dies eventually. Just a question of when and how."

She turned to look at me, eyes reflecting the soft glow of the instruments. "You've gotten harder since Ky died."

"Had to. Soft gets you killed."

"Hark's rubbing off on you."

"Worse fates."

She smiled, but it didn't reach her eyes. "Come here."

"I'm flying the ship."

"Autopilot's flying the ship. You're just pretending to be useful."

She wasn't wrong. I got up, crossed the three feet of space between us, and she pulled me down into her lap. It was awkward—the seats weren't made for two people—but we made it work.

"What are you doing?" I asked.

"Making sure you remember you're human. That you're not just some killing machine running on anger and revenge."

"I'm not—"

"Yes, you are. You've been running so hard, fighting so much, you forgot how to just... be. How to exist without an enemy to fight."

"We have plenty of enemies."

"We always will. But right now, in this moment, we're safe. We're alone. And I need you to be Nova, not some street soldier planning the next war."

I didn't know what to say to that. She was right—I had been running on autopilot, just like the ship. Moving from fight to fight, crisis to crisis, never stopping to actually process what was happening.

"I don't know how to just be anymore," I admitted.

"Then let me remind you."

She kissed me, slow and soft, nothing urgent about it. Just lips and breath and the taste of cigarettes. I kissed her back, letting myself sink into it, letting the tension drain from my shoulders.

"Better?" she asked.

"Getting there."

"Good. Now take me to bed."

*   *   *

The crew quarters were luxurious by our standards—actual beds with real mattresses, clean sheets, a door that locked. It felt weird, being in a space this nice. Like we were playing pretend, trying on a life that didn't belong to us.

But Trixx didn't care about the luxury. She cared about getting my clothes off.

"You're wearing too much," she said, pulling at my shirt.

"So are you."

"Then fix it."

I pulled her shirt over her head, revealing purple skin and glowing ink that pulsed brighter as my hands touched her. She wasn't wearing anything underneath—we'd been living in tactical gear for days, hadn't had time for shit like bras and modesty.

"You're beautiful," I said. Because she was. Every time I saw her like this, it hit me all over again how fucking lucky I was.

"I know," she said, that confident smirk playing at her lips. "Now get naked so I can appreciate you too."

I stripped fast, suddenly desperate to feel skin on skin. She did the same, and then we were pressed together on the bed, all that purple glow-ink making the room look like some alien dream.

"We almost died today," she whispered, hand sliding down my stomach.

"We almost die every day."

"That doesn't make it less scary."

"No," I agreed. "It doesn't."

She wrapped her hand around me, stroked slowly. I was already hard, had been since she kissed me in the cockpit. Her touch felt electric, every nerve ending firing at once.

"I need you," she said. Not want. Need. Like I was oxygen and she couldn't breathe without me.

"You got me," I told her. "Always."

I rolled her onto her back, settled between her legs. She was wet already, ready, body knowing what it wanted. I pushed inside slowly, watching her face as I filled her—the way her eyes went half-closed, the way her mouth opened in a silent gasp, the way glow-ink flared bright purple.

"Fuck," she breathed. "Yes."

I started moving, finding the rhythm we'd perfected over months together. Not too fast, not too slow. Deep strokes that made her gasp and arch beneath me. Her legs wrapped around my waist, pulling me closer, deeper.

"Harder," she demanded. Because Trixx never asked. She demanded. She took what she wanted.

I gave it to her. Pounding into her, the bed creaking beneath us, her nails raking down my back hard enough to draw blood. She liked it rough sometimes, liked the edge between pleasure and pain.

"Touch yourself," I told her, my own voice rough with need.

Her hand moved between us, fingers working her clit while I fucked her. I could feel her walls tightening around me, could feel her getting close.

"Look at me," I said.

She opened her eyes, met my gaze. Those eyes that had seen me at my worst, my most broken, and stayed anyway.

"I love you," I said.

"I love you too," she gasped. "Now make me come."

I shifted angles slightly, hitting that spot inside her that made her lose her mind. She cried out, her whole body tensing, glow-ink blazing so bright I had to squint.

"Nova—fuck—I'm—"

She came hard, her pussy squeezing me like a vice, her back arching off the bed. I kept moving through it, drawing it out, making it last as long as I could.

When she finally relaxed, breathing hard, I pulled out and flipped her over.

"Hands and knees," I said.

She obeyed without argument, getting into position, looking back at me over her shoulder with eyes that were still hazy with pleasure.

"You're not done?" she asked.

"Not even close."

I pushed back inside her from behind, gripping her hips, watching the glow-ink swirl across her back like living art. This position let me go deeper, harder, gave me leverage to really fuck her.

"Yes," she moaned. "Like that. Just like that."

I lost myself in the rhythm, in the feel of her, in the sounds she made. Everything else fell away—the war, the enemies, the future. There was only this moment, this connection, this desperate need to be as close to her as physically possible.

"I'm gonna come," I warned.

"Do it," she gasped. "Come inside me. Fill me up."

That did it. I buried myself deep and came hard, everything going white for a few seconds. Trixx collapsed onto the bed beneath me, and I followed, both of us panting, sweaty, glowing.

"Jesus," she said after a minute. "We needed that."

"Yeah," I agreed. "We really did."

We lay there in the afterglow, her head on my chest, my fingers tracing patterns on her back. The glow-ink responded to my touch, pulsing brighter wherever I touched.

"Do you think we'll survive this?" she asked quietly.

"This?"

"Everything. The war we started. The enemies we made. The revolution that's burning across the galaxy because we couldn't keep our fucking mouths shut."

"Honestly? I don't know. Odds aren't great."

"That's not comforting."

"You want comforting, don't ask me questions. I'm bad at lying."

She laughed, the sound vibrating against my chest. "That's fair."

"But," I continued, "if we do die, at least we die together. At least we die for something that matters."

"Starting a war matters?"

"Exposing genocide matters. Showing the universe what the Federation really is—that matters. Even if we don't live to see how it ends."

She propped herself up on one elbow, looked at me seriously. "You really believe that? That our deaths would mean something?"

"I have to. Otherwise what's the fucking point?"

"The point is staying alive. Being happy. Growing old together."

"That's not an option anymore. We crossed too many lines. Made too many enemies."

"There's always an option to run. To hide. To disappear."

"Is that what you want?"

She was quiet for a long time. Then: "No. I want to fight. I want to burn their whole fucking system to the ground and dance on the ashes. But I also want you alive. And those two things might not be compatible."

"Then we fight until we can't fight anymore. And whatever happens after that... we'll deal with it together."

"Promise?"

"Promise."

She kissed me, soft and slow, tasting like cigarettes and sex and something sweeter I couldn't name. When she pulled back, eyes were wet.

"Don't die," she whispered. "Please don't die."

"I'll try my best."

"That's not good enough."

"It's all I got."

* * *

We slept for about six hours, wrapped around each other, the ship's engines humming a lullaby. When I woke up, Trixx was already awake, watching me with an expression I couldn't quite read.

"What?" I asked.

"Nothing. Just... memorizing your face. In case."

"In case what?"

"In case we don't make it. I want to remember what you looked like when you were peaceful."

"I'm never peaceful."

"You are right now. Right here, in this moment. You look almost... happy."

I thought about it. "Maybe I am. A little."

"Good." She kissed my forehead. "Hold onto that feeling. We're gonna need it."

We got dressed, went back to the cockpit. Hark and Zeno were already there, looking at something on the screens that made them both frown.

"What's wrong?" I asked.

"We're being hailed," Zeno said. "Someone knows we're here. Knows we're coming."

"The mercs?"

"No. Different signature. Civilian vessel. Small. Just one person aboard."

"Could be a trap," Hark said.

"Everything could be a trap," I pointed out.

"Fair."

I looked at the comm request flashing on the screen. "Open the channel. Let's see who's calling."

The screen flickered, and a woman appeared. She was older—maybe sixty—with gray hair pulled back severe, wearing clothes that screamed money and power. Her eyes were sharp, calculating, the kind that missed nothing.

"Nova," she said, voice smooth and cultured. "I'm glad you decided to come."

"You're Sylla Reed?"

"I am. And you're late. I expected you twelve hours ago."

"We got held up. People trying to kill us. You know how it is."

"I do, actually. Which is why I'm impressed you made it at all. The Valkyrie Division doesn't usually let targets escape."

"We're not usual targets."

She smiled, and it reminded me of a shark. "No, you're not. Which is exactly why I want to hire you."

"For what?"

"For war, Nova. I want to hire you to help me destroy the Federation from within. To dismantle the black site network. To bring down the people who've been running the genocide operation for decades. To finish what you started when you leaked that data."

I looked at my crew. Trixx was tense, ready for anything. Hark was expressionless, waiting. Zeno was already analyzing the signal, probably trying to figure out if this was legitimate or a con.

"And why would you want to do that?" I asked. "What's your stake in this?"

"My daughter," Reed said simply. "She was taken by the Federation twenty years ago. Processed. Sent to one of those black sites you exposed. I've spent twenty years searching for her, fighting the system, trying to get her back. Now I finally have a chance. But I need help."

"Why us?"

"Because you're reckless enough to try impossible things. Smart enough to survive them. And angry enough to see it through. You're not soldiers or politicians or revolutionaries. You're street fighters who somehow stumbled into a war. And that makes you perfect."

"Perfect for what?"

"For going places I can't go. Doing things I can't do. Being the blade that cuts through the bureaucracy and bullshit and gets things done." She leaned forward. "I have money. Resources. Intelligence networks. But I don't have people willing to die for this cause. You've already proven you are."

"We're not dying for anyone," Trixx said.

"Then don't die. Live. Win. Help me tear down the empire that took my daughter and thousands like her. And when it's over, I'll make sure you're set for life. New identities. New lives. Enough money to disappear anywhere you want."

"And if we say no?"

"Then you keep running. Keep hiding. Keep waiting for the next assassin squad to find you. Because they will find you, Nova. Valkyrie was just the first wave. There will be others. Better ones. Until eventually you run out of luck."

She wasn't wrong. We couldn't run forever.

"We're listening," I said. "Tell us about the job."

Reed smiled, and for the first time, it looked genuine. "Dock at coordinates I'm sending now. We'll talk in person. And Nova? Welcome to the real revolution."

The transmission cut out.

"Well," Hark said after a moment. "That wasn't ominous at all."

"You think she's legit?" I asked Zeno.

"The signal's clean. No malware, no trackers. And I ran her name through my databases. Sylla Reed is real. She's a billionaire, major shareholder in half a dozen mega-corps, politically connected. Lost her daughter in 2338 during a Federation raid on a hybrid settlement. Story checks out."

"That doesn't mean she's not using us," Trixx said.

"Everyone uses everyone," I said. "Question is whether her goals align with ours."

"Do they?"

I thought about the black sites. The thousands of names. The harvesting chambers. All that death and suffering hidden away where nobody could see.

"Yeah," I said. "They do."

"Then we're really doing this," Trixx said. "We're joining a billionaire's private war against the Federation."

"Looks like it."

"Fuck it," Hark said, sparking a smoke. "We've done stupider shit."

"Have we?" Zeno asked.

"Probably not. But there's a first time for everything."

I set course for the coordinates Reed had sent. Whatever came next, we'd face it together.

Like we always did.

✦ ✦ ✦

CHAPTER 18

Empire of Ashes

The coordinates Reed sent led us to a mining station orbiting a dead planet. The kind of place corporations built, sucked dry of resources, then abandoned when the profits dried up. It looked like a skeleton—metal bones picked clean, floating in the void.

"Cheerful," Trixx muttered as we approached.

"It's smart," Zeno said, scanning the station. "No official registry, no traffic logs, no oversight. Perfect place for someone who wants to stay off the grid."

"Or ambush people," Hark added.

"That too."

We docked at the coordinates Reed specified—Bay Seven on the lower ring. The bay was clean, well-maintained, which was weird for an abandoned station. Someone was keeping this place operational.

The airlock cycled, and we stepped through into artificial gravity that actually worked. The corridor was lit, heated, pressurized. Not abandoned. Repurposed.

"Welcome," a voice said through hidden speakers. Reed's voice. "Follow the green lights to the conference room. And please, leave your weapons holstered. My security team has standing orders to respond to drawn weapons with lethal force."

"Friendly," I said.

Green lights appeared in the floor, leading deeper into the station. We followed, hands near our guns but not on them, every instinct screaming that this was a trap.

The conference room was unexpected—expensive furniture, real wood paneling, windows showing the dead planet below. Reed was waiting at the head of a long table, flanked by two bodyguards who looked like they ate nails for breakfast.

"Nova," she said, standing. "Ms. Trixx. Mr. Harkness. Mr. Zeno. Thank you for coming."

"You made it sound like we didn't have a choice," I said.

"You always have a choice. You chose to come. That tells me you're interested."

"Interested in not being hunted by professional killers," Trixx said. "That's different from interested in working for you."

Reed smiled. "Fair. Please, sit. We have much to discuss."

We sat. The bodyguards didn't move, just watched us with the kind of focus that said they could kill us before we cleared our holsters.

"First," Reed said, "let me show you what you've accomplished."

She activated a holographic display. News feeds from across Federation space appeared—riots, protests, military crackdowns. The data leak we'd released was spreading like wildfire, and the galaxy was burning.

FEDERATION COUNCIL UNDER SIEGE—PROTESTERS DEMAND ACCOUNTABILITY

BLACK SITE SCANDAL GROWS: 47 FACILITIES CONFIRMED, THOUSANDS STILL MISSING

HYBRID RIGHTS MOVEMENT EXPLODES: 200+ WORLDS JOIN CALL FOR REFORM

"Forty-seven confirmed black sites," Reed said. "That's forty-seven places where the Federation was systematically murdering and harvesting people. Thanks to your leak, the universe knows. And they're not happy about it."

"People are dying in those riots," I said. "We saw the reports. Federation troops shooting civilians."

"Yes. War is messy. Change is violent. But it's happening. For the first time in decades, the Federation is on the defensive. Their propaganda isn't working. Their lies are exposed. They're scared."

"And what do you want from us?" Hark asked.

"I want to finish what you started. The data you leaked exposed the black sites. But it didn't shut them down. The facilities are still operating. The prisoners are still there. Including, possibly, my daughter."

She pulled up a file. A young woman's face appeared—maybe twenty when the photo was taken, with Reed's eyes and a smile that looked like it could light up a room.

"Mira Reed. Taken in 2338 during a Federation raid on Settlement Epsilon-7. She was sixteen. I've spent two decades searching for her, bribing officials, hacking databases, following every lead. And I've gotten nowhere. Because the Federation buries its secrets deep."

"You think she's still alive?" Trixx asked.

"I know she is. Two months ago, I finally got access to a black site prisoner manifest. Her name was on it. Facility Theta-Nine, located in the Kronos Sector. She's there. She's alive. And I'm getting her out."

"Okay," I said. "What does that have to do with us?"

"Everything. Facility Theta-Nine is a maximum security detention center. Military-grade defenses, rotating guard shifts, off-grid communications. It's designed to be impenetrable. But you've proven you can do the impossible. You stole data from a Federation intelligence ship. You survived Valkyrie Division. You leaked information that started a galactic revolution. You're exactly the kind of people I need."

"To do what, exactly?" Zeno asked.

"To help me raid Facility Theta-Nine. Extract the prisoners. Document the atrocities. And burn the whole fucking place to the ground so they can never use it again."

The room went quiet. We looked at each other—me, Trixx, Hark, Zeno. Silently calculating the odds of survival. Coming up with numbers we didn't like.

"That's a suicide mission," Hark said flatly.

"It's a high-risk operation with significant potential for casualties," Reed corrected. "But it's not suicide. I have resources. Intelligence. A team of specialists who've been planning this for months. All I need is the final piece—people crazy enough to actually execute the plan."

"Why not hire professional soldiers?" I asked.

"I have. Twelve of them. Ex-military, top-tier training, experienced in black operations. But they're not enough. This job requires people who think differently. Who don't follow rules. Who see impossible odds and say 'fuck it, let's try anyway.' That's you."

She wasn't wrong. We were exactly that stupid.

"What's the pay?" Trixx asked.

"One million credits each. Plus new identities that even the Federation can't track. Plus sanctuary on any of my corporate holdings across the galaxy. You walk away from this—if you survive—and you're set for life."

"And if we don't survive?"

"Then your deaths will mean something. You'll be heroes who helped shut down the Federation's genocide machine. There are worse epitaphs."

"I've heard better pitches," I said.

Reed leaned forward, and for the first time, I saw the anger beneath her polished exterior. The grief. The rage of a mother who'd lost her daughter and spent twenty years trying to get her back.

"I'm not asking you to die for me," she said. "I'm asking you to fight. To take everything the Federation did to you—every loss, every injustice, every brother they killed—and turn it into a weapon. You started a war with that data leak. Now finish it."

. . .

We stepped out of the conference room to discuss. Reed had given us an hour to decide.

"She's insane," Zeno said. "Raiding a black site? That's like robbing Fort Knox while on fire."

"But she's right about one thing," Hark said. "We can't keep running. Eventually someone will find us. Might as well go down fighting for something that matters."

"Easy for you to say," Trixx snapped. "You've already lived your life. Some of us aren't ready to die for a stranger's daughter."

"It's not about her daughter," I said. "It's about all of them. Everyone in those facilities. Everyone the Federation disappeared. We exposed it. Now we have a chance to actually stop it."

"At what cost?" Trixx demanded. "Our lives? Is that worth it?"

"I don't know. But doing nothing definitely isn't worth it."

She stared at me, frustration and fear warring in her eyes. "You've already decided, haven't you? You're going, whether we agree or not."

"No. I'm not doing anything without the crew. We all go or none of us go."

"That's emotional blackmail."

"That's reality. We're family. We stick together."

Zeno was running calculations on his portable display. "If we're actually considering this... I'd need details. Schematics, guard rotations, security protocols. And I'd need Reed's specialists to be competent. One fuckup and we're all dead."

"You're seriously thinking about it?" Trixx asked.

"I'm thinking we don't have better options. Voss's people will keep hunting us. The Federation wants us dead. Even if we hide for years, eventually we'd slip up. Or get sold out. Or just get unlucky." He looked up from his screen. "At least this way we choose the fight. Choose the cause. Go out on our terms."

"If we go out," Hark added. "Reed's not wrong about us being good at impossible shit. We might actually pull this off."

Trixx looked at each of us, seeing that we'd already made up our minds. Seeing that she was outvoted but also understanding why.

"Fuck," she said quietly. "Okay. Okay, we do this. But on one condition."

"What?" I asked.

"After this job, we're done. No more revolutions. No more fighting other people's wars. We take the money, get our new identities, and we disappear. We find some quiet colony world and we live. Actually live. Together. Deal?"

"Deal," I said.

"You're lying," she said. "But I appreciate the effort."

She wasn't wrong. I was lying. Because I knew the truth—there was no walking away from this. Not really. We'd crossed too many lines, burned too many bridges. This life was all we had now.

But I could pretend. For her. For us.

. . .

We told Reed yes.

She smiled like she'd won something valuable. "Excellent. Let me show you what you're working with."

She led us deeper into the station, through corridors that got progressively more military-grade. Reinforced walls. Biometric locks. Armed guards at every checkpoint. This wasn't just a hideout. It was a command center.

"I've been preparing for this operation for six months," Reed explained. "Ever since I confirmed Mira's location. I've assembled a team, gathered intelligence, acquired the necessary equipment. All I was missing was the catalyst."

"That's us," I said. "The catalyst."

"Yes."

We entered a large room that looked like a military briefing center. Screens covered the walls showing satellite feeds, blueprints, troop movements. A dozen people were working stations—analysts, techs, coordinators. This was a full-scale operation.

"Jesus," Zeno whispered. "You really weren't fucking around."

"I never fuck around about my daughter," Reed said.

A man approached—mid-forties, military bearing, scar across his jaw that looked like it came from something sharp. "Ma'am. The new recruits?"

"Commander Saito, meet Nova's crew. They'll be joining the assault team."

Saito looked us over with the critical eye of a career soldier evaluating raw recruits. His expression said he wasn't impressed. "No offense, ma'am, but they look like street thugs."

"They are street thugs," Reed said. "They're also survivors, innovators, and impossible to predict. Which is exactly what we need."

"With all due respect—"

"Commander, I hired you for your expertise, not your opinions. These four have accomplished things your team couldn't. They stole Federation intelligence, survived Valkyrie Division, and started a revolution that's currently burning across sixty star systems. I think they've earned their place on this operation."

Saito's jaw tightened, but he nodded. "Yes, ma'am. When do we brief them?"

"Now."

The briefing took two hours. Saito walked us through every detail—the facility's location, its defenses, the guard schedules, the prisoner locations, the extraction routes. It was thorough, professional, and absolutely terrifying.

Facility Theta-Nine was designed to hold two thousand prisoners. It had a garrison of three hundred soldiers, automated defense systems, and was located in deep space far from any friendly reinforcements. Getting in would be hard. Getting out would be impossible.

Unless.

"There's a shift change every seventy-two hours," Saito explained. "That's when supply ships dock and prisoners are transferred. For fifteen minutes, the facility's defenses are at their weakest. That's our window."

"Fifteen minutes," Hark said. "To breach, extract prisoners, and escape."

"Correct."

"That's insane."

"That's the plan."

Zeno was studying the schematics. "The security systems are networked. If I can access the main hub here—" he pointed "—I can create a cascade failure. Blind their sensors, lock their blast doors, create chaos."

"That's your job," Saito said. "You'll go in with the tech team. Meanwhile, the assault teams breach here, here, and here—" he indicated three entry points "—and fight to the prisoner blocks. We extract as many as we can carry, plant demolition charges, and evacuate before reinforcements arrive."

"What kind of resistance are we expecting?" I asked.

"Heavy. The guards are veterans, well-trained, well-armed. And once they realize what's happening, they'll fight hard to keep us from the prisoners. Expect casualties."

"On both sides," Hark said.

"Yes."

"When do we leave?" Trixx asked.

"Forty-eight hours. I need time to finalize logistics, run the assault teams through their drills, and coordinate with our intelligence assets on-site." Saito looked at us. "Use that time to rest, train, and make peace with whatever gods you pray to. This operation is high-risk. Some of us won't make it back."

"Cheerful," I said.

"Realistic."

· · ·

Reed gave us quarters on the station—actual rooms with beds and privacy. Luxury compared to what we'd been living in. But sleep didn't come easy.

I stood at the window, watching the dead planet rotate below, smoking a Black Death and thinking about everything that had led me here. Ky's death. Vale's tyranny. The revolution. The black sites. It all connected, one choice leading to another, a chain of decisions that had brought me to this moment.

About to raid a Federation black site with a billionaire's private army.

"You okay?" Trixx asked. She was lying in bed, watching me with those eyes that saw too much.

"No. But I haven't been okay since Ky died. Maybe I'm not supposed to be okay."

"That's a depressing philosophy."

"It's the truth."

She got up, came to stand beside me. Her glow-ink was dim, peaceful. "We could still walk away. Tell Reed we changed our minds. Take what money we have and disappear."

"Could we?"

"Probably not. But I want to believe we could."

I put my arm around her, pulled her close. "After this job, we'll figure it out. Find somewhere quiet. Build something normal."

"You keep saying that."

"Maybe if I say it enough times, it'll be true."

"Or maybe," she said quietly, "we're both lying to ourselves. Maybe this is who we are now. Fighters. Revolutionaries. People who burn things down."

"Is that so bad?"

"I don't know. Ask me after we survive this."

My comm buzzed. Zeno.

"You watching the feeds?"

"What feeds?"

"Turn on the news. Any channel. It's getting worse."

I pulled up a news stream on my wrist display. The images were brutal—Federation troops opening fire on protesters, bodies in the streets, entire sectors under martial law. The revolution we'd started was turning into a war.

FEDERATION DECLARES STATE OF EMERGENCY: MARTIAL LAW ACROSS 89 SYSTEMS

DEATH TOLL RISES: 12,000+ CONFIRMED DEAD IN BLACK SITE PROTESTS

HYBRID SETTLEMENTS UNDER SIEGE: MILITARY DEPLOYING TO "RESTORE ORDER"

"Jesus Christ," Trixx whispered.

"This is our fault," I said.

"No. This is the Federation's fault. We just showed everyone what they'd been hiding."

"People are dying because of information we leaked."

"People were already dying. They were just dying quietly, where nobody could see. Now at least they're fighting back."

She was right. But it didn't make the guilt any lighter.

Another alert flashed across the screen. This one made my blood run cold.

NOVA DELEON NAMED TERRORIST: FEDERATION ISSUES GALAXY-WIDE WARRANT

BOUNTY INCREASED TO 50 MILLION CREDITS—DEAD OR ALIVE

My face appeared on the screen. Not Marcus Chen. Nova. My real face, my real name, broadcast across every system in Federation space.

"They know," I said. "They know who leaked the data. They know it was us."

"How?" Zeno's voice in my ear. "I encrypted everything, routed it through fifty different servers. There's no way they should've traced it back to us."

"But they did," Trixx said. "Which means someone talked. Or someone connected the dots. Either way, we're marked."

My comm buzzed again. Reed this time.

"I assume you've seen the news."

"Yeah."

"Then you understand that walking away is no longer an option. The Federation wants you dead. Voss's people want you dead. Half the bounty hunters in the galaxy are coming for you. Your only chance is to stay with me, under my protection, until we can get you new identities that work."

"And after the raid?"

"After the raid, you disappear. Permanently. I have resources on the outer rim, beyond Federation space. Colonies that don't care about warrants or bounties. You can start over there. If you survive."

"Always a catch," I said.

"There's always a catch. Forty-eight hours, Nova. Be ready."

She disconnected.

I looked at Trixx. At her purple skin glowing in the dim light. At eyes that had seen me at my worst and stayed anyway.

"Fifty million credits," she said. "That's a lot of money."

"Yeah."

"Someone's gonna try to collect."

"Probably."

"And we're about to raid a black site with our faces plastered across every screen in the galaxy."

"Yep."

She laughed, bitter and sharp. "We're so fucked."

"Completely."

"And we're doing it anyway."

"Have to. It's the only way forward."

She kissed me, hard and desperate, tasting like fear and determination. "Then let's make it count. Let's save those people. Burn that facility to the ground. Give the Federation something to remember us by."

"Assuming we survive."

"Even if we don't."

Outside the window, the dead planet kept rotating. Dead but still moving, still existing, a monument to things that used to matter.

We had forty-eight hours until we joined it.

✦ ✦ ✦

CHAPTER 19

Theta-Nine

The assault craft looked like something designed to kill efficiently and nothing else.

No windows. No comfort. Just rows of seats, weapon racks, and blast doors that could withstand small arms fire. Twenty-four of us packed in tight—Reed's twelve specialists, Nova's crew, and eight more mercenaries who looked like they'd been killing people professionally for decades.

Commander Saito stood at the front, his scarred face illuminated by red combat lighting. "Final briefing. We hit Facility Theta-Nine in ten minutes. Alpha Team breaches the north sector, extracts prisoners from Blocks A through D. Bravo Team takes south sector, Blocks E through H. Charlie Team—that's tech support—secures the control center and shuts down their defenses."

"What's our team?" I asked.

"You're with me on Alpha. Your skills are infiltration and chaos. I need both." He pointed to a holographic map. "We go in hard and fast. Fifteen minutes from breach to extraction. Any longer and reinforcements arrive. Questions?"

"What if we find Reed's daughter before the fifteen minutes?" Trixx asked.

"Then we extract her and keep moving. But she's not the priority. We're saving everyone we can carry." Saito's eyes were hard. "I know

Ms. Reed hired you to find her daughter specifically. But this operation is bigger than one person. Understood?"

We nodded. It made sense tactically, even if it felt cold.

"One more thing," Saito said. "These prisoners have been in captivity for years. Maybe decades. They'll be traumatized, confused, possibly violent. Don't expect gratitude. Expect chaos. Your job is to get them to the extraction ships alive. How you do that is up to you."

The pilot's voice crackled over speakers. "Two minutes to drop zone. All teams, prepare for combat deployment."

Around me, soldiers checked weapons, tightened armor, made peace with whatever gods they believed in. Hark was calm, methodical, loading magazines like he'd done it ten thousand times. Zeno looked terrified but determined, his cybernetic implants glowing as he ran final diagnostics on his hacking equipment. Trixx was checking her pistols, glow-ink pulsing bright purple with adrenaline.

I sparked a Black Death, took one last drag before combat. The smoke tasted like courage I didn't quite feel.

"You good?" Trixx asked quietly.

"No. You?"

"Scared shitless. But I'm with you, so at least we die together."

"Romantic."

"I try."

The assault craft shuddered as we approached the facility. Through the tactical display, I could see Facility Theta-Nine—a massive structure floating in deep space, armed to the teeth, designed to keep secrets buried forever.

We were about to dig them up.

"Thirty seconds!" the pilot shouted.

Saito stood at the breach door, combat rifle ready. "Listen up! This is what we trained for! We go in fast, we hit hard, we get our people out! Remember—fifteen minutes! Not a second more! Move with purpose, trust your training, and watch your corners!"

The assault craft latched onto the facility's hull with a metallic clang. Cutting torches ignited, burning through the external armor.

"Ten seconds!"

I stood, weapon ready, heart pounding so hard I thought it might explode. This was it. The point of no return. We were either heroes or corpses, and we'd know which in about fifteen minutes.

"Breach in three... two... one... GO!"

The door blew inward. Saito charged through, and we followed into hell.

•   •   •

The facility's interior was industrial—metal corridors, harsh lighting, the smell of recycled air and fear. Alarms were already screaming, red lights flashing, automated voice announcing "PERIMETER BREACH. ALL PERSONNEL TO COMBAT STATIONS."

We moved fast, weapons up, clearing rooms and corridors. The first guards we encountered were caught off-guard, still scrambling for weapons. Saito's team cut them down efficiently—three-round bursts, center mass, professionals working.

"Contact front!" someone shouted.

More guards poured in from a side corridor, armor and assault rifles, ready for war. The corridor lit up with plasma fire. I dove behind a support pillar, returned fire, felt rounds impact the metal inches from my head.

"Grenade!" Hark shouted.

I saw it bounce down the corridor—small, black, deadly. I lunged sideways just as it detonated, the blast wave slamming me into a wall. My ears rang. Smoke everywhere. Someone screaming.

"Move!" Saito yelled. "Through the breach! Keep moving!"

We pushed forward through the smoke and bodies. One guard was still alive, reaching for his weapon. Trixx put two rounds in his chest without breaking stride. No mercy. No hesitation. This was war.

"Charlie Team, report!" Saito shouted into his comm.

"We're pinned down at the control center!" Zeno's voice, stressed. "Heavy resistance! I can't access the systems while dodging bullets!"

"Hold position! We're coming to you!"

We diverted, running through corridors that all looked the same. Behind us, I heard more explosions—Bravo Team hitting their objectives. The whole facility was a warzone now.

We found Charlie Team trapped in a corridor, taking fire from automated turrets. Two mercs were down, bleeding. Zeno was behind cover, trying to hack the turrets remotely while lasers carved chunks out of the walls around him.

"I need thirty seconds!" Zeno shouted.

"We'll give you ten!" Saito responded. "Suppressing fire!"

We opened up on the turrets, plasma and bullets hammering their armor. The turrets swiveled, targeting us, and suddenly I was diving again as bolts melted metal where I'd been standing.

"Twenty seconds!" Zeno yelled.

"Work faster!"

A turret's targeting laser found Hark. He tried to dodge, but the bolt caught him in the shoulder, spinning him around. He went down hard.

"Hark!" I scrambled toward him.

"I'm good!" He was back up, left arm hanging useless, but still firing his rifle one-handed. "Takes more than that to kill me!"

"Ten seconds!"

The turrets were shredding our cover. We couldn't hold much longer.

"Five seconds!"

One of the mercs caught a burst, armor failing, body hitting the floor.

"Now!"

The turrets went dark. Zeno was in their systems, shutting them down one by one. We pushed forward, into the control center.

The room was full of screens showing every corner of the facility—prisoner blocks, guard stations, the other assault teams fighting their way through. Zeno immediately started working, hands flying across keyboards, implants glowing as he interfaced directly with the facility's network.

"I'm in! Shutting down automated defenses! Opening blast doors for Alpha and Bravo Teams! Locating prisoner manifests!"

"How long to find Reed's daughter?" I asked.

"Searching! There's thousands of files! Give me a minute!"

"We don't have a minute!"

Outside the control center, I heard boots. Heavy ones. A lot of them.

"They're coming!" Trixx was at the door, watching the corridor. "Big group! Maybe twenty soldiers!"

"Hold them!" Saito ordered. "Zeno needs time!"

We set up a defensive position—using consoles as cover, angles of fire covering the entrance. This was going to get ugly.

The first Federation soldier who rounded the corner caught three rounds from different angles. He dropped, and his buddies learned to be more careful. They started using grenades, smoke, trying to flush us out.

"Got her!" Zeno shouted. "Mira Reed! Prisoner Block F, Cell 247! She's alive!"

"Block F is in Bravo Team's sector," Saito said into his comm. "Bravo Leader, priority target in your zone—Cell 247, prisoner name Mira Reed. Extract her first!"

"Copy that," came the response. "We're taking heavy fire but we're close!"

An explosion rocked the control center. Part of the wall blew inward, and Federation troops poured through the breach. Close quarters now. No room for tactics, just shooting and moving and trying not to die.

I dropped two soldiers, then a third. Trixx was beside me, her pistols flashing, purple glow-ink making her look like some avenging demon. Hark was propped against a console, firing one-handed, every shot counting.

"We need to fall back!" Saito shouted.

"Can't!" Zeno yelled. "I'm downloading the prisoner files! Need thirty more seconds!"

"We don't have thirty seconds!"

"We need this data! It's proof! Without it, the Federation can deny everything!"

Saito cursed, started firing faster. We were being overrun. Too many soldiers, too many guns, not enough cover.

One of our mercs went down. Then another. The Federation was winning.

"Twenty seconds!" Zeno said.

A grenade landed near my feet. I tried to kick it away but wasn't fast enough. The blast lifted me off the ground, slammed me down hard. Everything went white, then red, then I couldn't hear anything except ringing.

Trixx was pulling me up, her mouth moving, shouting something I couldn't hear. Blood on her face. Maybe mine. Hard to tell.

"Ten seconds!"

The Federation soldiers were at the door. One kicked it open, started spraying automatic fire. Saito took a round in the leg, went down. Still firing from the ground, the crazy bastard.

"Done!" Zeno had the data chip, was disconnecting. "I got everything! Let's go!"

"Plant the charges!" Saito ordered, struggling to stand. "We torch this whole fucking place on our way out!"

Hark pulled out the demolition pack, started setting timers. "Five minutes!"

"That's not enough time!"

"It's what we got! Move!"

We ran, carrying our wounded, fighting through corridors that were collapsing as the charges went off. Behind us, I heard Federation soldiers screaming, calling for backup, trying to stop the facility from tearing itself apart.

We made it to Prisoner Block A. The doors were open—Zeno's hack had worked. Inside, hundreds of people were stumbling out of cells, confused, terrified, some too weak to walk.

They looked like ghosts. Skin pale from years without sunlight. Bodies thin from malnutrition. Eyes hollow from trauma. This was what the Federation did to people it wanted to forget.

"Everyone move!" I shouted. "We're getting you out! Follow us to the ships!"

Most obeyed. Some just stood there, catatonic. We had to physically carry them.

My comm crackled. Bravo Team. "We've got the primary target! Mira Reed is secured! But we're cut off! The Federation sealed the corridor! We can't reach extraction!"

"Where are you?" Saito demanded.

"Block F, north corridor! They've got heavy weapons pinning us down!"

"Hold position! We're coming!"

We diverted again, this time herding prisoners toward the extraction ships while a fire team went to help Bravo. I went with them—couldn't leave people behind.

Block F was a nightmare. Bodies everywhere—prisoners and guards mixed together. Smoke so thick I could barely see. The sound of gunfire echoing off metal walls.

We found Bravo Team behind a makeshift barricade, surrounded. They had maybe fifteen prisoners with them, including a woman who looked like a younger version of Sylla Reed.

"Mira?" I asked.

She looked at me with eyes that had seen too much. "Who are you?"

"Your mom sent us. We're getting you out."

"Mom's... mom's alive?"

"Very alive. Very pissed. Very determined to get you back. Now get behind me and stay low."

We laid down suppressing fire, burning through ammunition, trying to buy time. The demolition charges were ticking down. Three minutes left.

"We need to move!" Saito shouted. "Now!"

We broke cover, ran for it. The Federation soldiers tried to stop us, but we had momentum and desperation. Hark threw his last grenade, taking out a heavy weapons team. Trixx provided cover fire while we evacuated prisoners through a side corridor.

Two minutes left.

We made it to the extraction bay. The assault crafts were already loading—prisoners cramming in, soldiers helping them aboard, everyone moving fast because we all knew what happened in two minutes.

"All teams, sound off!" Saito ordered.

"Alpha Team, seventy percent casualties, mission complete!"

"Bravo Team, mission complete, primary target secured!"

"Charlie Team, data recovered, facility rigged to blow!"

"Load up! We're leaving!"

The last prisoners boarded. We jumped on just as the facility started shaking—the charges going off in sequence, tearing through critical systems.

The assault craft detached, engines burning hard, putting distance between us and Theta-Nine.

"One minute," someone said.

We watched through the viewscreen as the facility tried to hold together. Then the main charges detonated, and the whole structure tore itself apart. Secondary explosions rippled through the sections. The reactor went critical. And Facility Theta-Nine—home to two thousand prisoners, three hundred guards, and the Federation's darkest secrets—became an expanding cloud of debris.

"Facility destroyed," the pilot confirmed. "All assault craft accounted for. We're clear."

The assault craft erupted in cheers. Soldiers hugging each other, crying, laughing. We'd done it. Against impossible odds, we'd actually done it.

I looked at the prisoners crammed into every available space. They weren't cheering. They looked shell-shocked, overwhelmed, unable to process that they were free.

Mira Reed was crying silently, face in her hands. Twenty years as a prisoner. Twenty years thinking she'd die in that place. And now she was free.

Trixx collapsed next to me, exhausted. "We did it."

"Yeah."

"I can't believe we did it."

"Me neither."

Hark was getting his shoulder treated by a medic, cursing every time they touched it. Zeno was staring at the data chip like it contained the secrets of the universe. Which, in a way, it did.

"Casualties?" I asked Saito.

"Eight dead. Twelve wounded. Out of twenty-four." He shook his head. "Heavy losses. But we saved six hundred and thirty-two prisoners. And we destroyed a facility the Federation said didn't exist."

"Worth it?"

"Ask them." He gestured to the prisoners. "But yeah. I think it was worth it."

My comm buzzed. Reed.

"Tell me you found her."

"We found her. She's alive. She's here."

Silence on the line. Then: "Thank you. Thank you so much."

"We'll see you at the rendezvous."

.　.　.

The trip back took four hours. Reed was waiting when we docked, surrounded by medical teams and support staff.

The moment Mira stepped off the assault craft, Reed ran to her. They collided in the middle of the bay, holding each other, both of them crying, twenty years of separation ending in a single moment.

"I looked for you," Reed sobbed. "Every day. I never stopped looking."

"I know," Mira whispered. "I knew you would. I knew you'd come."

I turned away, giving them privacy. Trixx took my hand, squeezed it.

"We did good," she said.

"We did something."

The prisoners were being processed—medical exams, food, clothes, counseling. Most of them were in shock, unable to believe they were really free. Some kept asking if this was real or another psychological test the Federation was running.

It took hours to convince them that yes, this was real. Yes, they were safe. Yes, the facility was destroyed and could never hurt them again.

Reed found us in the mess hall, eating the first hot meal we'd had in days. Her eyes were red from crying but she looked happier than I'd ever seen her.

"I don't know how to thank you," she said.

"The million credits is a good start," I said.

She laughed. "Already transferred. Along with bonuses for everyone. And the new identities I promised. You're officially dead as far as the Federation's concerned. New names, new histories, new lives."

"What about the prisoners?" Trixx asked.

"I'm taking care of them. Medical treatment, rehabilitation, transportation to wherever they want to go. It'll take months, maybe years, but they'll have the chance to rebuild their lives."

"And the data?" Zeno held up the chip.

Reed smiled. "That data is about to become very public. Every news outlet in the galaxy is going to see proof of what the Federation's been doing. Facility locations, prisoner counts, names of officials who authorized it. The entire conspiracy exposed."

"They'll come after you," I said.

"Let them try. I've got resources they can't imagine. Lawyers, politicians, corporate allies. And now I've got proof. They can't suppress this. Not anymore."

She pulled up a holographic display. News feeds from across the galaxy—our raid was already making headlines.

FEDERATION BLACK SITE DESTROYED: 600+ PRISONERS FREED

SHOCKING FOOTAGE FROM FACILITY THETA-NINE: EVIDENCE OF SYSTEMATIC TORTURE

WHO ARE THE RAIDERS? MYSTERY TEAM EXPOSES GENOCIDE OPERATION

"You're heroes," Reed said. "Anonymous heroes, but heroes nonetheless. The galaxy's talking about nothing else."

"Heroes don't usually have fifty million credit bounties," I pointed out.

"Not anymore. The Federation quietly rescinded the warrants an hour ago. Too much public pressure. You're no longer wanted criminals."

"We're not?"

"Nope. You're free. Free to go anywhere, be anyone, live however you want." She smiled. "Congratulations. You survived."

I looked at my crew. At Trixx with her purple skin and fierce eyes. At Hark with his arm in a sling and that sardonic smile. At Zeno surrounded by his computers and impossible dreams.

We'd survived. Against every odd, we'd actually survived.

"So what now?" Trixx asked.

"Now?" I sparked a Black Death, tasted freedom for the first time in my life. "Now we figure out who we want to be when we're not running for our lives."

"That might take a while," Hark said.

"We got time."

Reed left us to our celebration. Around the station, six hundred and thirty-two former prisoners were learning what freedom felt like. Across the galaxy, the Federation was scrambling to contain the scandal. And somewhere out there, Ky was smiling.

We'd done it. We'd actually done it.

Started a revolution. Exposed genocide. Freed the prisoners. Survived.

Not bad for a street kid from Nova Block Six-Nine.

✦ ✦ ✦

CHAPTER 20

New Horizons

Two weeks after we destroyed Facility Theta-Nine, I was standing in the observation deck of Reed's station, watching ships come and go, thinking about everything that had happened.

We'd done the impossible. Started a revolution. Exposed genocide. Freed six hundred prisoners. Survived long enough to spend the money we'd earned.

And somehow, I felt emptier than ever.

"You're brooding again," Trixx said, walking up behind me. She wrapped her arms around my waist, rested her chin on my shoulder. "You've been doing that a lot lately."

"Just thinking."

"About?"

"About what comes next. We got our freedom. Got our money. Got new identities. We could go anywhere, be anyone. So why do I feel like something's missing?"

"Because you're addicted to the fight," she said simply. "You spent your whole life running jobs, chasing revenge, fighting the system. Now that you've won, you don't know who you are without an enemy."

She wasn't wrong.

The galaxy had changed in the two weeks since the raid. The footage Zeno downloaded—combined with the testimony of six hundred freed prisoners—had sparked protests on every Federation world. Not riots this time. Organized resistance. People demanding investigations, reforms, accountability.

The Federation was on the defensive. Three high-ranking officials had resigned. The Council had launched a formal inquiry into the black site network. Vale's conviction was being reviewed— his connections to the genocide operation making his crimes look even worse.

We'd actually changed something.

But what did that mean for us?

"Reed wants to see us," Trixx said. "All four of us. Says she has a proposition."

"Another job?"

"Probably. You know her type. Doesn't stop until every wrong is righted and every secret is exposed."

"Should we hear her out?"

"Do we have a choice? We're bored as fuck and you know it."

She was right about that too.

· · ·

Reed's office was on the top level of the station, with windows showing the void in all directions. She was standing at her desk, looking at holographic displays showing news feeds from across the galaxy. Mira was with her—still thin, still recovering, but alive and getting stronger every day.

"Nova," Reed said as we entered. "Thank you for coming. All of you."

Hark and Zeno followed us in. Hark's shoulder was healing but he still moved stiff. Zeno looked healthier than I'd seen him in months, like having a purpose agreed with him.

"You said you had a proposition," I said.

"Direct as always." Reed smiled. "Yes. I want to hire you again."

"For what?"

"To finish what we started. Facility Theta-Nine was one black site out of forty-seven. The data Zeno recovered showed us where the others are. I want to shut them all down."

"That's a war," Hark said flatly. "One facility nearly killed us. Forty-six more would definitely finish the job."

"I'm not asking you to raid all forty-six. I'm asking you to help me coordinate a larger operation. I've been reaching out to resistance groups, activist networks, independent security contractors. People who want to see the Federation held accountable. But they need leadership. They need someone who's actually done it before."

"You want us to train insurgents," I said.

"I want you to lead them. Show them how to fight smart, not just hard. How to expose the Federation's crimes without getting killed in the process. You've proven you can do the impossible. Now teach others to do the same."

"Why us?" Trixx asked. "You've got military contacts, professional soldiers. We're just street criminals who got lucky."

"You're survivors who understand what it means to be powerless. You fight for the people the system forgot. That's not something I can buy with money or train with military discipline. That's what makes you perfect for this."

Mira spoke up for the first time. "You saved my life. You saved six hundred lives. There are thousands more waiting in those other facilities. They deserve the same chance we got."

It was a good pitch. But it was also a commitment. A choice to keep fighting instead of walking away.

"We need to discuss this," I said. "Can you give us a few hours?"

"Take all the time you need," Reed said. "But Nova? The galaxy is watching. What you do next matters. Not just to me. To everyone."

* * *

We gathered in our quarters—the four of us, like always, making decisions that would probably get us killed.

"I'm out," Trixx said immediately. "I did my part. Ky's avenged. Vale's in prison. The black sites are exposed. I'm done fighting other people's wars."

"It's not other people's war," I said. "It's our war. We started it."

"No. You started it. I just followed because I love your stupid ass and didn't want you to die alone."

"And now?"

"Now I want to live. Actually live. Not just survive between battles. I want a house on some colony world where nobody knows our names. I want mornings without checking for assassins. I want to get old with you without wondering which fight will be our last."

She was tearing up. I'd never seen Trixx cry before. Not really. Not like this.

"I can't keep doing this," she said quietly. "I can't keep watching you throw yourself at impossible odds and praying you come back. Eventually the odds catch up. Eventually you don't come back. And I can't... I can't watch you die, Nova. I can't."

I pulled her close, held her while she cried into my chest. Felt my own eyes getting wet.

"I don't want to die either," I said. "But I can't walk away. Not yet. There's too many people still trapped in those facilities. Too many names in Zeno's database. If we don't help them, who will?"

"Someone else. Anyone else. Let them be the heroes. We've done enough."

"Have we?"

She pulled back, looked at me with red eyes. "You tell me. When is it enough? When are you satisfied? When will you finally say 'okay, I've done my part, time to live for myself'? Because if that day never comes, then we don't have a future. We just have a countdown until you get yourself killed."

Silence. Heavy and suffocating.

Hark cleared his throat. "For what it's worth, I'm with Nova. I'm too old to retire. Might as well die doing something useful."

"That's because you're already dead inside," Trixx snapped.

"Probably. But at least I'm honest about it."

Zeno was quiet, staring at his hands. "I... I want to help. Those files I downloaded, they have names. Thousands of names. People who've been prisoners for years, decades. Some of them are hybrids like us. Some are political dissidents. Some are just unlucky people who saw the wrong thing at the wrong time. If we can save them..."

"We can't save everyone," Trixx said.

"No. But we can try. And isn't that better than doing nothing?"

"Doing nothing keeps us alive."

"Does it? We've spent two weeks hiding here, pretending to be normal, and we're all miserable. Maybe this is who we are now. Maybe we don't get normal lives anymore."

Trixx looked at each of us—Hark with his cynical acceptance, Zeno with his idealistic hope, me with my stubborn refusal to quit. She saw that she was outvoted. That this was happening whether she agreed or not.

"Fine," she said. "Fine. We do this. But on one condition."

"What?" I asked.

"After we shut down these black sites, we're done. No more wars. No more revolutions. We take our money, we disappear, and we live. For real this time. No compromises."

"Deal," I said immediately.

She shook her head, a sad smile on her lips. "You say that so fast. Like the words don't cost you anything."

"They cost me everything. But I'm saying them anyway."

"Because this is who you are. A fighter who can't stop fighting. And I'm the idiot who loves you anyway." She kissed me, hard and desperate and sad. "Let's do this. Let's save the galaxy. And then let's see if we survive long enough to regret it."

. . .

We told Reed yes.

She had the operation planned within days. We'd travel to different systems, meet with resistance cells, coordinate attacks on black sites across Federation space. Hit them all simultaneously so the Federation couldn't reinforce or evacuate. Overwhelming force, multiple fronts, maximum chaos.

It was ambitious. Probably impossible. Exactly the kind of stupid plan that somehow worked.

"You'll be based on the Outer Rim," Reed explained. "Beyond direct Federation jurisdiction. I've purchased a ship for you—fast, armed, with quarters for a crew of four. Your home and headquarters."

"You bought us a ship?" Zeno asked, eyes lighting up.

"Custom built. Military-grade engines, civilian exterior, enough firepower to fight your way out of most situations. Consider it a company vehicle."

"What's it called?" I asked.

Reed smiled. "That's for you to decide. She's yours."

We went to see it in the hangar bay. It was beautiful—sleek black hull, curved lines, aggressive stance. Bigger than the Caprice but not by much. Built for speed and survival.

"She's perfect," Trixx said, running her hand along the hull.

"What do we call her?" Zeno asked.

I thought about Ky. About how he'd always talked about wanting to see the stars, to travel beyond the Verge, to be free. He never got that chance. But maybe we could honor his dream.

"Kyrie," I said. "We call her Kyrie."

"After your brother?" Reed asked.

"Yeah. He wanted to fly. Now he will. In a way."

Reed nodded, understanding. "The Kyrie it is. May she carry you safely through whatever comes next."

•　　•　　•

We spent a week outfitting the ship. Zeno filled it with computers and equipment. Hark stocked weapons and ammunition. Trixx made the quarters livable. I learned how to fly her—learning her quirks, her limits, how she handled in combat and in calm.

The Kyrie was faster than anything I'd ever flown. Responsive. Almost alive. She felt right in a way the Caprice never had.

"You're gonna get us killed in this thing," Trixx said, watching me run flight tests.

"Probably. But we'll look good doing it."

"That's not comforting."

"It's not supposed to be."

Our first mission was three jumps away—a Federation black site in the Kronos Sector, smaller than Theta-Nine but still holding two hundred prisoners. We'd be coordinating with local resistance, providing tactical support and extraction.

It was dangerous. Probably stupid. Exactly what we did best.

The night before we left, I found Trixx on the observation deck, staring out at the stars.

"You okay?" I asked.

"No. But I will be."

"We don't have to do this. We could still walk away."

"No, we couldn't. You'd always wonder. Always feel guilty. Always know you left people behind." She turned to me. "So we do this. We save them. We fight this war. And when it's over—if we survive—we find that quiet colony world and we live. Really live. Deal?"

"Deal."

"Promise?"

"I promise. After this war, we're done. We disappear. We be normal."

"You're lying."

"I'm trying not to."

She kissed me, soft and sad and perfect. "I know. And I love you anyway. That's my curse."

"Mine too."

.   .   .

The next morning, we boarded the Kyrie. Hark took his station at weapons. Zeno at communications and sensors. Trixx at co-pilot. Me at the helm.

Reed was on the comm. "The resistance cells are ready. They're waiting for your signal. When you arrive in Kronos Sector, you'll be the tip of the spear. Everything depends on you."

"No pressure," I said.

"None at all. Good luck, Nova. To all of you. May you return safely."

"We'll try our best."

I fired up the engines. The Kyrie hummed to life, powerful and eager. Through the viewport, I could see the void—infinite, dangerous, full of people who needed help and enemies who wanted us dead.

"Everyone ready?" I asked.

"No," Hark said.

"Not at all," Zeno added.

"Absolutely not," Trixx agreed.

"Good," I said. "Let's go anyway."

I punched the thrusters. The Kyrie shot forward, out of the hangar, into the black. Behind us, Reed's station shrank to a point of light. Ahead, the jump point beckoned—a doorway to the next fight, the next mission, the next impossible thing we'd somehow survive.

My comm buzzed. A message from an unknown number. I opened it.

Text only. Two words: *Stay vigilant.*

No signature. No source. Just a warning from someone who knew who we were and what we were doing.

"Everything okay?" Trixx asked.

"Yeah. Just someone wishing us luck."

"We're gonna need it."

The jump point approached. One more second, and we'd be gone—leaving behind everything we knew, everything we'd been, launching into something new and terrifying and necessary.

I thought about Ky. About Vale in his prison cell. About six hundred freed prisoners starting new lives. About thousands more waiting in black sites across the galaxy, hoping someone would remember them, hoping someone would care enough to fight.

We were that someone.

Four criminals from a space station slum. A driver, a hacker, a killer, and a woman who deserved better than all of us. The Federation called us terrorists. The resistance called us heroes. The news feeds called us *Galactic Trap Lords*—shadow warriors striking from the dark.

We were just trying to survive. And maybe, along the way, save a few people who couldn't save themselves.

"Jump in three," I said. "Two. One."

The Kyrie hit the jump point. The stars stretched to lines. Reality bent and twisted. And we were gone, racing toward whatever came next.

Behind us, the war we'd started continued burning.

Ahead, the war to finish waited.

And somewhere between, we'd figure out how to survive long enough to actually live.

Maybe.

Probably not.

But we'd die trying.

✦ ✦ ✦

EPILOGUE

Federation High Command, Three Weeks After Theta-Nine

The man in the pristine white uniform studied the holographic display with cold calculation. Forty-seven black sites. Thirty-two compromised or destroyed in coordinated attacks. Fifteen still operational but exposed.

Billions of credits lost. Decades of work undone. Thousands of assets freed or killed.

All because of four criminals from a space station slum.

"Sir," an aide said nervously. "The Council is demanding answers. They want someone held accountable."

"Someone will be," the man said. His name was Admiral Kaine, and he'd run the black site program for fifteen years without a single leak until Nova DeLeon had exposed everything. "But first, we deal with the source of the problem."

"The crew?"

"Not just them. Sylla Reed. The resistance cells. Everyone who thinks they can challenge the Federation's authority. We're going to make examples. Bloody ones."

"The public—"

"The public has a short memory. Give them six months and they'll forget. Give them a new enemy to hate and they'll forgive us anything." He pulled up a file. Nova's face appeared—young, angry, dangerous. "But first, we remind these insurgents what happens to people who defy us."

"What are your orders, sir?"

"Activate the Ghost Protocol. I want every intelligence asset, every black ops team, every resource we have hunting these four. I want them found. I want them broken. And I want their heads delivered to me personally."

"Sir, they have Sylla Reed's protection—"

"No one is untouchable. Reed will learn that lesson soon enough." He smiled, cold and terrible. "The Federation has survived for three centuries. A few idealistic criminals won't bring us down. They'll just teach us to be more careful about who we eliminate next time."

He closed the file. Nova's face disappeared.

"Spread the word," Kaine said. "The Federation doesn't forgive. The Federation doesn't forget. And anyone who helps Nova DeLeon and the crew will share their fate."

The aide saluted and left.

Kaine turned back to his displays, already planning. The black site program was damaged but not destroyed. They'd rebuild. Quietly. Carefully. And this time, there would be no leaks.

Because the Federation's work was too important to stop.

And a few thousand disappeared prisoners were a small price to pay for galactic order.

.   .   .

.   .   .

✦ ✦ ✦

To be continued in

GALACTIC TRAP LORDS

Book Two: Ashes & Iron

✦ ✦ ✦

✦ ✦ ✦

ABOUT THE AUTHOR

Lampert x Griffin Urban Universe™ brings authentic street narratives to the final frontier. Blending the raw energy of urban fiction with epic space opera, this debut trilogy introduces readers to a universe where the struggle for survival spans galaxies—but the heart remains rooted in the block.

Blood in the Stars is the first book in the Galactic Trap Lords trilogy.

www.ingramcontent.com/pod-product-compliance
Lightning Source LLC
Chambersburg PA
CBHW051537260626
47170CB00003B/983